Launch Me to the Stars, I'm Finished Here

Also by Nick Gregorio

Rare Encounters with Sea Beasts and Other Divine Phenomena

With a Difference (with Francis Daulerio)

This Distance

Good Grief

Praise for Nick Gregorio

"Get sucked into the vortex that is Gregorio's knack for intrigue. Leave yourself unapologetically starry-eyed, morphed into a celestial body comfortably rooted in a fumbling humanity. Nick shakes loose your shallow pretensions with a ride through your own nostalgic future."

Claire Hopple,
author of *Echo Chamber*

"Nick Gregorio once again catapults us to outer space with his latest novel, *Launch Me to the Stars, I'm Finished Here.* Tender and grounded, the story takes the reader on a journey through the minefields of navigating mental health struggles in a way that is both genuine and engaging. As always, Gregorio showcases his unique ability to craft characters you can't help but root for within his taut and lyrical prose, and he builds to an ending that is as wonderful as it is well-earned. *Launch Me to the Stars* is certainly in its own stratosphere."

Jane-Rebecca Cannarella,
author of *Thirst and Frost*

"*Launch Me to the Stars, I'm Finished Here* is a beautiful meditation on the distances we go for the ones we love. Call it sci-fi if you want, but behind the spaceships and talk of theoretical physics is an outstretched hand to anyone struggling to keep going. A reminder that we matter. Gregorio navigates the greatest expanse to bring us something essential, leaving us with a sense of wonder and hope for the days ahead, wherever they may be."

Francis Daulerio,
author of *Joy* and *With a Difference*

"*Launch Me to the Stars, I'm Finished Here* is both cosmic-suburban heist adventure and profound exploration of mental illness, friendship, and family. Funny, exciting, and heartfelt—don't miss this."

Stephanie Feldman,
author of *Saturnalia*

LAUNCH ME TO THE STARS, I'M FINISHED HERE

a novel

---

by Nick Gregorio

Trident Press
Boulder, CO

ISBN: 978-1-951226-18-3

Cover art by Kevin Sampsell

Published by Trident Press
940 Pearl St.
Boulder, CO 80302

tridentcafe.com/trident-press-titles

For anyone leading that deep, dark despair on a merry chase.

Let's all of us keep on running, yes?

Hang on tight and survive.

—Captain James T. Kirk

The way I see it, every life is a pile of good things and bad things. The good things don't always soften the bad things, but vice versa, the bad things don't always spoil the good things and make them unimportant.

—The Eleventh Doctor

We all have to make decisions that affect the course of our lives. You've gotta do what you've gotta do. And I've gotta do what I've gotta do.

—Dr. Emmett Brown

Beyond the Farthest Star

1.

Everything was blue.

The walls, the furniture, Loonsfoot's white lab coat.

Blue from the device in the center of the room, humming, spinning, which would, according to Loonsfoot, tunnel through the universe and give them a glimpse of Regis-132.

Astrid had only seen a photo of the place.

Grainy, blurry. A field. A building in the distance. Pink skies. Not the kind of pink from a sunset, but in place of the blue on a clear day. The tall grass, almost violet. Sort of glowing, shimmering somethings at the tips of the blades. And the building, or tower, or monolith, out of focus. Bulbous but sleek. Rounded but geometrically complex. Maybe not even built. Grown.

Loonsfoot, over the increasing noise from the machine, said, "You put on your sunscreen, yeah? The amount of energy getting pumped out of this thing will—"

"Put off about as much radiation as the sun on a summer day," Astrid said. "SPF 50, even under these." She tapped the goggles that were definitely going to leave creases on the bridge of her nose, her cheek bones. Didn't matter how many bunion cushions she stuck onto them. Happened every time. She'd bought sunglasses almost as big as the goggles from the dollar store just so she wouldn't have to explain the marks to Cassie. The sunglasses were hideous. She'd lied about them being in style. Lied that she'd needed to borrow the bunion cushions because of her school's ridiculous dress code's shoes. Lied about where she was. Lied about how well the therapy sessions with Loonsfoot had been going.

And Cassie believed all of it.

Which made it easier.

And worse.

"Fabulous," Loonsfoot said, louder now that the humming had shaken bits of plaster and dust into her red hair. Loonsfoot always seemed to have something in her hair, or on her clothes, or smeared on her face. Even the first time they'd met she'd had Doritos-orange dusted into the corners of her mouth. "Switch on the collider for me, yeah?"

Astrid, in front of a panel of dials, switches, glowing glass pimples ringed in silver, clicked on a finger grease-discolored exclamation point-shaped toggle labeled "The Switch Only to be Switched Once So Instructed" with masking tape and Sharpie. The rig could've come straight off the original *USS Enterprise* set. Wooden looking, painted black, chipping on top. Hotrod red on the sides. But that was where the comparison ended. Otherwise, there was a jellyfish of wires, cables, and plugs hanging from the bottom, spilling onto the floor, fanning out in a hundred directions to other panels, consoles, and power sources—all connected to integral systems, according to Loonsfoot. All certainly, most definitely, running on some form of electricity, according to Astrid.

Fireworks of sparks from a rat's nest of wire.

The humming now a steady rumble.

Smoke alarm bleeping, bleeping, bleeping.

Loonsfoot running this way, that, tweaking that, this.

Astrid watching. Following instructions that were yelled over the sound. Turning a dial to maximum output. Flicking a series of switches. Needing to catch her breath as the machine made everything a deeper blue than before. A shade deeper than that.

She wasn't sure. Couldn't be. But when she was young, she had asked Cassie about the feeling in her belly during her fourth birthday party.

Same one from Christmas morning.

Walking through the front gates of the Magic Kingdom that one time.

Plugging earbuds into her ears and dancing home from school.

Getting picked up from school early to catch a matinee before Cassie had to work the night shift at the diner.

Cassie had said, "Butterflies."

That.

Astrid had that.

Those.

Maybe.

The house could've fallen down around them and all the work they'd done, and Astrid wouldn't have noticed. Bolts of energy could've gotten burped out of that machine, blowing holes through walls, the ceiling, the floors, and there would've been nothing but the lightness in her gut. That thing could've atomized them both and she wouldn't have been afraid to go.

Except, this time, she wouldn't have necessarily wanted to per se.

If that were it though—the big it-it—she'd hope a beam of blue would blow open her stomach first, so she could see them. The butterflies. Dancing in the air as the house came down.

But nothing collapsed.

There was no violent reaction from the machine that, according to Loonsfoot, was tearing a hole in the universe to give them a glimpse of another world. Aside from its foundation-shaking energy output, anyway.

At least not before Loonsfoot came into view, waving her arms, snapping her gloved fingers in front of Astrid's goggles, saying something that could've been anything.

Astrid was bumped aside.

Light hip check, a wink, a smile.

And Loonsfoot went to work.

Like the way Astrid was taught to play *Space Invaders*, and *Galaga*, and *Asteroids* at the arcade in Sea Isle City that had probably been turned into condos by now. Day trip to the beach, hotdogs at the arcade, body surfing as the sun set, McDonald's on the ride home.

Butterflies.

Loonsfoot took Astrid's hand.

Pointed toward a red button on the console, nodded.

Astrid balled up a fist, hit the button.

And.

Silence.

The heat was everything.

Sweat under Astrid's arms, on her forehead. Underneath her lead apron. Just enough for her to begin involuntarily inching toward the front door because she'd have to sprint through the light and the heat to get to the one leading out back.

Loonsfoot said, "Wait. This is normal."

"But—"

"I don't want you to miss this."

Loonsfoot had a habit of using phrases like that. There was always something coming that Astrid couldn't miss, shouldn't miss. Their first session together, not all that long after the hospital, Loonsfoot had said, "No one wants you to miss what comes next." Astrid had said, "What comes next?" And Loonsfoot had said, "You'll have to wait and see."

Since then, there hadn't been much reason to ask what was so fantastically unmissable. There was always something. And something after that. And something else after that. And before Loonsfoot that hadn't very often been the case.

Loonsfoot said, "Wait."

And, "Wait."

And, "Keep waiting."

Butterflies.

Goosebumps.

Loonsfoot saying, "Want a magazine or something?"

Then, the middle of the room wasn't there anymore.

A hole.

To somewhere else.

No tower.

But the grass, the glowing bulbs. A forest of orange-trunked trees topped with mushroom caps, misting the air with silver and gold, which shimmered, shined in the suns—there were two of them. Both red and enormous in the pink sky. Everything visible ringed in an electric blue, pulsing, sparking energy band.

Butterflies still.

Something else too.

Better.

There was never a better before.

Not since, maybe, her big-girl bed. Or first place at the science fair. Or Cassie waking her up when it was still dark out, walking her to the window and whispering, "Snow day," in her ear before wrapping her up in blankets and blankets and plopping her on the couch for a movie marathon.

But no.

Never this.

Then, flash.

Pain.

In her arm.

Her back.

The back of her head.

There was a smell.

Grass, but smoky.

Dirt, but chalky.

Before Astrid opened her eyes, maybe what was in her nostrils was Regis-132. The smells from an alien world. Or, a world where Astrid was an alien.

She'd made it.

She sat up.

Opened her eyes.

But there was no more violet grass.

No puffs of clouds racing across the real-time time-lapsed sky.

No tower in the distance, shifting, spinning, changing shape, a thing that wasn't made but just was.

Just an Astrid-shaped hole in the front door. Splinters of wood. The wind through the new green leaves on the trees around the house. The static of traffic on 309 not a half-mile away. Loonsfoot yelling something like, "Christ on a crutch," or "Cheese n' crackers," or "Jesus H. Christmas cards," running toward her, framed in the hole Astrid had put through the door.

Then she saw it.

Her arm bent in the wrong direction at the elbow.

And everything hurt again.

A nub of bone pushing the skin bright white—a whitehead ready to burst, haloed in black, purple, green, and yellow.

"Can I get you something," Loonsfoot said. "A cookie or something? For your blood sugar?"

"I thought you were a doctor," Astrid said through that deep, teeth-hissy ache from a fresh injury pain-pain.

"By now you've gotten through most of the list and should know I'm not that kind of doctor either."

Loonsfoot cupped Astrid's cheeks in her palms, began chanting, "You're okay, you are going to be okay," like a mantra. Like she was talking to someone else.

Astrid wasn't sure who Loonsfoot could have been talking to with her red face and wide-open eyes and gritty, sweaty skin. But that level of concern certainly couldn't have been for Astrid. They had gotten close, sure, but only Cassie had ever spoken to her like that.

"You need to fix this for me," Astrid said through her teeth.

Loonsfoot gave Astrid the look she'd seen all too often during her stint in the hospital. Wrinkled forehead. Eyebrows like a second and third frown. Lips pursed. Eyes glassy.

Like Astrid was stupid. Ridiculous. Like she had no idea, really, why she had done what she'd done.

Tried to do.

She'd had every ounce of clarity and understanding she could've gotten before she did what she did.

Why wasn't a question.

"Stop that," Astrid said.

"Stop what?"

"That. Fix the face, please."

Loonsfoot rolled her eyes, asked if Astrid could stand.

Astrid told Loonsfoot about the bills. The second, third notices. The collection agency threats. Minimum wage. Cassie's tips. Rent. Credit cards.

Loonsfoot shushed her, said, "You're not stupid. Does that hideous thing look like a sprain or something?" gagging a little toward the end of her question.

Astrid couldn't stop herself from being pulled to her feet.

Gave up on trying to pull away from Loonsfoot's grip on her good hand.

There was nothing but stars blinking, blinking in the corners of Astrid's vision. All over Loonsfoot maneuvering the radiation vest around the break, up and over Astrid's head. On the side of Loonsfoot's car, the interior through the windshield—everything speckled with white.

The phone in Loonsfoot's hand. "Call your mom. She can meet us at the hospital."

Astrid pushed the hand away.

"Cut the shit, Amy," Loonsfoot said.

Stars.

Constellations glazed on Loonsfoot's face.

Silence.

Deeper than the moment before the machine blew.

Maybe the sound of the dead-black of space that thing was supposed to have gored a hole through.

Then Astrid said her own name.

Loonsfoot shook her head. "That's what I said."

The stars were brighter, forced Astrid to blink them away when she reached for her phone in her back pocket with her good arm.

Loonsfoot started the car.

Said nothing.

Kept her eyes straight ahead, staring, staring.

Astrid put the phone to her ear, used the time between the ringing and the hello to stitch an adequate story together in her overloaded mind.

2.

Cassie hated working overnights. Hate wasn't strong enough a word, actually. If overnights were a planet, Cassie would enjoy watching a Texas-sized meteorite crack that fucker in half, sending all the coffee-guzzling, bender-weaning, shitty-tipping, smoked-out, hipster-ish, 3AM weirdos into the black of space.

All the coffee she had to drink made it impossible to sleep. Blackout curtains drawn, television on mute, Neil deGrasse Tyson discussing the eventual heat death of the universe in her failing earbuds—nothing worked. Not even counting the glow-in-the-dark stars, which had lost most of their glow since Astrid had stuck them to the ceiling when she was a little girl, worked anymore.

"Twinkle, twinkle plastic stars, get me to sleep or I'm heading to the bar." She laughed at that one. Then she threw off the covers, pulled on her jeans, and went to the kitchenette.

"May as well," she told the coffee maker. Dumped the pot dregs she'd made that morning, last night, whenever it was she'd last made fresh coffee, into a mug. The microwave hummed and buzzed and flickered, and Cassie kept her distance. If the thing blew, it wouldn't be in her face. New microwave? About a hundred and fifty bucks. Okay, doable.

Facial reconstructive surgery? Three to five-grand depending on what needed doing.

Wasn't going to happen.

Couldn't happen.

Otherwise, goodbye, apartment. Catch you later, staggering good looks. So long, however much tuition remained after grants, scholarships, and financial aid every semester to keep Astrid in the black at the University of Pennsylvania in the fall.

She thought, Spock, dying of radiation poisoning at the end of *The Wrath of Khan*.

Vader, helmetless in *Return of the Jedi*.

Schwarzenegger and his ballooning, depressurized face in that dream sequence on the surface of Mars in *Total Recall*.

The microwave bleeped, went black. Looking at her reflection in the microwave door, maybe she'd throw in a nose job. She'd wanted one off and on since high school. And if one day the microwave exploded her face, why not? She'd already be out the entire cost to look human again anyway. She and Astrid would just work overnights at the diner together. A little vanity never hurt anybody. Especially when, at that point, she and Astrid would need to look pretty for tips.

She kept the stack of mail on the table at arm's length. Used one eye, kept it on the upper left corner of each envelope, used her mugless hand to flick through the pile. Electric bill. Water bill. Best Buy ad. Something from John Walsh.

It was a check.

Obviously it was a check.

She wedged a thumb under the flap, pushed through the static tear. Opened up a millimeter's worth of a papercut. Of course she did.

And, of course, it was a check.

She buried the envelope beneath the mail pile and padded the six feet into the living room.

On the couch, Cassie flicked through the fifteen television stations she could afford. Then opened a drawer in the IKEA coffee table. Rows and rows of DVDs. Everything from *Flight of the Navigator* to *Enemy Mine. The Fifth Element* to *Gattaca. 12 Monkeys* to *Stargate.*

Choice made, the state somewhere between awake and barely conscious achieved, the next sip of coffee was cold and stank of burn, but she drank it anyway. Once she slid closer to the awake side of the spectrum, Bruce Willis was drooling and Brad Pitt was raving with his walleye.

Cassie had to shut the movie off.

Astrid had never been a slobbering wreck—except when she was a baby, but that's what babies do. But tucking that DVD back into the coffee table, there was nothing but the things she'd seen her daughter do that she'd never wanted to see her daughter do, or remember her doing ever again.

Phone in hand, maybe she'd text Astrid, ask how her day was going. Ask if she wanted to hang out at the diner for coffee once Cassie's shift started, tell her they could sneak up onto the roof again. But maybe Astrid would see that as something less than sincere. Like she was an obligation that needed to be taken care of. Like she was a burden.

Cassie clapped her phone down onto the coffee table.

She could text Willa and ask how things were going. Willa would never tell Astrid about the call. Willa would give a report, and Cassie wouldn't have to sit in her apartment all day waiting for Astrid to come home, waiting to go back to work after lying around in bed with her eyes closed in that headspace-timesuck where people get those falling dreams. The space where hours were more like four and a half minutes.

But she didn't need to text Willa.

Willa called.

"Astrid's headed to the hospital."

Blood.

Pills.

Bleach.

She'd stopped eating.

She walked into traffic.

She drove off a bridge.

She jumped off a bridge.

"It's not what you think."

"Should've led with that, Will," Cassie said trying to catch her breath. "Sorry for the tone, but Christ."

"She was hit by a car, Cassie."

When she was thirteen, Astrid would zone out when her day didn't go the way she'd planned it to go. She would walk into things, step on things, be totally oblivious to everything. She'd fallen down a flight of five steps because she'd stepped out into empty space. She'd stood at the top of an escalator, her Chucks squeaking on the metal plate as the belt kept nudging her forward, telling her to get moving. Then she'd walked across Bethlehem Pike without looking both ways, or watching for the walk signal, or doing anything she was supposed to do before putting herself in front of oncoming cars.

"On purpose?" Cassie said.

"I don't think so, no," Willa said. "She promised. A lot. And she's been doing really well. I don't think we have to—I don't think you have to worry about that right now."

"You can say 'we.'"

"I don't think we have to worry about that right now."

"Why—why didn't she call me?"

"None of it made much sense. She sounded really hurt, may have just called the last person who called her."

Cassie didn't say anything. Sniffed back her runny nose, cleared her throat. "Which hospital?"

Willa told her.

There was silence on the line, Willa waiting for her to say something.

Anything.

"If I could pull it off, you'd eat for free at the diner every night. Every morning. Afternoon. Whatever."

Cassie heard Willa's smile over the phone. "You guys have good chicken parmesan sandwiches there."

"The best," Cassie said.

Cassie pocketed her phone, grabbed her keys, took a look at her reflection in the glass of the microwave door.

"You need some sleep, Cass." She made a face, said, "And you need to last until I hit the lottery, microwave."

Leaving the apartment, Astrid must have had a good reason to call Willa first.

Opening the car door, Astrid mustn't have been thinking straight.

Starting the car and pulling out of the parking lot, Astrid was in an accident.

It was an accident.

That was all.

3.

Willa outright refused to wear the standard plaid skirt portion of the school uniform. The word uniform itself denoted one outfit. Not one for people with penises and another for people with vaginas. That was how she'd put it to her father at the start of the school year, in an attempt to make him as uncomfortable as possible, anyway. Classic Ken Baumgartner. Talk about real things, especially genitalia—didn't matter which sort as long as the words were coming out of his teenage daughter's mouth—and he'd get all sweaty and red.

But Willa didn't have the strength to say anything after he'd picked her up, and, once again, mentioned she looked like a boy. At a time like this, no less.

After Astrid's call.

After calling Cassie.

After texting Ken, asking him for a ride to the hospital even though her car was parked in the student parking lot. Snotty, red, and puffy, standing out front of school. Hands too shaky to get her car door unlocked, much less drive. Head too light to not need a wall to lean on.

Yes, even then, her khakis made her look like a boy.

She kept her sweating palms on her thighs as they drove. Tried concentrating on leaving handprints on her pants instead of whatever Ken was saying.

But she snapped back to herself once she heard him ask what she knew he'd ask once she'd admitted to herself she couldn't drive and needed him to pick her up, considering the circumstances under which she needed to do so. "No," she said. "It's not that."

"How can you be sure?"

"Because she's better now."

"Do people ever actually get better from that?"

"Do people ever stop talking about things they don't understand when they have no intention of ever actually learning about what they're talking about?"

Willa watched her father stumble over what he was trying to say next. The stunted vowels, the cut off syllables. The frustration showing in the wrinkles of his forehead. Before long, he'd start to yell. Instead, he said, "I'm just asking. It's just—"

There it was. Ken trying to make himself look like the concerned father. Not the judgmental, faux-rational mansplainer he was.

"It's just what," Willa said.

"I don't want you to be in denial of anything."

"Feel free to expand on that, Dad."

Ken squirmed in his seat, said, "You know what I mean."

"Nope. No idea. Please, go ahead."

"Jesus. I just don't want it to come as a shock if she... succeeds one day."

Willa said nothing.

Kept her eyes out the window. Focused on nothing. Just the blur. The world in fast-forward. Moving around her. Like Astrid had said. A while back. After she'd done what she'd done.

Ken pulled the car up to the Emergency Room entrance, said he'd go park and meet her inside.

"Cassie's meeting me here," Willa said. "She'll take me back to my car."

"And then you'll come home."

Willa didn't say anything for a moment. Figured the silence would be enough. But then she said, "Vagina," and got out of the car. She didn't look back, allowed herself a smirk at the thought of Ken's face heating up, filling with blood. That would do her just fine until the next time she and her father got into it.

She heard Cassie before she saw her.

At the desk, asking questions, talking, talking.

Being Cassie.

So Willa waited. Based that decision on the same principle that made her refuse to just walk on in through their apartment door, or not just assume she'd be invited when they'd make plans, or always pay at the diner even when Cassie said it was on her every now and again. She was a guest, not family.

But then, Doctor Barbara Loonsfoot.

Disheveled, bursting through the women's room door as if she were on that show Ken watched over and over again, and kept saying is still relevant, still funny, and still the best sitcom ever made. Willa had told Ken that every problem in every episode could've been solved with a cell phone.

"Well, they didn't have cell phones then," he'd said.

"Then how is it still relevant, Dad?"

She would never tell Ken that, yeah, it's funny. But seeing something like that in real life—from Astrid's therapist, no less—didn't give Willa much confidence in the woman's skills. No matter how many accolades she had been able to dig up on the internet. Or the way Astrid had taken to her so quickly. Or how much Cassie had been in support of all of it. None of it made Willa warm and fuzzy about Astrid's supposed uptick and outlook.

Willa couldn't wait any longer. She crossed the room full of sick-looking, hurt people. People coughing behind masks. People wrapped in gauze dotted with red. She put a hand on Cassie's shoulder. She leaned against the counter with a cocked eyebrow, and a pair of pursed lips, every expression directed at Loonsfoot.

The conversation didn't lag. While the receptionist was doing whatever receptionists at hospitals do with papers, and clipboards, and pens on chains, Loonsfoot said things like, "It was a really positive session."

And, "We worked through quite a bit today."

And, "I think she's working her way to a really good place."

And before Cassie could say anything, Willa said, "So how'd she get hit by a car?"

Cassie said, "Willa."

Loonsfoot said, "Crossing the street. Saw it from the office window. Nearly dove through the glass when it happened."

"Did you get a license plate? You can find out anything about anyone with a license plate if you know where to look." She'd heard that somewhere. Mr. Sigmund's tech class, maybe. Or Garrett trying to impress Astrid during fourth period lunch.

Cassie said, "Willa," stretched out the A. She turned, asked Loonsfoot if she could excuse them for a moment. And once Loonsfoot wandered away, Cassie said something about Loonsfoot being eccentric, almost bizarre, but she was doing what all the other therapists couldn't.

"We don't know that."

"No. You're right. But, Christ, what else are we supposed to do?"

Loonsfoot tripped over a crutch, landed in an old lady's lap, knocked a stack of magazines onto the stamped-flat carpet, kicked the crutch she'd tripped over into the air and into a man holding a paper cone of water, soaking his shirt.

On the floor, hair all in her face, Loonsfoot said, "I'm sorry, but that was a pretty fantastic chain of events. Everybody okay? Well done, everyone."

Willa watched Cassie read the look on her face. "Okay, so, eccentric was the wrong word, okay?"

"Are you sure you're okay with this?"

"I'm not sure about anything. I'm not okay with anything."

Then there was nothing.

Cassie's eyes looking back and forth between Willa's, left, right, left, right. The blue of Cassie's irises. The black of her pupils. But Willa couldn't keep her eyes where they were because there was the counter to consider. The carpet. Loonsfoot reading a magazine with a rope of hair in her mouth. The sound of casters over a plastic chair mat. The receptionist giving them Astrid's room number, saying, "She just got out of surgery. She won't be awake for a while yet."

Cassie went to work chewing on the inside of her mouth. Tick, tick, ticking her fingernails on the countertop. She cleared her throat, said, "Any good magazines around here?" She shook her head before she even finished her sentence. "Sorry, I'm not the best in stressful situations..."

The receptionist was already working on something else.

And Cassie went to work on her fingernails, making snapping sounds as the whites tore away between her teeth.

Willa went to the water cooler, filled a cone, was careful not to spill while she handed it over to Cassie.

Sitting, sipping, Cassie said, "Why do you think they have cones instead of cups? Is it more economical? Is it a statement? Like, 'We're a paper cone hospital, we disapprove of cups.'"

Willa nodded, shrugged, and listened as Cassie couldn't keep herself from talking.

4.

They tried to keep it together so they wouldn't worry one another, even though that's exactly what they were already doing. So they wouldn't make themselves think for a second that there was any sort of judgement being passed, even though they couldn't help themselves.

So they would spare themselves from letting anything get out of hand.

Like tears.

Or choked-through sentences.

Or apologies.

Or grandiose statements and promises none of them could possibly live up to, despite, right then, being absolutely certain they could.

They'd have to.

For each other.

For her.

And her.

And her too.

There were explanations, and reasons, and excuses. There were definitions of compound fractures, and spiral fractures, and ligament damage. There was the unusual nature of the injuries and their inconsistencies with traditional car accident damage—but the doctor had certainly seen stranger things. There were doctor's orders they all took one way or another to mean one thing or another.

They were in bed, and in a chair next to the bed, and leaning against the wall a few feet from the bed, and they couldn't put all the pieces together because they didn't have all the information. And if they didn't have all the information, how could they trust one another. And if they couldn't trust one another, and one of them had wanted to die, the others would wish they were dead if the one who'd tried to die had died.

They were talking.

And laughing.

They were relieved.

And scared shitless.

And none of them had anything to say to anyone else because what was left to say?

They all wanted to move past this.

To live.

But how they'd live would be dictated by circumstances not a single one of them could control.

And that left holes in their conversations.

Enough room to hear nothing but machines.

And footsteps down the tile hallway.

And the sounds of three sets of lungs pulling in air.

The quiet was good for that at least. The reassurance.

5.

Everything was happening too fast.

It was the pain meds. The post-surgery cotton stuffed between Astrid's ears. Cassie and Willa and Loonsfoot coming in and out, and in and out of the room. Snacks. Juice. Coffee. DVDs. Sharpies for the cast.

She'd felt like dancing. Hadn't felt like doing that since long before the first time she had to spend a few nights in a hospital bed. Then her arm was bent the wrong way, and she was lying in a pile of garbage.

Loonsfoot had seen the whole thing. Ran outside, was too panicked to catch the license plate.

Astrid had complicated things, calling Willa first, telling her she'd been hit by a car out front of Loonsfoot's office. Loonsfoot had said so on the way to the hospital. Told her the least complex lie was the best lie, pulling into the Emergency Room parking lot. Told her they were well beyond simplicity now. That things would get difficult. And that she'd need to make up a license plate number for the cops.

And Loonsfoot, as usual, had turned out to be correct.

Astrid couldn't keep much straight.

Willa gave her looks. Knew something was off. Had to. She always knew. And she wouldn't look at Loonsfoot. At all.

But Astrid could blame the pain meds, or the post-surgery cotton. For the time being at least.

Once it was Astrid and Cassie, just the two of them—no Willa to watch quietly and speculate about the holes in the story, no Loonsfoot feeling the need to go over everything that had happened again and again—Astrid laid back into her pillow and took a deep, slow breath.

Cassie kept her eyes on the television, said, "*Pacific Rim: Uprising* sounds a little porny, doesn't it?"

She wouldn't go home. She'd call out of work. Stay with Astrid overnight. Wouldn't mention the bills they were going to get slapped with. Wouldn't ask how the hell she'd gotten herself hit by a car dancing across the street. Wouldn't say she couldn't remember the last time she'd seen Astrid dance. Or mention that it must've been beautiful. And goofy. But mostly beautiful.

"We're in public, Mom."

"Just the two of us in a closed-off hospital room is not public, kid. And there's no way a movie called *Pacific Rim: Uprising* is not not going to get a porn parody. It's low-hanging fruit."

"And that was a double negative."

"See what I did there?"

"With the double negative or the scrotum reference?"

"You saw what I did there."

"Also, porny is not a word."

"Did I say it?"

"Yes."

"Were you picking up what I was putting down?"

"Yes."

"Then porny's a word."

"That's...that's not how it works."

Cassie went from porn parodies to Godzilla movies. From Matthew Broderick to Denzel Washington. From Saturday Night Live to *Caddyshack*. And from Bill Murray to some skeevy men's website that posts mostly photos of boobs and butts, and uses Murray as their de facto mascot—then back to porn parodies.

Despite Astrid's cotton-head, the ache inside the plaster L she'd be lugging around a while, Willa's suspicion of Loonsfoot, and Loonsfoot...being Loonsfoot, she watched Cassie talk. The way she moved her hands. The shapes her mouth made. Her nose scrunching, unscrunching. Her eyebrows dancing. How she asked if Astrid knew what she meant, or if she got it, or if something was, "Crazy, right?" only when their eyes were locked—which wasn't ever for very long.

But long enough.

Cassie talked, talked. Through the nurses coming in, checking on Astrid, asking if she was in any pain, if she needed anything, if she wanted a snack or a drink. Through Astrid's phone buzzing, buzzing with text messages from Loonsfoot, and Willa, and Garrett on the bedside table. Through the glimpses of her feet sticking up from beneath the hospital sheets again, and the itch from the hospital gown against her skin again, and the electric whine from the boxy television bolted to the wall again.

"I ever tell you the story about how you ate as a little girl?" Cassie asked.

Astrid, mouth full of Oreo, mumbled through saying, yes, she had, so please not again, dusting the sheets with black crumbs.

Cassie nodded.

Didn't ignore the yep, heard that one before.

For once.

The ache in Astrid's arm bubbled up a bit.

She wouldn't tell Cassie that she could've sat through that story again. The one where she was stuffing her face with Vienna Fingers. Crumbs everywhere. Doughy wad of sugar and cream filling tucked to the side of her mouth. Singing. "Get Ready" by the Temptations. Head rocking back and forth, she sucked back that clump of cookie. Got it lodged in her throat. Cassie had to hook the tan colored ball with her finger and pull it out. And as soon as Astrid caught her breath, she was singing again.

"You were such a happy kid," Cassie said.

Were.

It was in Astrid's head. It had to be. The electricity shooting from her elbow, up past her shoulder and into her jaw, down to the tips of her chewed-away fingernails.

Pain from a word.

Not a real thing.

Maybe for Astrid's brain, though.

That thing did what it wanted.

Cassie said she was sorry. "I didn't mean to use the past tense to make some sort of horrible statement or anything."

Astrid kept herself from wincing, showed her teeth, said, "It's okay."

They didn't talk much after that.

For a while.

Astrid counted heartbeats in her elbow.

Maybe the counting would let her to drift off to sleep.

Then, "So."

Astrid said, "Buttons."

They laughed. At another thing Astrid used to do a thousand years ago.

They laughed just long enough for Astrid to catch Cassie's cue that she was faking. Three quick drags of air at the back of her throat. Like she was choking. Or morphing into a cartoon.

Astrid brushed the crumbs off her sheet.

Wanted to jam a finger into her cast and scratch.

Eventually, Cassie said, "So how's everything going, by the way?" tapping two fingers just above her temple. "Up there?"

Astrid had to catch herself from stumbling through a sentence.

In through her nose.

Out through her mouth.

"Good."

"Just good?"

"Better than good before I got here. Sunny day. Really think I got somewhere in session."

"Doctor Loonsfoot said, yeah."

"Yeah."

"She's been helping?"

"Yeah. Far as I can tell, yeah."

Cassie said good, good, stared up at the television for a beat, two. Long enough that Astrid almost went into specifics about how Loonsfoot's sessions were helping even though she had nothing specific she could say.

Cassie said, "The dancing part before the botched vehicular manslaughter sounded like the opening to a John Hughes."

"Right?"

Astrid gave up a big smile for that one. But she couldn't tell if it was the real thing. Not for sure.

"Was it you?" Cassie said.

"What do you mean," Astrid asked, breathing in through her nose, out through her mouth.

Cassie's hand in Astrid's, she asked, "Was it you? Or the meds? Or an epis—"

"It wasn't that."

There it was. The thing Loonsfoot had warned her about. The complex lie. Having to combine an untrue thing with the butterflies.

The dancing and singing in the street. That definitely wasn't her. Hadn't been forever. It was good back then though. It was good and she had to lie about it happening now. Say she'd been hit by a car. Hope Cassie didn't really, deep down believe Astrid hadn't walked into traffic on purpose.

But maybe she'd gotten too close to the Coulomb barrier and set off the explosion accidentally on purpose. For attention. For a reason to ask for more help. For no other reason than she'd wanted to be dead.

That wasn't true.

Couldn't be.

Could be.

But couldn't.

Hand squeeze. "You're sure?"

"Absolutely."

Cassie was all pursed lips, and a crinkled forehead, and pulsing jaw muscles.

"Episodes are different," Astrid said. "I wasn't all make-outy. I'm all make-outy before things get really bad."

Loonsfoot had said that the best lies are the simplest. But sprinkling them with some truth makes them sing.

Face slack, voice flat, Cassie said, "As much as hearing that you weren't all horned up makes me downright giddy, you were dancing." A shift in tone. Brighter. Louder. "That's new. New-new. Well, old-new."

Eyes stinging, bottom lip poking out a bit, Astrid said, "Maybe that was me."

Harder hand squeeze. "I so hope so, kid."

Cassie leaned in, kissed Astrid on the forehead.

Remote in her good hand, Astrid turned toward the TV.

Silence again.

For a while.

Just the deep, electric ache shooting through Astrid's body.

Star Trek.

One of the good episodes.

Astrid listened to Cassie replace "Man" with "Woman" in Captain Kirk's opening monologue. Leaned back into her pillows. Watched the *Enterprise* zip across the starry black.

Watched Cassie watch.

Watched her mouth move, whispering the lines she'd memorized.

Watched the corners of her mouth curve into a smile with a dumb joke from Doctor McCoy.

Responded to texts from Willa. Read the ones from Garrett but couldn't quite find words good enough to type into her phone.

Read through a thread from Loonsfoot.

All caps and exclamation points. That they'd done it, they'd done it. That they can really do it, that they'll make it. A still of the wormhole in the middle of the room from one of the GoPros. According to Loonsfoot, it lost its inertial integrity. According to Astrid, it simply blew up.

Then, a list: Reinforced titanium plating. Two sets of welding gear. Precision tools. Iridium. A thermo—

Cassie grabbed Astrid's hand, told her to watch this part, that she needed to watch this part.

Kirk.

A line about exploring for the sake of it.

The *Enterprise* in the black.

That black.

Astrid used to stare up into it.

Let it confirm for her she was nothing.

Make what she wanted to do seem simple.

But now she watched Cassie watch the ending, hum the final musical flourish.

"What's it mean to you, Mom?"

Cassie turned, smiled, said, "Hope."

Astrid saved the photo of the wormhole to her phone. Made it her home screen. Zoomed in, zoomed out. Stared.

And stared.

And then.

Then she found her face in the image, her reflection in the glass. She squeezed Cassie's hand, and echoed that iconic flourish as if to say, "It's me. I'm right here."

6.

Willa outright refused to eat at McDonald's. Most of their food couldn't technically be called food. Food referred to as "food product" was, in order to obtain such a classification, made with more non-food additives than actual food. Pink paste. Sawdust. Soy biproduct. Ground-up bone. No, Willa would not eat anything from that menu.

But she dug through Astrid's purse for fifteen bucks at the counter. Only found six. Threw in the rest herself. She filled Astrid's cup with a Coke/Barq's blend. Carried the cup and the tray of food to a table. Went and grabbed handfuls of ketchup packets, plopped them beside the French fries. Then helped Astrid eat her lunch.

"I'm going to ask for more hours," Astrid said.

"Stop it."

"Seriously, I'm going to pay you back."

Eyes on eyes, Willa said, "You don't need to pay me back for anything."

"I'm serious. Every cent."

"Will you stop?"

Before she had been admitted the first time, Astrid talked, talked too. Like Cassie.

WebMD had gotten Willa to begin to question her own sanity after searching for whether or not that sort of manic conversation was a symptom of oncoming episodes. Made her start to believe that, maybe, she had more in common with Astrid than she thought she had while she was sitting next to her hospital bed and waiting for her to wake up. She'd written notes, speeches about how Astrid wasn't really alone, that most people were dealing with deep, dark pits of thoughts and feelings, and everyone, always, had a place, had value.

But that was all bullshit, feel-good nonsense that only people who don't suffer from assorted forms of mental illness ever believed.

Willa, watching Astrid shovel a handful of fries into her mouth, had nothing to say. No encouraging words. No lines of poetry about how humans are all sunflowers—tall, beautiful, things people paint pictures of, and photograph, and keep in their gardens. Nothing inspiring to put in a letter, or a text message. Nothing to say, if there was even anything to say anymore anyway.

So, she answered texts from Garrett. Another one asking how Astrid was. If there was anything he could do. If she was upset with him for any reason. If sending flowers to her apartment would be appropriate. If Willa was with her right then.

Willa deleted "Idiot," and "Leave me alone," and "Just wait for her to text you," and typed, "She'll be home later today." She sent the text on its way and maybe cracked her screen, whopping her phone facedown onto the table.

Orders were tapped into registers. People were asking for extra special sauce, and more salt on their fries, and no onions on their Quarter Pounders. Willa's legs shook up, down, up, down, up, down.

Then she took a deep breath, said, "Astrid, there's something—"

The face from across the table had heard everything Willa was about to say before. Questions from Cassie. From the doctors. Even from Loonsfoot.

It was a tired face.

Bored.

Sick to death of all of it.

Willa reached across the table, wiped a glob of ketchup from Astrid's cheek with her thumb. "One fry at a time is fine."

"I'd be a hot mess without you, wouldn't I?" Astrid chomped into her burger while texting, the phone pinched between the bar of plaster across her palm and her fingers.

"Who's that?" Willa said.

Astrid spat, "Garrett," as if she'd been waiting to be asked who she was texting.

"Tell him hello for me."

"That'd be weird."

"Yeah, it would. Never mind."

Willa hadn't cracked her screen—she would've had to deal with it until she was due for an upgrade in a year or two if she had.

Garrett didn't waste time—probably alone in his filthy bedroom, crusty socks all over the place, in nothing but three-day-old boxers. He responded in seconds. A second. Astrid hadn't texted him, no. Not since yesterday. Had she said something? Should he text her?

Mouth full of sawdust, soy biproduct, and some beef, Astrid said, "Who's that?"

"My dad."

"And how is Ken?"

"You know Ken."

"Kind of dumb, pretty racist, scared of gays, balding, and getting soggy around the midsection." Their voices were almost harmonized, working their way through a chorus Willa had been belching out since the start of high school.

They laughed. Loud. Hard. Enough to get most people in the restaurant that Willa couldn't bring herself to call a restaurant to stare at them.

Willa stood, said, "Are you not entertained?"

Astrid said Willa's name, covered some of her face with her good hand. And Willa waited. Waited. Posed, arms spread wide, standing in front of a dozen strangers, Willa waited for Astrid. Because if Astrid did what she used to do—before everything—then everything else was fine. Would have to be. There'd be evidence. Clear cut. She was fine.

Astrid climbed up onto the table, which almost made Willa hold her hands out just in case, just in case. "Soylent Green is people," Astrid said, her voice loud, shrill, peppered with horror movie gurgles.

They laughed through the manager stopping at their table, telling them to keep it down or take it outside.

Laughed through the rest of Astrid's lunch.

Laughed on the way out the door. Down the steps into the parking lot. Across the lot to Willa's car. In Willa's car.

Then Astrid was texting again.

Texting not Garrett.

Texting, texting.

"Mom. Seeing how work is," Astrid said.

"Tell her hello for me."

"She says hi."

Key, ignition. Shifting from park to drive. Pulling through the parking lot and into the lane that formed a perpetual loop around the shopping center. Willa would not text Cassie. Would not ask Astrid if she was really, actually texting her mother.. Because Astrid was fine. She'd been in an accident. What had happened before was a one-time thing. It was being taken care of. Willa and Cassie and Astrid were a team. With Loonsfoot on the B-squad. Willa would not text while driving. She would follow the rules of the road. She would use her signals to give other drivers plenty of notice of her upcoming turns.

"Keep going straight, Will, I have an appointment," Astrid said.

"Cassie didn't tell me you had an appointment."

"She must've forgotten. You know what her schedule can do to her. Sorry."

"So, Doctor Leary's office then?"

"Doctor Loonsfoot's."

"Right."

"Left, actually. On Haws."

"Yeah, no, I know. I was just—"

Astrid was all teeth. She winked. First the left eye, then the right.

Willa outright refused to allow herself to begin questioning every shift in Astrid's schedule. Astrid had proven she did not need to be under constant surveillance. She was trustworthy, and concerned for her own wellbeing as much, if not more so, as Willa and Cassie were. She had an appointment, and Willa would get her there on time. That was how Willa would help her friend.

Willa asked about Garrett. And UPenn. And whether or not she would be gracing Garrett with her presence at the prom. And once she pulled up in front of Loonsfoot's home office, she gave Astrid a hug, a kiss on the cheek. Then watched her walk up the glittering sidewalk path, up the steps. Waved when Astrid waved and was ushered inside by Loonsfoot.

She would not text Cassie about the change in schedule, Cassie was busy. Always busy.

She would trust Astrid because Astrid deserved it.

She would drive home, do her homework, read a book, maybe watch television in the family room if she felt up to it.

She would not take a photo of Loonsfoot's license plate.

But Willa didn't listen to a single thing she told herself she would or wouldn't do.

The Paradise Syndrome

7.

Everyone was so nice.

Mostly because they didn't know.

Not about the ambulance. The stomach pump. The hospital stay. The stint in in-patient care.

If they'd known, Astrid wouldn't have been Astrid anymore. She would have become Astrid with an asterisk. The one that almost died. The crazy one. The suicide risk. The manic depressive. It wouldn't have been their fault. They'd never lived lives quite like Astrid's.

Still, they couldn't know.

But they couldn't keep it from administration. If they had, no graduation. No UPenn. No scholarship. No future. Not the future Cassie and Willa, and Astrid too, were pulling for anyway.

Astrid had completed every missed assignment, assessment, and project. It was part of the deal, and she had done better than anyone else could have. Finished every single thing. No muss, fuss, nothing. She'd been sick.

Sick-sick.

Ill.

So, now, at school, not a single student was given the chance to have thoughts go crawling through their minds that Astrid had given up on her cocktail of meds and, maybe, thrown herself in front of that car. The car that didn't exist. The car that forced its way out of Astrid's mouth because her arm had been on backward and the truth would have sounded second-extended-hospital-stint strange.

Instead, most of her classmates had brought their own Sharpies.

"How are you feeling? That must have been so scary," Gemma from the crew team said, her eyebrows up and arched. She signed in lime green.

"We were so worried about you," Lyla from student council said after hugging Astrid a little too hard for Astrid's surgically repaired arm. She signed in orange.

"Think of how many more signatures you could've fit on this thing if your leg had been broken," Ken from the Honors Society said, smiling, making Astrid laugh. He signed in pink.

Hayley from AV signed in blue. Brian from Adventure News, the school's morning news report, signed in purple. Even Mr. Hogan, Astrid's AP English teacher, signed her cast in red—which he'd tended to use all over most of her classmates' papers.

But then there was Garrett.

Garrett signed in black.

The most visible non-color on the cast.

It glowed through the rainbow of Jenny, and Mitch, and Jordan, and Tamara, and Izzy, and Ron, and Yan, and Dannie.

Garrett Frank.

His hair was always a mess. In a good way. Windblown, curly, everywhere. Astrid had to stop herself from running her hands through it. But not because she was make-outy.

No.

She wasn't that.

Couldn't be that.

But because, look at it. When he smiled, asked her if he could sign, he was teeth, and hazel eyes, and more black dots of stubble than any of the other boys in the graduating class.

And Astrid couldn't say much more than she was sorry she hadn't texted him as much as she would have liked. She had definitely meant to.

"You don't need to apologize," Garrett said. "Sorry for texting so much."

"You don't need to apologize either."

If they'd left together right then, Astrid would kiss him on the way to his car. Would pull him into her. Wouldn't bother flinching with the pressure on her cast tucked between them because everything would be his eyelids blurred into one cyclopean rim of beautiful eyelashes beyond the tip of her nose, his hair smelling like a full day of not caring what it looked like, his mouth tasting like his cucumber-mint chapstick.

But maybe that would be the start of something.

Something bad.

And maybe she'd really do it this time.

The one time.

The last time.

She'd never see Regis-132. Never get to ask why the hell Loonsfoot had given it such a stupid name. She'd never get to come back, bring Cassie and Willa to her new home. All because she'd ignored the signals.

"So," Garrett said.

"So."

"You going to the Green on Friday night?"

"I'd heard it was happening. Haven't been formally invited yet though."

She'd been invited to the Green. Invited to sit on, around, all over the eighteenth hole at the Flourtown Country Club—which just so happened to butt up against Kelly Straub's parents' backyard. She was never invited by Kelly though. Never her. And Astrid had never gone even when she had been tangentially invited. It wasn't because of Cassie. Or some fear of getting caught by groundskeepers. Or maybe needing to run drunk across the perfect grass to Haws Road, having to hide behind strips of bushes until the cops took whoever they were able to nab back to the station.

It was the electric fingers when the beer mixed with the Lamictal. The tug in her belly when the liquor soaked in, sent her scrambling for a toilet. That sense she'd gotten every now and then—driving late, in the dark-dark, knowing that one day someone would drive the same road, and Astrid would have never existed to them.

To anyone.

She'd be nothing but rubber atoms buried beneath layer after layer after layer of new road, and those atoms wouldn't even be her's. Only an extension of her. As meaningless and memorable as a drive to work.

Alcohol did make her funny though. So she'd heard. All that talk about being useless, purposeless, nothing. Apparently it was hilarious. Dark, but hilarious.

Garrett ran his hand through his hair for the hundredth time. "Would you want to go to the Green? With me? Formally?"

He'd slathered cucumber mint on his lips. Astrid could smell it. Almost leaned forward a little for a sniff.

"Yeah," Astrid said. "Yes. That'd be nice."

She squeezed her fist around the plaster in her palm while Garrett said all sorts of things. Words that would be italicized if someone were to write an accurate transcript. Odd, capitalized bits of words. Exclamation points. Lots of them. But his words were nothing but sounds in the ache. Up, down Astrid's arm. From the tensed forearm muscles into her neck, her jaw. Spreading into her ribs, her guts.

She should've told him she was busy. She should cancel. But he was already gone. And the ache faded. Burned off. Cooled.

And it was just Astrid in the hall again. Alone. In front of the plate glass front wall of the administration offices. Hairline shiny with sweat from the pain. Gut fluttering from the butterflies again.

No, nothing she'd agreed to would lead to anything but more butterflies.

It would take some occasional bouts of convincing herself she was fine, she was totally fine, sure.

But she had a job to do, so—at least for now—she would revel a bit beneath the distraction of what needed doing.

So she waited.

Waited.

Watched Mrs. Mullen wind her way around desks, push through the swinging waist-high door in the counter dividing the room in two, then pull open the glass door to the hall. Astrid said hello and waved just before Mrs. Mullen turned down the hall and headed toward the women's room.

Then Astrid moved. Took the same course Mullen did. Through the slowly closing glass door. Past Principal Asher's empty office. Past the receptionists. She smiled, said she had an appointment. They called her hun, told her she could go on back and wait. And in Mullen's office, behind her desk, Astrid used the office phone and dialed the number Loonsfoot had texted her.

She cleared her throat when a woman picked up, said, "Hello, this is Mary Mullen from Wyndmoor Academy Preparatory School's guidance office. I'm calling to schedule a formal visit to the astrophysics labs for one of my students."

Astrid pinched the phone between her ear and shoulder. Reached her good hand into her purse. Pulled her new ID. The one with her hair tucked underneath a short blonde wig, a pair of stylish glasses hanging from the bridge of her noise, eye-penciled freckles dotting her cheekbones. "Josephine Whittaker."

She pretended to write, said, "Mmhmm."

And, "Okay."

And, "She's looking forward to it too."

She hung up. Needed to sit a minute to catch her breath. She hadn't been that winded since opening night of *Arsenic and Old Lace* her freshman year. But once the butterflies, and the urge to throw her arms up and whoop cleared, she left everything the way she found it. Traced her footsteps through the office. But, before heading back out into the hall, she handed a note over to Miss Ginny.

"Everything okay?"

"Yep. Just a full day consultation I've been putting off."

"You're doing so well. We're all so happy to see you back and healthy. Take care of yourself. I'll make sure Mr. Asher gets this."

Astrid did what she was supposed to do when people thought they'd said a nice thing.

She showed her teeth, said, "Thank you, I really appreciate you saying that."

Astrid barely heard Miss Ginny's next question. But she had an answer for it regardless.

"Nope," she said. "Mixed up my days. My appointment with Mrs. Mullen is tomorrow, not today."

The ache in her arm was deep, pulsing. She'd overdone it, stressing the muscles beneath her cast after Garrett had gone.

Or maybe she hadn't.

Maybe she was making it up.

She was already making plenty of things up.

Out front, Willa was where she said she would be, leaning against one of the pillars holding up the overhang running over the sidewalk where kids would wait for their buses or their rides home. She was hazy, ethereal-looking in a cloud of exhaust from a passing school bus. But she was waving, smiling, pushing herself away from the pillar as if she hadn't been bored of waiting for Astrid. Which never happened. Willa was a lot of things, but she would never usually present herself as bright and upbeat.

"What?" Astrid said.

"What, what? I'm happy to see you?"

Astrid could almost see the question mark worm its way out of Willa's mouth, like she should never be asked about the intent of her words. That was more Willa. Not the toothy, cheery, higher octave-voiced version she'd been since the accident.

Willa walked to Astrid, looped her arm through the corner of her cast. Watermelon and island hibiscus in her hair. The slow in and out of her ribs against the cast. The faintest whine of her deviated septum at the end of each breath.

And, for a minute, there was nothing but the two of them. Like they were in Loonsfoot's photo. In the violet grass tipped with glowing bulbs. The living tower way off in the distance. The fast-forward sky.

"This is weird," Astrid said.

"A little, yeah. Whatever, I still love you. Shut up about it."

"Yeah, me too. Weirdo."

They walked to Willa's car without saying much.

Astrid started, stopped, started, stopped sentences with cut-off monosyllables, to which Willa, every time, said, "What?"

Using Willa's words, Astrid said, "What, what?"

Then, nothing.

Just the ache. Real, not real, didn't matter.

To be sure, though, Astrid made it real. Squeezed her fist until her teeth were hot.

Willa said, "What?"

And Astrid said, "What, what?"

8.

Chris showed up at the diner as soon as he'd gotten out of work. That time of day, the number of early-birders low, Cassie took him to the manager's office. They were quick, and quiet, and, after, Cassie said, "I should give you a pager."

It was the only way whatever it was Chris and Cassie were could work with her schedule, with Astrid. The parking lot out back before the late-nighters stumbled in. The women's room if Dante had come back from Gainesville to check on things by holing himself up in the office, leafing through bills, searching for things to bitch about. Once on table four in the dark after a rat scare when they'd had to close overnight before the exterminator showed up in the morning. They'd had coffee in the stillness and quiet after, watched the cars on 309 stream by in white and red ribbons of light.

Working the way she did, time moved differently for Cassie. Normal people knew what day it was, how much longer they had to wait for this or that. They had the luxury of long, boring days. Cassie couldn't place the name of a day to the last time she'd done laundry, had to smell-check her pits when there was a possibility of she and Chris meeting up. Couldn't say if she was thirty-three or thirty-four for sure. If she was hot in the car, it was summer; shivering, winter. And it was all flitting by. Like her father said it would, Cassie on his lap, showing her how to use a Mickey Mouse flipbook. The faster he flipped, the faster Mickey's little story would end. She'd never believed him when he'd told her the same principle could apply to real life. Didn't want to have to believe him even now.

"Cass?" Chris said, like he'd been repeating himself.

"A pager would be too obvious, wouldn't it."

The way his forehead wrinkled when he cocked his eyebrow made Cassie stuff her hands into her pockets, her workpants still unzipped, unbuttoned. She would have run a finger over the scrunched skin, his eyebrows, his cheekbones otherwise. Then everything would've started over, and she'd miss out on some tables. But, if she got her tables, she'd have to watch other, less interesting sets of eyebrows wrinkle less beautiful foreheads.

Chris said her name again.

She couldn't avoid this anymore. Wouldn't.

She tucked in her shirt, closed her pants, tied her apron back on. She said, "Look," and "Listen," and "It's like this," but stopped herself before saying anything real. Every way she was going to begin was all daytime television, and bad romcoms, and *Friends*. And no one wanted to come off like *Friends*. "I maybe don't need to work as much as I do," she said, standing over him, hands on her hips. "I did. Before. Still need to work a lot now, too. Just not this much. I think about that a lot."

That forehead again. Eyes looking up into Cassie's. Voice soft, smooth, saying, "I'm not sure what you mean."

"Can we switch places? I feel like I'm lecturing you."

Chris stood, motioned for Cassie to sit. Went to the door, leaned his back against it. He folded his fingers together, hung his arms slack, his hands together at his crotch, like Cassie used to see people do in church, fake praying.

"This isn't ending, by the way," Cassie said pointing back

and forth between them."That's not a thing that's going to happen, okay?"

A smile incapable of hiding behind lips. Eyes searching the orange tiles on the floor.

"That's not to say that it's a permanent—never mind. Okay, I'm pretty much afraid all the time."

"Of me?"

"God, no." Palm to forehead. "That's not to say you're not mysterious or—never mind. Astrid is. She's—she's not like you and me. She's different. Not in a bad way. Okay, in some, one or two, not-so-great ways, but nothing indicative of heinous character flaws or anything like that. She's special. And I'm scared for her. And I need you to know some stuff if we're going to be more than diner sex. But it's probably going to be mostly diner sex because I'm pretty sure I'm a coward. I think."

Chris said, "I don't think you're a coward," like people do on television. It didn't make Cassie roll her eyes or grind her teeth. It made her laugh a bit—but in a good way.

"I am, though," she said, after diner sounds seeped their way under the office door. "I definitely am."

She talked fast. Faster than usual. Stumbled over her words. Kept herself in check by staring at a trampled-over piece of gum that had been flattened black over the last ten or so years. It might have been hers. No way to tell. Ten years. A million footsteps, crushing whatever was left of the person it came from onto shoes, tiles, the carpeted floor in the dining room. It couldn't even be considered gum anymore, but it was everywhere, and it carried little bits of the chewer around with it. Until, maybe, that person was smeared all over this place with nothing to show for it but an atom-thin stain that wasn't coming up unless the tiles were ripped from the cement.

Chris was Chris during all of it. If words about what the hell he was still even doing there were floating behind his eyes, he didn't show it. He nodded. Put his hands in his pockets during the sad bits. Crossed his arms over his chest when he asked questions. Never once did he try to offer some kind of canned advice that would have forced Cassie to pull out her eyeballs and roll them across the floor to adequately show her distain for his words.

"I guess the thing I'm aiming toward here is, I have no idea what I'm doing. Astrid's seeing a new therapist and that seems to be working out pretty well for her. The accident was scary, but she's good, she's okay. So, everything's good. Like, really good. But that feels bad."

"How or why does or should that feel bad?"

"Ever hear the stats concept of regression toward the mean?"

"I almost flunked stats junior year."

"So, it's basically like, everybody's got a baseline. Everybody's is different too. Life at that baseline is fine. But it never stays there. It'll rise into the good or great section of the line graph, but it can never stay up there, and, typically, it'll take a dive below the baseline to make up for the difference to even things out in order to get back to baseline again. Eventually. My baseline's been low for most of my life. Astrid's has been even lower. But it seems like we're on an uptick. Or maybe I just think it's an uptick because I don't ask any questions because I don't know what questions will do more damage than good."

Chris squatted in front of Cassie's chair, leveled his eyes with hers. "Cassie, you've got a great kid. A great kid with some issues. But the whole part about having a great kid means to me you're doing everything you're capable of doing, and what you're capable of doing is nothing but good."

Cassie pulled her eyes from his. Went to the little blonde hairs on his hands. His bitten fingernails. His soft, white palms. "You're a good guy."

"And I'll keep trying to prove that to you as long as you'll let me."

"That was a bit much."

"I thought so too."

They laughed. Kissed.

But when Chris pulled away, his eyes were looking past Cassie. Something behind her.

She turned, watched Astrid and Willa staring at their phones, standing at the front counter in grainy black and white.

Cassie and Chris hissed curses, stifled nervous laughter with their hands, gestured to one another to check if they were put together properly enough to go back out into a world that disapproves of sexual intercourse in food service establishments.

"Stay here," Cassie said.

"What, until they finish their food? I tutor nights."

"Just—shh." She reached for the door handle. Turned back to Chris. "You know, you're pretty hot when you're stressed."

"Will you just go, please?"

Cassie opened the door, squeezed herself through the smallest sliver of space she could manage, and shouted, "Hi," as she slammed the door back into place.

Astrid and Willa in their school uniforms, smiling. Cassie had hated wearing those things every day. Bitched about it, wrote op-eds in Adventure News about it. But, Astrid in the plaid skirt, white golf shirt, Willa in the shirt, a pair of khakis, Cassie could see the parental appeal. They looked like children. Difficult as kids could be, there wasn't much left of that.

Cassie pulled her phone from her back pocket, held it up to them. Astrid said "Mom" with five or six more Os than the word required, Willa held a hand up. It was a bad photo. And Cassie would most definitely get it printed and framed. "Table for two, mademoiselles?"

Astrid asked for the finest table in the place. Her French accent was getting better but was still awful.

"Lead zee way, I inzeest" Cassie said. And, with Astrid

and Willa heading into the dining room, she looked over her shoulder to the camera hanging over the entrance and nodded.

Astrid said something in a tone Cassie hadn't heard too often. Higher than her usual pitch, the words were spat rapid fire. Something about her cast. All the people who'd signed it. But by the time Cassie had registered that Astrid had turned back around to show her what she was talking about, she had taken too long to break herself away from trying to remember the last time she'd heard that level of excitement in her daughter's voice—just before it happened, maybe when she was little? Astrid was already looking over Cassie's shoulder at Chris sneaking out of the half-open office door.

"Mr. Hogan?" Astrid said.

"Uh, hi, Astrid," Chris said. "Cassie?"

But Cassie couldn't speak. Was focusing on Astrid's eyes. Her mouth. The color in her face. For something. Anything. Fluttering eyelids. Crinkled nose. Shaky chin. Any indicator that could help her figure out how she needed to respond.

She could have told Chris he was banned from the diner, insist he tell her who the hell he thought he was going into the manager's office like that.

She could have told the truth. Like she'd been meaning to but hadn't just yet because how could she ever naturally bring that up in conversation. She couldn't, so she didn't.

She could have just continued to stand there staring at her daughter's face, completely ignoring every word that was being said to her.

But then, Astrid smiled. A real one. The kind without teeth that was more contentment than joy. The one she used to have on her face all the time when she was younger, sitting in the patch of sun that filtered into the apartment on a Saturday afternoon. "I'm happy for you, Mom."

Astrid hugged her then. Kissed her cheek. Walked back to the table, to Willa. Sat down with that smile still on her face.

"I'm happy so many people signed your cast," Cassie called over to the table.

"Me too," Astrid said. "Now delete that awful photo you took, please."

Cassie went through the motions of deleting the picture but didn't delete anything. She absolutely never would. How could she? It was the precursor to a good moment. A really good one. Chris waved, said he'd call later, and made his way out the front door. The diner was bright, warm. The adult contemporary playing softly throughout the place wasn't awful. The entire time Cassie ran tables around Astrid and Willa, she couldn't help but watch her daughter speak, laugh, whisper, eat, drink her coffee. And whenever Astrid would notice her, Cassie's eyes went to the window. Watched the blue sky outside, hoping for someone else's baseline to come crashing down. Not Astrid's. Not her own. And if a metorite's orbit just so happened to be collapsing up there beyond that blue, hopefully it would smash someone else's world to pebbles.

9.

Willa couldn't have outright refused to go to the second largest mall in the country when Astrid asked if she'd help her pick out a new outfit for the Green. Even if the place was more or less a massive hub for human traffickers—it was on the news, verifiable. Even if it had been forever since they'd done something as ordinary as going to the mall. Like, since they'd needed to be dropped off out front of the TGI Friday's that was now a Bone Fish Grill and told to meet there at nine sharp. Back when they'd shopped pretty much exclusively at Justice, Claire's, and Aéropostale.

But, walking from this store, that store, next to Astrid talking fast—fast, fast—about school, and next year, post-college, and about how excited she was for Cassie and Mr. Hogan, Willa needed to keep herself from grabbing her friend by the shoulders, shaking her, and telling her to cut the shit. Instead, needing to ask vaguely probing questions about how she was really feeling—like, really feeling—and having to live with answers like, "I feel great, Will," and "I think I've really turned a corner," and "Why would I lie to you?" made Willa make nasty comments about the pace other people kept while walking the mall. And it wasn't just Astrid's tone of voice, or the speed at which she spat out random thoughts and factoids. All signs, by the way, that pointed directly to a person who suffers like Astrid not being okay—Willa wasn't a psychologist, but she'd done the research. It was more that she was being told sorry, to hold on a second, as Astrid responded to text messages and .gifs from all the lovely people at school. It was Willa texting Gemma, and Lyla, and Garrett to see if they were really texting Astrid and getting a "Nope," a "No why?" and a "Yep." And it was tapping out a lengthy message to Cassie while waiting outside the dressing room, deleting it, typing it again, and deleting it again, while having to constantly tell herself that, no, it would not be okay if she were to rifle through Astrid's purse for her phone to see who she was actually talking to.

No, Willa wouldn't do that. She would drop Astrid off at her apartment, go home, drink Ken's fancy Scotch from the blue bottle, and fall asleep after screaming into her pillow for a while. That was exactly what she would do. Because despite the initial, gleeful rush spending time with Astrid the way they used to spend time together gave her, Willa couldn't assign a positive label to her friend's behavior as much as she couldn't have ditched the trip to the mall. And when Astrid kicked open the dressing room door, strutted out in a sundress and a pair of fake Doc Martens, and said, "Do I look beautiful or what?" Willa did what Astrid was doing.

She faked it.

She smiled, said, "Yes, of course, darling," replaced the R with an H.

"Liar. I think the yellow washes me out."

"I'm just impressed you got into that thing so quickly with your cement arm."

"I guess I'm just used to getting used to things."

Willa was such an asshole.

She almost said it out loud.

Instead, when Astrid was back in her jeans and t-shirt, Willa hooked her arm into the L of Astrid's cast, and kept it there during checkout, the pattern they took around the clothing racks on the way out of the store, back out into the mall.

She kept the conversation light. Said, "Excuse us," when they maneuvered around meandering shoppers. Told Astrid she would look nice in that one, and that one, and that one whenever they stopped for split seconds to check out window displays. Didn't put up a fight when Astrid offered to pay for Tony Luke's in the food court. Laughed, deep and real, watching Astrid cross her eyes, chomp into her soggy, Cheez Whiz-soaked cheesesteak. Took photos of her with caked yellow lips, a mouth stuffed with bread and chipped meat. Sent the photos to Cassie.

And, once all the food wrappers were crumpled and stuffed into the bag, once the straws in their paper cups were pulling up nothing but air and little shards of ice, Willa laid her arm across the table, opened her palm.

Astrid put her good hand in Willa's.

They weaved their fingers together the best they could and laughed a little.

Willa said, "I'm sorry"

"For what?" Astrid's response was quick, easy. Like she was about to hear Willa apologize for spitting out stats of how many children are picked off and sold from the King of Prussia Mall every year, or facts about what happens to the cows before they're turned into cheesesteaks, or an estimated amount of fecal matter smeared onto the tables per square inch based on a ballparked number of how many people used the food court restrooms per hour compared to the national average percentage of people who don't wash their hands after pooping.

"That you've had to get used to so many things," Willa said.

Silence, a long hand squeeze. "Thanks."

"Are...do you get lonely?"

"Sometimes. Not recently."

"How come?"

"Because I'm not the only person who's ever thought my thoughts."

"Like, statistically speaking?"

"No. Like, literally." Another squeeze. "I'm not alone. And that helps."

There was nothing for a bit. Just people around them chewing or talking too loudly. Other people laughing, enjoying themselves. It was more than likely not a moment Willa would keep in her mind long after that afternoon, but, Astrid's hand in hers, sitting in a warm patch from the skylights that were keeping the air-conditioned chill off Willa's bare arms, it was certainly a good one.

"Ready?" Astrid said. "One more thing to pick up."

Of course she'd parked on the exact opposite side of the mall from where their last stop was, but Willa wouldn't mock a lady for keeping her kid on a coiled, plastic leash. Wouldn't comment on all the boys their age walking about in public wearing sweat suits looking as if they'd splashed bleach all over themselves before leaving their houses. Wouldn't spit out a single, critical thing about anyone or anything. She was lost listening to Astrid. Watching people flow through the space. Noting how amazing it was, despite all of the horrible things that had happened and could maybe happen, that people could walk, and talk, and be in a smelly place filled with breath, and skin, and sweat. There was something beautiful about that.

But then, in Macy's, when the cashier called Astrid Miss Welch instead of Miss Walsh, handed back a shiny, fresh credit card, and a lovely pantsuit over the counter, Willa bit into a fingernail until it pulled deep enough that she could taste metal.

"What's the suit for?"

"Interview at UPenn on Wednesday."

"I thought you got in already."

"It's for a scholarship. Ready?"

Back through the mall, on the way to car, there was nothing but chewing slivers of nail to dust and listening to Astrid go on and on about things that didn't matter. Nothing mattered anymore. And sending a text to Cassie wasn't the only thing Willa would do. She would have to do much more than that because something was definitely, very wrong, and she couldn't prove it without mounds of evidence.

10.

There wasn't much stopping Astrid from getting where she needed to go.

The blonde wig.

The glasses.

The new name.

All of it pulled Astrid out of her body, stuffed Josephine Whittaker in.

Serious.

Confident.

Unwilling to give much more than a toothless smirk, a cocked eyebrow.

Standing outside of herself, next to Josephine, watching her check in for her tour of the astrophysics labs.

"Yes, I'm here for my tour," Astrid said in a tone of voice she assumed a person like Josephine would use.

Said, "I'll be able to use the equipment, yes? The other universities I've visited allowed me full access."

Said, "I'd like very much to attend UPenn in the fall, yes. I hope it will suit my needs."

Josephine Whittaker was a very accomplished student. GPA near a 5.0 considering all of her Advanced Placement courses. A rower, a volunteer, a Student Ambassador to Australia, Tahiti, New Zealand, and Fiji. An intern and lab assistant at the Hayden Planetarium for the past two summers. Courted by every major university with notable astrophysics departments—Berkeley, Harvard, MIT to name a few.

But Philadelphia was home.

And if she could find a school that was suited well enough to meet all of her needs in order to stay, she'd stay

Loonsfoot had put all of that material together. Got her hands on letterhead and certificates. Created Josephine's online presence. But the ridiculous, all-day photo shoot she'd put Astrid through made it all real.

There was Josephine teaching a class of Tahitian students.

There was Josephine in a lab coat giving a presentation on quantum physics and theoretical wormhole dynamics.

There was Josephine with Neil deGrasse Tyson.

That one was a bit much.

But associate professor Jim Maguire, Josephine's tour guide, was stuttering through his greeting, shaking hands with Astrid and Loonsfoot, saying how nice it was to meet them, and he hoped he would do the department justice, and of course she would be able to get her hands dirty in the lab—so to speak.

Astrid had seen herself do things like this before.

Become someone else.

Because herself wasn't good enough.

She had to be the first student in class with her hand up, waving, while nearly spitting out answers to questions.

Needed to be the one giving an acceptance speech for being elected class president.

Had to offer advice to her classmates as debate club chairperson despite herself.

But Josephine made all those Astrids look like kindergarteners. It made her heart beat at three times its normal rate.

Made her pits damp.

Made her want to trade places with this person.

Forever.

Sit Astrid in the back corner of her brain, give her all the fond memories she would need, and leave her there. It'd be better that way.

"What can you tell us about your research into quantum tunneling?" Loonsfoot said, her voice low, calm, slow. Her wig was straight, brown with blonde highlights. She'd ditched her glasses for a pair of brown contacts. Wore a tan pantsuit. Called herself Doctor Whittaker.

"Well, obviously we're not CERN," Maguire said. "So, most of our research is in simulating theoretical models as opposed to conducting those experiments in real-world settings."

Loonsfoot turned to Astrid, said, "Hmm."

"Hmm," Astrid said, lips pursed, arms folded across her chest. "So practical experimentation is essentially a non-starter here then."

"That—that's not exactly true," Maguire said. He ushered them into a lab filled with electron microscopes, white boards turned gray with erasures, devices of shapes and sizes that suggested maybe Astrid had overstepped. "Theoretical astrophysics and quantum dynamics is certainly something we have been focusing on more recently in an attempt to muster up some new funding sources, but, for what it's worth, we were the ones who discovered the Earth-like Exoplanet that was featured on ABC and CBS a few months back. That was big find."

Astrid almost called it Regis-132, but said, "Mmm. HATS-44b."

Maguire snapped his fingers, said, "That's the one."

"Interesting."

"You know your stuff."

Loonsfoot cut in, sounded put off. "Of course she does."

"I didn't mean to—"

"Of course you didn't," Astrid said, exchanging a stern look with Loonsfoot.

"Um, right this way." Maguire turned, walked toward the

steel doors at the far end of the lab.

Loonsfoot was smiling big, wide, her eyes were full orbs of excitement, her thumbs were up. She mouthed something like, "Brilliant," or "Fantastic," or "Amazing."

Astrid returned Loonsfoot's gestures, let the butterflies flutter around inside her belly.

There were so many of them these days.

But she couldn't let herself get used to them.

Wouldn't.

Astrid watched Josephine and Doctor Whittaker follow Maguire.

Listened as they all discussed the merits of M-Theory, the multiverse, the possibility that Earth is just one of an infinite number of possible Earths, most of the rest of which would never have been able to form properly according to even the slightest alteration to that universe. In the next lab, Maguire talked about his research, some of his publications. Talked about how he is currently writing a paper that could totally revamp M-Theory based on his most recent computer models.

"What do you think, Josephine? Do you think there's another you out there somewhere?"

Astrid cleared her throat, said, "M-Theory is bunk, professor. You've all been moving the bar for decades. First you said you'd have some definitive theories in the 80s. Then the mid-90s. Then the early 2000s. But all you're really able to tell us is that there could be something out there beyond our universe...but what? I focus more on getting to places we can actually see."

"Well stated, Josephine," Loonsfoot said.

"I know."

Then, nothing.

Just a stark white room.

Maguire's heavy breathing.

The beads of sweat on his upper lip.

The butterflies in Astrid's gut.

"So," he said. "What happened to your arm there?"

"An unfortunate accident in attempting to breach the Coulomb barrier in a quantum tunneling experiment," Astrid said. "At Harvard."

Loonsfoot had needed to cut the sleeve of Astrid's new suitcoat to make room for her cast. It had made Astrid's stomach twist considering how much she'd put on her credit card for it. Not that it mattered.

Maguire swallowed.

Hard.

"Sorry to hear that. So, this lab is the rare and experimental metal—"

"Professor Maguire, may I have a word? Privately," Loonsfoot said.

"Of course. Josephine, please feel free to take a look around."

Once Loonsfoot and Maguire were gone, once the lab doors had swung themselves shut, Astrid let Astrid take over.

The butterflies were different.

Heavier.

More frantic.

Like they were trying to burst out of her stomach and escape.

The photo saved on Astrid's phone showed her what she was looking for. A gleaming silver clump of metal that looked to be a cross between crumpled aluminum foil and T-1000 after Arnold had blown a hole in his face in *Terminator 2*.

With her finger, Astrid ran along the side of a steel case labeled Noble and Precious Metals.

She passed Palladium.

Osmium.

Platinum.

Rhodium.

Rhenium.

Silver.

Nearly passed by the Iridium.

There was a slot for a key.

She pulled anyway. Got nothing but a click, click, click for each of the three tugs she gave the little metal hatch.

She kept her eyes on the lab doors, went into her coat pocket.

Loonsfoot had taught her how to use it. Made Astrid practice using the lock pick on the new front door at the lab—a title Loonsfoot insisted they began calling the rental property. Willa had called twice in the time it took for Astrid to unlock the new door. Left two voicemails, a string of texts. Astrid had forgotten to call her back. But at least she'd been at the diner when Cassie, out of nowhere, sat at her table, asked how she was doing—Willa had to have texted Cassie about the lack of responses. Astrid had needed to flex, and push, and pull at her casted arm to stop herself from being furious that Willa had been checking up on her.

Astrid got the pick to turn the lock holding the metal door in place without much effort.

She pocketed every wad of Iridium from the locker.

Closed it.

Locked it.

And the moment she tucked the lock pick away, Loonsfoot exploded back into the lab. "I've never been so insulted in my life," she said. "I won't waste another second in this two-bit, second-rate, trumped-up state school, much less a single red cent. My daughter could teach circles around you, you clown."

Loonsfoot mouthed, "Got it?"

Astrid nodded, said, "I knew it the moment we walked in here. What sort of self-respecting Ivy League University doesn't focus on proper experimentation and research?"

Arm in good arm, Astrid and Loonsfoot strode back through the labs, their chins up, their heels clicking-clacking.

Behind them, Maguire said please, and asked what he had done, and said he was so sorry for anything untoward he may have inadvertently said.

They didn't bother to say anything else through the hallway toward the lobby.

They ignored the woman at the front desk.

Threw the glass front doors open.

Click-clacked down the cement steps onto Walnut Street.

And Astrid's butterflies were back.

The light ones.

The ones she wouldn't forget.

Couldn't.

Astrid went right on 33rd Street. Loonsfoot, left.

The duffel bag was still waiting for Astrid inside the dumpster behind the Starbucks. She slung it over her shoulder, wondered what sort of drink a woman like Josephine would order on her way around to the front of the building.

"Venti Strawberry Açai Refresher," she said to the barista, a little bit of Josephine still puffing her way out of Astrid's lungs.

She'd done enough right then to heed the "Customers Only" warning hanging over the restrooms, paid for her drink and made a beeline for the women's room.

Replacing the suit pants with jeans was easy enough. Maneuvering around her cast made the rest difficult.

But when Astrid stuffed Josephine into the duffel, it was as if something had drained out of her. Something powerful and good and right. And there was a hole where Josephine had been.

Astrid thanked the woman who called for Josephine to pick up her drink, and did her best to ignore the looks she got with her actual hair, without her glasses.

She sipped her drink out front. Decided maybe Josephine wouldn't have gone for such a fruity drink, but Astrid liked it just fine.

Despite the Josephine-shaped void in her, the butterflies were still fluttering, fluttering.

But they eased with every pull from her straw.

Then Loonsfoot pulled up, said, "Still have it?" through the open passenger window.

Astrid said she did.

By then butterflies were a cement block.

She could barely bring herself to respond to anything Loonsfoot said on the way home, much less contribute anything further to the conversation.

"What's the matter," Loonsfoot said moving her eyes from the road, to Astrid, to the road.

"Nothing," Astrid said. "Just not feeling very well at the moment."

"Maybe it's whatever's in that drink."

Astrid watched the road pass beneath the car through the window.

Static.

Nothing.

"No. I think it might something else."

II.

Cassie cooked while Willa whispered. Kept saying, "Yeah?" every time Willa stopped mid-sentence, held her finger up.

The pipes whining through the walls, the shower hiss from the bathroom, Willa would start back up again. About the texts, the phone calls, the supposed interview at UPenn.

"Willa—"

"Shh."

Cassie lowered her voice, said, "We have to start trusting her. We have to give her at least that."

"Did you know about this UPenn thing?"

"This is the first night I've had off in months, Will." Cassie pulled the lid from a pot on the stove, stirred a serving spoon through rice. Sprinkled sea salt onto asparagus sputtering in a pan. Opened the oven, flipped the London Broil with a pair of tongs. "She's the most proactive kid on the planet. If she says she had an interview, she had an interview. I'll follow up with her about it, I promise."

"What about the Miss Welch thing? When did she—" the pipes, the shower, "—when did she get a credit card?"

Cassie clanged the pot lid back into place. "How do you know it was a credit card?"

"I don't, not for sure. I just—"

"I appreciate everything you're doing. I couldn't have asked for a better friend for my daughter, for me. But you can't do this to yourself, and you certainly can't do this to Astrid."

"I'm doing this for Astrid."

Cassie gave Willa's forehead a quick peck. Told her she knew that. Said she appreciated her for that. Really. And when the pipes gave up their singing, the water quit with its white noise, she said, "But we have to stop now."

Muffled, Astrid spoke through the bathroom door. Something about needing ten minutes. Something about getting out of Cassie and Mr. Hogan's way.

"It's sort of ridiculous she only needs ten minutes to get ready," Cassie said. "Natural beauty's a bitch for those who don't have it."

Willa said nothing, went to the couch. Flipped through a copy of whatever novel Astrid was reading.

Cassie would have to make up for this. She hadn't exactly snapped at Willa, but enough was enough. Since the hospital, since Chris, since learning to use her casted up arm better than Cassie could use her own un-plastered limbs, Astrid was dancing to cloying electropop music in her room again. Was reading nearly a book a day. Was talking about her sessions with Loonsfoot over the phone on Cassie's breaks.

So, for once, Cassie was cooking for someone. Even though, maybe, it should've been for Astrid.

She slammed the oven door shut.

Checked the timers, the food.

Went to the couch, pushed Willa's legs out of her way, flopped down on the cushion next to her. "I blame you," she said.

"Yeah, me too."

Cassie held up her hand, waved it about, said, "Smell that? Smells good, right? I can cook, man. I'm really good at it. And that smells like the dumpster out back of Michael's Diner right about now."

"Sorry."

"Oh, shut up. I don't really blame you."

"You shut up."

Cassie didn't say anything. Sat, stared at the television, the *Star Trek* marathon she'd left on for most of the week. Waited.

A click. A low hum with an octave playing underneath. The hair dryer.

"Everybody's got secrets," Cassie said. "Christ knows I've got a bunch. You do too, don't you? And I think Astrid deserves some of her own too."

"Yeah, but—"

"Pardon the sports metaphor, but you and me have been playing defense for Astrid for so long that it feels like we've forgotten how to give a shit about ourselves. Your hackles are up all the time. I barely ever sleep."

"If we don't watch out for her, though, no one will."

"She will. She was hit by a car. That's the truth. She didn't throw herself into traffic, she didn't lay down in the middle of the road. It was a freak thing, and we, you and me—"

"I. You and I."

"Whatever. You and I need to acknowledge that maybe Astrid's go at killing herself was a freak thing, too. A one off. A thing that she's actively treating in her own way, after our help—our way—showed her what she really needs."

"Maybe."

"I'm not going to tell you anything about what happens when Mr. Hogan comes over for dinner tonight, same as you're not going to tell me about anything you guys are going to get into at the Green. We need to let Astrid tell us what she needs to when she needs to."

The hairdryer clicked off. Astrid went from the bathroom to her bedroom with a "Just a couple more minutes."

Cassie stood, pointed to the television. "This is a good one."

"Is it?" Willa said.

"Sure. If people like you look at it the right way."

"People like me?"

"The uninitiated."

Willa nodded.

Cassie went back to the oven, the stove, the cabinets for plates.

"You're pretty smart, you know that?" Willa said from the couch.

"I do know my *Star Trek*."

The food didn't smell the way it did a few minutes ago. The garlic, the pepper, the butter, the meat, it was all good again. Cassie would save some for Astrid. Maybe for steak and eggs in the morning before her shift. She could fry the frozen potatoes with peppers and onions too. She would do it before Astrid woke up. Maybe it would even pull her out of bed, the smell. Maybe waking up with that in her nostrils could be Cassie's contribution to her day. A small part of whatever she had planned for tomorrow.

Cassie barely heard the knock at the front door.

But Astrid's voice, her feet thumping across the carpet, all of that was front and center. It was bright, exciting, almost as if Cassie's eyes would have caught some lens flare if she'd turned around in time. It was a sound she would put in her memory banks if she were the *Enterprise*'s onboard computer.

When she finally took her eyes off the oven, there was Astrid in yellow. Her feet in a pair of Chucks. Her hair wavy, shiny. Her teeth white.

And there was Chris. With flowers.

Astrid wrapped Cassie up, kissed her. Told her they'd be home late. She and Willa sang, "Hi, Mr. Hogan. Bye, Mr. Hogan," and laughed their way out the front door, out to the parking lot.

Chris pushed the door closed, said, "Hi."

"Hi."

"These, uh," Chris went for the cabinets with the bouquet. "These are for you."

"I don't have a vase. A vahz. Whatever."

"Fair enough." He pulled down a drinking glass. Filled it with water at the sink. Stuffed the stems into it, spilling water all over the counter. "Sorry."

Cassie's face hurt. "I do believe I shall ravage you now."

"Before dinner?"

"Let's call dinner dessert."

Cassie went to Chris, and she was able to keep her attention on him the entire time.

12.

Willa wasn't going to smoke any weed tonight.

But the smell was nice.

And, sitting in a lawn chair in the dark, just outside the ring of light from the tiki torches—even though she said no, no, no—she pinched the blunt between her thumb and index finger, took a hit.

Then another.

She had to.

If she was going to be there. If she was going to be nice to people she had actively avoided since her first day of freshman year, if she was going to keep her eye on Astrid and Garrett all night—Astrid's hand reaching for his arm whenever he said something that could've been considered funny if whomever he was speaking to hadn't already labeled him a moron, the way he looked at the grass when he was embarrassed, or maybe trying to come off as shy—Willa would need it.

She would have to hit it again on its next pass after watching Garrett hand Astrid his cup, Astrid taking a sip.

"Shit."

She'd keep more in her lungs longer.

Sarah, Lily, and Grace—one holding smoke in her lungs, another letting it steam from her nostrils, and the third with the blunt to her lips—all made faces at Willa. Like, "Are you okay?" with their eyebrows, lips, or a hacking cough.

"No, yeah, no," Willa said. "Drug test is next month. Forgot it was April."

Lily asked really, her voice muffled, the word coming out gray.

"Not really, no." Willa would not text Cassie. Everything would be fine. Nothing could or would go wrong. Astrid was smart, Garrett was a capital-N nice guy according to the yearbook, the school paper, everybody who had ever hung out with him ever. It'd be fine.

The blunt came back Willa's way. She brought it to her lips, pinched her eyes closed from its heat.

"I didn't know you smoke," Grace said.

"Glaucoma."

Sarah said, "Seriously?"

Willa smiled, shook her head, got a little spinny. "Just when I'm nervous."

"You're funny," Grace said. "I didn't know you were this funny."

"Yeah," Lily said. "You're always with Astrid. Which is awesome, she's great. But still. You should hang out with us more."

Willa laughed. "I think you're just high."

"Takes a lot more than this anymore. Also, you're high."

The torches were burning slow. Dancing orange women with smoke hair. People talking, laughing, drinking, and not making a sound. The grass so green-green that Willa's toes were wriggling from the tickle of the blades through the soles of her Keds. Beyond the halos of light around the flames, the light they cast, the golf course faded into the black, a sheet of mist creating a barrier that was solid, liquid, gaseous, roiling, almost pulsing to the music from the speakers set up in the space between Kelly's backyard and the eighteenth green. Couples wrapped up in each other walked into the mist as one creature, disappeared into the trees.

"So, what's your deal?" Grace said.

Willa cleared her throat. "What do you mean?"

"Like, who are you, Willa? You can't just be Astrid's friend. You're so much more than that. We're all so much more than that."

Lily said, "Grace is, in fact, high."

Astrid, not far away but far enough, her hair drifting in the breeze in slow motion, her teeth catching the light from the torches, her eyes the way they always were. Sad. But not a deep, dark sad. The tired sort. The hasn't-slept-properly-in-years kind.

Willa would do what Cassie told her.

She would tuck her phone into her back pocket and leave it there.

She would leave Astrid and Garrett to themselves.

Because Grace was totally right, Willa was more than that.

And she told them so. Told them about Ken, and how she couldn't stand the guy but has to at least be civil with him because her mother just couldn't take any more awful dinners.

About the crew team. How she was counted on to steer the boat so they wouldn't go careening into another team's oars. Or the retaining walls along the sides of the Schuylkill River. Or one of the Girard Avenue Bridge abutments.

That she used to read. All the time. Kept a book in her back pocket, or in her wristlet where everyone else would keep their makeup. She couldn't remember the last book she'd read that hadn't been assigned by Mr. Hogan.

There was no Willa Baumgartner. Just Astrid's friend Willa. Just angry Willa. Just snappy, miserable, short, opinionated, annoying Willa. Just the Willa that everyone already knew about.

And that was all.

Grace's mouth hung open. Her forehead lumped into shiny rolls.

"Sorry," Willa said.

"You're intense," Lily said.

"Intense Willa."

"That's your new nickname," Sarah said. "Intense Willa. Or, or Willa the Intense."

Willa gritted her teeth, sat back in her chair, said, "What was my nickname before?"

There was nothing for a moment. Just some song from Post Malone, or one of the other dozen or so laconic-voiced copycats. Laughter. Talking.

"No one's ever given you one," Grace said. "I don't know anyone who's hung out with you outside of school. And I know a lot of people. Sell weed to most of them."

"That's the spirit, Grace," Willa said. "Already an entrepreneur. You should design an app, make payment and delivery easier on everyone involved."

"I did actually. Still working out the bugs, but—"

"Jesus Christ."

"See?" Sarah said. "Willa the Intense."

They were all red, watery eyes, and teeth, and deep coughs, and aching stomachs. They couldn't catch their breaths. And all of them, Willa too, were almost going to pee themselves.

"Seriously, Willa," Lily said. "You should hang out with us more."

"Yeah," Grace said. "You probably won't be seeing much of Astrid anymore anyway."

"Garrett's a girlfriend guy," Sarah said. "Committed."

Willa pushed herself out of her chair, stood, nearly fell into a tiki torch. She couldn't help but collapse into the grass despite her valiant effort to not cause a chain reaction that would burn down the Flourtown Country Club, and it was funnier than hell. And the cool, prickly tips of the grass made her want to avoid pulling herself upright for the rest of her life.

Until she said, "Shit."

Pulled herself off the ground.

Stood.

Needed to dig her toes into her shoes to keep her balance.

Sarah, Lily, and Grace said, "What?" Then told each other to stop saying things at the same time, they were seriously going to ruin their jeans.

The mist had taken over most of the Green. Turned the tiki torch flames into the glowing orbs of glass at the tops of streetlights. Turned people into shadows, all of them bringing cups to their formless faces, or groping at each other, melting into one another.

But there was no Astrid shadow.

No Garrett.

Willa fired of a round of f-words, pulled a torch from the ground, stabbed the flame into the grass until the dark spot they'd been sitting in was full black. She had no idea why, of course, but it helped the panic subside a little.

Sarah, and Lily, and Grace said, whoa, and chill, and wow.

Sarah said, "They're probably just hooking up."

Lily said, "She's a big girl."

Grace said, "Here," held out what was left of the blunt.

Willa told them they didn't understand, couldn't understand.

She kept blabbing, blabbing, blabbing, trying to get her legs to chase after Astrid, but they didn't want to go after Astrid. Of course they didn't.

But Willa needed them to.

But she shouldn't need them to.

She said, "Fuck this," and trudged off through the gray and into the black.

13.

Astrid kissed Garrett first.

Used her tongue first.

Pushed clothing aside to touch bare skin first.

Her fingers in the tuft of hair on the small of his back. Feeling for the ridges of spine where his back dipped into a groove in the center. Put a finger in his bellybutton. They both laughed at that, all chuckles and lips and beer breath.

And there was nothing else.

It didn't matter that she hadn't responded to Loonsfoot's texts since UPenn.

Didn't matter that, even though she couldn't prove it, there seemed to be an uptick in men in black suits floating about at the bookstore, driving black cars around the neighborhood—maybe searching for her, the Iridium, Loonsfoot.

And no, she shouldn't have finished Garrett's drink.

Yes, that was a mistake.

But she pushed it all down, out of the way.

Because of Garrett's hand on her ass.

Because he let her push him against a tree, press herself into him.

Because he would bite her bottom lip every so often in the best way.

There was an electric tingle in her fingertips, her toes.

Her vision softened the edges of everything when she opened her eyes to see if he'd opened his eyes. She leaned her knees into him, wouldn't be able to stay standing otherwise.

It was her medicine.

The beer.

They were creating new things.

Nasty things.

Making Garret's eyebrows look angry. Forcing his teeth to bite harder as if to tell Astrid to stop.

Making her fingers hook into the waistband of his jeans. The buzzing fingertips, fingernails brushing over hair.

Her cement arm tucked between them, she squeezed the plaster bar in her palm, flexed all of the muscles from her wrist to her shoulder.

She sucked back air, deep, hard with the pain.

Garrett pulled away from her. "Did I hurt you?"

The electric fingers, the dull edges of everything became more solid while her ache settled in.

"No," Astrid said. "But I can't have sex with you on the Green."

Garrett, dazed, hair mussed, said, "Me neither."

Straightening herself, Astrid said, "I'm sorry. I'd just heard that Kelly and her friends have sex on the Green during these things, and I won't have sex on the Green."

She could.

Would.

Would lay down in the patch of clover cropping up around the roots of the tree, hike up her dress. Or let Garrett do it. Either way.

She flexed in her cast again.

The roots and dirt and dead leaves would wreck her new dress.

Astrid had defined make-outy for Cassie not all that long ago, but hadn't quite walked her through a deep dive of the phenomenon. If she were there, she'd pull Astrid aside, gentle, kind, say, "Pretty sure you didn't mention sex in the woods as one of the synonyms of make-outy."

"I've never done it out here, if that counts for anything," Garrett said.

Astrid flexed again, stopped herself from going after him again, said, "I just sort of assumed. They're your friends, too."

"I know," Garrett said, shrugged. "But do you and Willa do all the same things all the time?"

The hospital.

The therapy.

The meds.

The lies.

The theft.

The world away from all of it, out there past the stars.

"We used to," Astrid said. Her fingers were shaking now, the ache in her arm deep and constant.

"I used to, too," Garrett said. "But we're leaving soon. It's like, if we're all leaving each other, all of us trying to be the same doesn't make much sense to me." He sat down, wedged himself between two arms of tree root.

He was less Garrett then. He'd practiced this. May have been waiting for someone to give him a reason to give them his reasons. Every movement, sigh, pause, facial expression, rehearsed for a Garrett in a mirror.

Astrid took a breath. In through her mouth, out through her nose.

She went to him, sat between his legs.

Took his hand with her good arm, pulled it in front of her and laced her fingers with his.

After Garrett finished talking, Astrid said, "I practice my speeches, too."

They were shaking shoulders and aching cheeks from the laughing for a bit. Garrett's ribcage bumped into Astrid's back, Astrid's back bumped back. Her world was still blurry, her fingers were still electric—she'd have to wait a while for all that to subside—but it didn't matter then.

Until it did.

Until Astrid had to say, "I do that all the time, actually."

Until she needed to grit her teeth waiting for Garrett to ask her what she meant by that because he didn't quite understand.

Astrid was a liar.

A fake.

A poseur.

She didn't deserve to be sitting with him.

Didn't deserve any of the signatures on her cast.

Certainly not Cassie's loopy handwriting. Or Willa's jagged scrawl.

The only one that should've been on that arm, maybe, was Loonsfoot's. She, at the very least, knew exactly what Astrid was.

And what she was was awful.

It was impossible that Cassie and Willa didn't see that. They had to be lying about it. To her. To themselves.

Astrid reached back, put her hand through his Garrett's hair, pulled him toward her.

The talking had made his breath a little stale.

But it was good.

Honest.

But then he pulled away from her.

She moved to kiss him again.

"I'm not sure what you meant before," he said, stopping her. "You feel like you have to practice everything you say before you say it? All the time?"

"I just can't be like everyone else," she said. "I wish I could be, but I can't. That's all."

He was nothing but lips again.

Until he was talking into her mouth.

Until his words weren't muffled once he pulled away from her—wait, and wait, and what.

They had agreed, Astrid, Cassie, and Willa, that no one

needed to know anything. That it was no one else's business but theirs.

But Astrid hadn't told them the real, actual truth in however long.

And whenever she'd told her truth, it shifted into something else days, hours, minutes later.

Whatever was real wasn't.

Whatever wasn't was.

It didn't matter.

But something had to.

So, she talked.

She talked about how she used to pull her own hair out in clumps. How she'd ground her teeth bloody in her sleep until they chipped, cracked. How, when she crossed a bridge, or stepped off an elevator on the upper floors of a tall building, there was nothing but what would be running through her head on the way down. If there would be any regret. If she'd flail her arms and legs trying to catch the air, trying to float safely to the sidewalk or the water. Maybe she'd sail off into the pink sunset as some new kind of human. Or if she would just open her arms, eyes, and watch whatever was below her rocketing its way up to her. If the autopsy would reveal she was stuffed with adrenaline, thrilled about the whole thing.

If Cassie would be better off. Open her own restaurant—Chez Cassandra. Have another kid. One who wasn't so fucked. Forget about Astrid all together.

If Willa would make new, better friends. Fall in love. Write a book. Discover new and wonderful scientific principles. Move to Hollywood to make movies. Wind up so busy and so happy that Astrid would never have existed to her.

One way or the other, Astrid wouldn't ever see any of that happen. But, a lot of the time, she wouldn't mind figuring out a way to find out what would become of them without her.

Garrett's face didn't change through any of it. He was

either unfazed, horrified, or holding back tears. Or a combination of the three.

Astrid had only ever met one person whose face suggested they had any business hearing about any of this. One face that knew. And Astrid had spent most of the past few days ignoring her.

"I swallowed a bottle of pills," Astrid said. "I threw most of it up but needed to get the rest pumped out. My stomach and esophagus were wrecked for weeks. I spent some time at a psychiatric hospital in New Jersey. My mom and Willa came as often as they could, but it was in a supervised area—like we were in a zoo. I don't remember too much of that year. Sophomore year. Once I came home, we went to therapist after therapist, all of whom said I should go and find the right doctor who would work best for me when things started not to work out with them. Didn't find one that worked until about six months ago."

Garrett's eyes shifted. Sad looking, glassy. His forehead was wrinkled, his lips were pressed flat. He nodded.

Lamictal.

Lunesta.

Buspirone.

Aciphex.

Alka-Seltzer.

Abilify.

Nexium.

Zyprexa.

Latuda.

Lithium when things were really bad.

"I shouldn't have taken your beer. That was a mistake. But I really like you, and I was nervous, so I drank it. It wasn't your fault. Not even a little. So please don't think it was."

Silence.

Bugs zipping around in the dark.

Rustling somewhere out there. Maybe an animal. Maybe people.

Garrett's fingers were still tied up in Astrid's.

That couldn't be bad.

"So, I think that's it," Astrid said.

Then she said, "Thanks."

Then she said, "Sorry."

Another long stretch of forever.

Sound.

Wind.

"Wow," Garrett said. "That's a lot."

"I know. I didn't mean to unload like that, I just thought—"

"No, yeah, I understand. So, no one else knows? How could no one else know?" Garrett pulled his hand away from her.

Astrid stood, brushed off whatever was clinging to the back of her dress. "My mom worked it out with school. I finished everything I missed over that summer so I wouldn't be behind. Officially I had mono—that's what people were told kept me out so long."

Garrett pulled himself up. Scratched the back of his head. "I'm really sorry you have to deal with all that. It's not fair."

He got it.

He did.

Of course he did.

Astrid needed to give people like him more credit. He was going through stuff too. Everyone was. He understood the need to keep things from people. To have to be dishonest to keep up appearances.

He got it.

"No, it's not fair. But I'm okay right now."

A beat.

Two.

Garrett said, "You want to go back and get a soda or something?"

"I kind of want to stick my finger in your belly button again. I liked the way you laughed when I did that. Sorry if that's weird. That's weird, right?"

He smiled, rubbed the back of his head. "I'm kind of thirsty."

Astrid nodded. "Yeah, me too."

Garrett's feet scraped through the brush, the dead leaves left over from last fall. That swoosh-swoosh sound moving away from her.

So crunchy.

So dead.

Astrid went through her purse, said, "Wait, I think I dropped my keys somewhere."

Garrett turned. Swoosh-swoosh, stop. "Do you need help finding them?"

Astrid turned on her phone's flashlight, scanned the ground. "They're around here somewhere."

"Okay," Garrett said.

Crickets.

Literal ones.

"I'll meet you at the coolers then?"

Eyes on a circle of moonlight on the dirt, the grass, the leaves, the tree roots, Astrid said, "I'll be there."

She looked for her keys that were already in her purse until the swoosh-swooshing faded, until she was alone.

No Garrett.

No Willa.

No Cassie.

No one else.

A bunch of names on her arm.

Sam.

Jerry.

Kurt.

Who were they?

Astrid heard her name.

Not far.

Not really close.

Willa probably.

Astrid dabbed her eyes with a tissue from her purse. Fixed

her mussed hair, tied it back. Blew her nose. Straightened her dress. Gripped the plaster bar in her palm until she had to wipe her eyes again with her used tissues.

Her name again.

Definitely Willa.

Not Bobby.

Or Meg.

Or Dennis.

There would be so many questions. And none of Astrid's answers would work the way Willa needed them to. Everything after that would be about how and why she needed to find Astrid in the woods. About what she was doing out there even though Willa wasn't an idiot.

Astrid could find her way out of the goddamn woods.

Her name again.

Louder, closer.

Who the hell were Lenny, or Jim, or Christina?

Astrid again.

This time it wasn't a call. It was a yell.

Willa would never be anything but angry in this situation.

Cassie wouldn't be able to give much more than one of her couch talks. Always hopeful, always nearly whispered. Always off the mark, always teetering toward a dead damn complete misunderstanding.

Loonsfoot.

On Astrid's arm.

The picture of Regis-132 on Astrid's home screen.

The pinks, the violets. The glowing bulbs.

Standing in the long-dead leaves, the spring grass, the patch of clover, Astrid made the phone call.

Over the line, "Oh, terrific timing," Loonsfoot said. "So glad you called."

"What else do we need to get for the machine?" Astrid said, keeping her voice low so Willa, getting closer, closer, couldn't hear her.

14.

American Spirits burned slower.

That's what the kid behind the counter at Wawa told Cassie anyway.

When Astrid was younger, Cassie smoked Kools. Then switched to Camels. And then, even after sitting through a PowerPoint on the dangers of smoking featuring photos of blackened lungs, tracheal rings, toothless mouths, presented by her eleven-year-old daughter holding a laser pointer, Cassie kept a pack of Camel Blue in her apron at work—for emergencies.

This wasn't an emergency per se. It was more a celebration. And celebrations counted too. The celebratory smoking was damn near reaffirmed under the starlight and moonglow. Every celestial body in the sky outshone the storefronts and streetlamps for Christ's sake. Even still, on the walk back from the convenience store, Cassie had tacked this emergency contingency clause onto the mental list of smoking rules stored rent-free in her brain in case Astrid ever caught her smoking again.

Everything was...she wouldn't use the word perfect. Everything was walking back to a cramped apartment to sit outside on the stoop smoking cigarettes with a boy whilst staring into space thanking the stars for the lightheadedness and the luck. And that was all it needed to be.

The food she'd cooked had gotten cold in the kitchenette while she and Chris spent most of the night in the bedroom. And the best parts weren't the ones that she would've normally considered the best parts. Watching the hair on his chest move with his ribs while he spoke. His hand running along her naked hip while he wasn't waiting his turn to talk. The rumble from his belly that neither of them were willing to do anything about right then. His eyes just watching her, glittering in the dark.

They'd eaten eventually. But it hadn't mattered that the microwave had sapped every ounce of moisture and sucked the flavor out of every fleck of seasoning—dinner was delicious. It wouldn't last, but she wasn't urged to cringe with his loud chewing, or the faces he'd make trying to clear a hunk of meat from between his teeth with his tongue. She'd bring it up eventually, but none of it had even prompted a chuckle from her.

Chris's still being in the apartment, sitting on the couch, reading one of Astrid's books didn't force Cassie into making something up about not feeling well, or having to get up early for work, or having to run to her poor, ailing father's bedside.

Instead, she held the pack of cigarettes over her head, said she had the power in the best Dolph Lundgren she could muster, and asked if he could run to the closet for the beach chairs.

They didn't say much.

Not at first.

They smoked. Watched the gray coil up and away from the cherries, disappear into the air, into the stars.

Then, "What are you looking at up there?" Chris's legs were crossed, his shoe danced to whatever beat was running through his head.

"Did you know," Cassie said. "That if you were in a shuttle that increased its velocity to the speed of light at a pace that wouldn't liquify your bones, a forty-year round trip to the center of the galaxy, relative to you and your crew, would equate to a thousand years in relative Earth-time?"

Smile. Smoke. "I did not know that."

"Now you do."

"Isn't that theoretical though?"

"Sure it is. But everything's theoretical until somebody goes and does it. That somebody could be anybody. Could be you."

Chris's chair groaned while he uncrossed, recrossed his legs. Left over right this time. "Not me, no. But that's very hopeful of you. Very optimistic."

Cassie took a long drag from her cigarette, tapped a half inch of ash onto the cement. "We don't get a lot of that around here. But we try."

Nothing but the sound of cars on the road.

"I'm sorry," Chris said.

"Nothing to be sorry about." Cassie reached out, squeezed Chris's arm. "But thanks."

"Nothing to thank me for."

"Sure there is. Astrid and I don't have much. When something good comes around, we are very grateful. You're good. And I am grateful."

Cassie said it was cute when they stubbed their cigarettes out at the same time. Said no when Chris asked if she wanted to go back inside. Looked back at the sky, said sure when he held the pack of Spirits out to her.

"So," he said in a cloud of smoke. "You like space."

"No, I love space. Actually, I love possibility. Limitless potential." She lit her cigarette. It was good. She sank herself deeper into her chair.

"Like *Star Trek*?" Chris said.

"You like *Star Trek*?"

"No, but I scrolled through your Netflix queue. Says a lot about a person."

"Snooping through people's Netflix queues says a lot about a person too."

There was more coughing than laughing, but the laughter was definitely in there somewhere.

"When Astrid was born, my dad put us up here. Kept it from my mom for a little while. But all I had were bargain bin DVDs and this little girl who loved watching the *Enterprise* zip through deep space. Maybe it was the theme song, I don't know. But we would watch together, and we would go on the away missions with Kirk, Spock, and McCoy, and Astrid would giggle every time I laughed at the horrible supporting cast, and it wouldn't matter if I had to eat baby food, or if Astrid couldn't sleep through the night, or if we were always sick, or if we felt like we were the only two people in the universe. Things were bad. But we could always fly between stars at, like, a thousand and twenty-four times the speed of light—that's warp eight, by the way—and, for fifty minutes at a time, it was me and her, you know...boldly going."

The road noise.

The creaking of rusty beach chairs that hadn't been on a beach in years.

Chris breathing.

"So, yeah," Cassie said, dragging from her cigarette, releasing a jet of gray into the air. "Infinite potential."

Chris began saying something. Something sweet, complimentary, somehow not sticky, sugary, but Cassie didn't catch the second half of his sentence. She said, "Shit," flicked her cigarette into the parking lot. Let whatever smoke was left in her lungs out through her nostrils.

Willa's car nearly jumped the parking block.

Caught in binoculars of white, eyes squinting from the headlights, Cassie stood, waved, spoke through her teeth. "Hi, how was the night? I thought one of you was going to let me know when you were on your way home."

Willa slammed her door shut, pointed at the still-smoldering cigarette on the black top, and said, "Astrid's going to kill you."

There was nothing Cassie could say. She'd been caught.

"Look, the cigarettes were a one time—"

"And I have been calling. For an hour."

The passenger door opened, but it wasn't Astrid stepping out of the car. Some scraggly-haired kid with a black eye.

"Who's that?" But Cassie was already through the front door, at the kitchen table, at the coffee table, in the bedroom.

She picked up the facedown phone, saw all the texts, the missed calls.

She didn't read a single one.

Didn't bother to see who called.

None of the messages, none of the notifications would be from Astrid anyway.

Cassie, through the front door, down the steps, her hands crumpling the front of the kid's shirt, said things to him that would prompt a call to the police if he were to tell his parents about any of it.

"Garrett's an idiot," Willa said. "But he agreed to help me find Astrid after I punched his stupid eye in."

"For the record," Garrett said. "I would've helped before the punch. Hi, Mr. Hogan."

Chris stuffed his hands into his pockets, waved.

And, through all of it, Cassie saw Astrid in the woods, laying in the leaves, foam around her lips. Astrid in the Wissahickon river, stones tied to her neck, arms. Astrid at the Falls Bridge, leaping into the air.

It had never mattered that Cassie always had good points to make, could wrap them up with flowery words, gussie them into profound speeches.

She took a breath.

Another.

A third.

Then, "My keys are on the coffee table, Chris."

15.

Astrid stuck to the woods until she couldn't anymore.

Cut behind the Acme, and the community pool.

Underneath the 309 overpass.

Past the Oreland Inn, the smokers who'd been forced outside—miserable and wrinkled, standing in a cloud of gray, watching Fox News on the deck television.

Over the train tracks.

Through the basketball courts.

Behind the dumpsters that used to belong to a pizza place that had been burned down for the insurance payout.

Once she reached the tree line, she couldn't see the house deep in the woods; the rental—the lab—but there was a glow. Pale blue flickering through the trees, shrubs. Still a ways away, barely visible from the road.

She waited.

Stepped into the dark at the sight of headlights.

Kept an eye on the road, watched a black car roll past. Slow.

It was nothing.

Just a car.

Had to be.

Still, Astrid almost retraced her steps.

Almost went home.

Almost.

Explaining this to Cassie, to Willa, would be the same as trying to tell them all the ways her brain often misfired, sent signals ping-ponging around her skull to all the wrong parts in this lobe or that lobe, that lobe or this lobe. They'd never be unkind. They'd nod, blink away the sheen in their glassy eyes, say all the things they'd learned to say from all their research. That they were there for her.

But there—where they were, how they lived—just wasn't good enough.

Not their fault.

No one's fault.

Astrid just wasn't meant to live here.

So she followed the glow into the woods.

The blue beacon that could take her somewhere else.

Away.

In the dark, the blue light did something to the woods. Morphed tree bark into smooth, off-white stalks that reached up into the starry black. Capped the new trees with solid circular masses instead of branches and leaves. Even the stars shifted position with the strobing light, dotted the sky with new constellations. The dirt, the leaves, the fallen branches and sticks were near purple, more a webbed network of sentient forest than random, dead litter.

But once Astrid stepped through the tree line into the clearing, the lab was just a broken old house.

The path that led to the dirt road which led to an actual road was just gravel and leaves with a pretty blue tint.

The trees were just trees. Alive, but alone. Standing tall, stiff, without any ability to understand there were hundreds of others like them just feet away. Their limbs were all tangled, and they could never know that closeness.

But there was Loonsfoot.

On the porch.

Waving to Astrid wearing big rubber gloves. A welding mask pulled up and away from her face. A leather apron slung over her neck, looped around her back, tied in a knot at her waist. Clunky black boots on her feet. "Sure took you long enough to get here," she shouted.

Astrid was about to say she wasn't in the damn mood, but stopped herself when Loonsfoot was clapping those gloves together, smiling—before the mask slung down covering her face.

Up the creaking porch steps.

Following Loonsfoot through the new front door.

Taking the goggles handed to her, strapping them over her eyes.

Listening, but not really.

"I don't have a ton of time tonight," Astrid said.

Voice muffled behind the welding mask, Loonsfoot said, "Just wanted to show you something is all. Won't be long now."

"Until what?"

"Regis-132, my dear."

Astrid crossed her arms, leaned back against the wall in the foyer.

Flat metal face, a rectangular tinted glass eye moving from Astrid to the doorway into the blue, to Astrid, back to the blue. "They can get more Iridium," Loonsfoot said. "If that's what's been bothering you. It's a naturally occurring metal. It's not like we took a lump of Einsteinium, and they'd need to make more." She reached up, lifted her mask. "Also, Einsteinium doesn't create the antiprotons necessary to safely breach the Coulomb barrier. Have you ever seen *Raiders of the Lost Ark*? We'd melt like the Nazis at the end without Iridium. Just one more reason, as if we really need another, not to be like Nazis."

Through the goggles, the flickering blue was almost alive.

And so close.

The rubber strap around her head was already making Astrid aware of the pulse in her temples, squeezing her nose sore. "Why couldn't we have just ordered it?"

Loonsfoot's put her hands on her hips, shrugged. "Where's the fun in that?"

"We have the money, don't we?"

"Of course we do. But we have to use that sparingly. It shines a light where light need not be shone."

Loonsfoot used her arms for emphasis, as punctuation, as if she'd developed her own bizarre sign language. Willa and Astrid used to speak like that. It had been a while. Astrid forced her lips closed to keep her smile inside her face. "So I shouldn't have bought my suit with it, then?"

"Definitely not. But, when a rookie, do as rookies do, I suppose. Just quit it. Speaking of which—" Loonsfoot spun, charged into the blue, cut right, and was gone.

Nothing but clinging, clanging, and questions to no one about where she'd put this, that.

An ah-ha!

More metal scraping across the bare concrete slab in the back room.

Mask lifted away from her face, Loonsfoot thumped back into the foyer and handed over a manila envelope. "Next job, if you choose to accept it."

"You keep mixing up phrases and references. It's distracting." She pinched the envelope's metal wings together and opened the flap.

She took a breath. Reached in.

Paper, plastic, booklets, sharp corners of cardstock.

She pulled it all out at once.

Stiff, matte business card. Chief Operating Officer, Amanda Roman, Regis Technologies, LLC.

Pennsylvania Driver's License. Roman, Amanda M, born 11/15/1985, eyes: blue, height: 5'8", organ donor, and a photo of Astrid with red hair.

Purple Discover card in Amanda's name.

Regis Technologies, LLC company credit card in Amanda's name.

Regis Technologies, LLC checkbook in Amanda's name.

"You've been keeping busy, then?" Astrid tucked her second new life back into the envelope, folded it in half, stuffed it all into her purse.

Loonsfoot clapped her gloved hands and waved Astrid into the next room.

In the spare room, in the blue, it was just a frame. Pointy, diamond shaped, propped up on a series of sawhorses. A panel wired into a control console casting the pulsing blue all over the room, all over Loonsfoot, all over Astrid.

Astrid lifted her goggles, let the plastic dig into her forehead.

"You should keep them on," Loonsfoot said.

"I like it better this way."

Arms held out in front of her, presenting the thing in her best Vanna White, Loonsfoot said, "I call it the *Rippa*."

Astrid could almost see the rest of the machine build itself over the frame.

Rivetted panels.

Welding burns.

Cockpit hatch with a porthole.

An Aztec pattern in the metal hull.

Rippa in the *Enterprise* typeface.

"Wait," Astrid said. "*Rippa* as in Kelly Ripa?"

"Don't be ridiculous." Hands on her hips again. "As in we're going to rip a hole in spacetime and be the first to step foot on another world. A better world. Also, yes, I did find *Live! With Regis and Kelly* to be an absolute delight."

Bathed in blue, Astrid took a breath.

Another.

A third.

Then, "You need to promise me that this is all real. Willa and my mom think I'm getting better—that I'll be cured someday or whatever—but I'm pretty sure all the bad stuff's volume is just turned down right now. It keeps bubbling back up. I'm keeping it under control. Mostly. With this. With a few other things, too. But I want to believe in all of this so badly."

Loonsfoot lifted her mask.

Moved across the room.

Pulled off her gloves.

Both hands on Astrid's shoulders, she said, "Belief has nothing to do with fact. I've seen this place for myself. I could almost feel the breeze through the portal. You have the picture I sent, yeah?"

Astrid chewed at the inside of her mouth, wiped her nose with her good hand. "Yeah."

"No matter how hard people like you and me try, we can't stuff ourselves into the spaces most of the population can so easily slide into. It doesn't mean we're sick, or strange—it doesn't mean we have to resent people for that ability either. It just means we're different, and we see the world differently. Maybe we see it for what it actually is as opposed to what we're asked to believe it could be. And, if you ask me, that makes us special. We have an opportunity here to find a place we can make wholly our own. A world that would only be limited by how far we can stretch our imaginations. Maybe, one day, if we do this right, we can show everyone that people like us hold the same intrinsic value as everyone else—that just because we're not meant for this place doesn't mean we don't have a place. Maybe if we can save ourselves, we'll be able save other people who struggle so much worse than we do. We can find meaning by giving people hope. And at that point it would be cyclical. Hope without its ugly alter ego. Despair won't be able to find us out there. Also, we'd be spacetime travelers, and that in and of itself sounds really fucking cool, doesn't it?"

It did sound fucking cool.

And shiny and brilliant, and all of the other descriptors Loonsfoot used while talking about what they would need, how they could get it, and how they would most certainly, definitely have a bit of fun along the way while doing it.

And in the blue, in front of a shell of a spacetime vessel, Astrid wiped her eyes.

It wasn't the despair's volume ramping up, up, up in her brain.

It was the opposite.

The good one.

And even though texts and calls from Willa, and Cassie, and Garrett kept popping up on her phone, and even though she needed to leave right that second, and the second after that, she kept her eyes on the photo Loonsfoot had sent her. The colors. The life. The glimmering blubs on the grass.

And only one thing pried her imagination away from her future home.

A word.

Repeated when Astrid said she didn't quite hear Loonsfoot right then.

"Uranium," Loonsfoot said.

16.

They were quiet for a good long while once they unlocked the apartment door, took seats on the couch, at the kitchen table, on the floor in front of the coffee table. But then there were questions. Breathy, calm, sweet sounding at first.

What happened?

Did anything else go on that needed to be talked through?

Why walk alone, in the dark, after hours of no communication at all?

The answers were short, almost whispered into a pair of folded hands in a lap draped in yellow.

But they weren't enough. Not even close. There was no excuse, after everything, to just go off and not tell anyone anything.

They weren't trying to keep tabs on anyone.

No one lost trust in anyone.

But it was nothing short of disturbing, needing to be in touch while not being able to be in touch while one of them was making an active choice not to reach out.

They should have reached a point by now that nothing would stop them from telling any one of them anything.

Where they were.

What they were doing.

If they needed anything.

Help.

But then, "You didn't tell me about Mr. Hogan until I pretty much walked in on you."

And, "You had no right to come after me on a hunch—Garrett didn't do anything to deserve being punched in front of all of his friends."

And, "I know you guys are in constant communication with each other about me."

Astrid, pacing around the room, talked about trust and how there was a total lack thereof if they weren't willing to, at the very least, give her the space she needed to process her life in her own way. She had been nothing but honest with them with the things they needed to know.

But, they asked, what about the second interview, and what about the suit, and what about the credit card and being called a different name at the mall?

"I set up a private visit to the counseling center at UPenn because what if Loonsfoot wouldn't be available if there was some sort of crisis? I wanted to look nice, and I've been saving up for a suit, and, yeah, I'd gotten a credit card to begin building up my credit score—I needed to offer you at least some relief, Mom. UPenn isn't cheap regardless of scholarships and loans."

Then Willa said, "You talk about Loonsfoot too much. It's odd. A little more like some bizarre friendship than an appropriate patient/therapist relationship."

Then Cassie said, "Loonsfoot is working for Astrid, and we need to be supportive of that."

Then, "That woman needs a therapist herself—she's fucking nuts."

Then Cassie.

Then Willa again.

Then Astrid slammed her bedroom door shut.

"Willa, I think you'd better head home."

"Are you serious?"

Cassie sat at the kitchen table.

She squinted as headlamps beamed through the window as Willa pulled her car out of the parking lot.

She put her head down.

Eventually she slept.

A Private Little War

17.

Astrid was Amanda Roman, COO of Regis Technologies, LLC.

Became Amanda Roman after Loonsfoot had stuck her in a chair at the lab. Slathered on eyeliner thicker than Astrid ever would have applied it herself. Eyeshadow to add a little smoke. Concealer, bronzer, a bit of pink on her cheeks—but not too much. Lipstick, red, matte. Tucked her hair into a wig cap. Pulled on the monofilament-based red hairpiece. Parted it here, there, two, three times before settling on what she'd said was the most fiercely business appropriate.

In the mirror, Loonsfoot behind Astrid with her hands on her shoulders, Amanda had been more Astrid than originally expected. Like this person was a future Astrid. The one she'd given up on more times than she could count. The one she had been absolutely certain she would never see.

But then Loonsfoot had called her Amy again, smiling, glassy-eyed in the mirror next to Astrid's someday face. And Astrid had needed to squeeze the plaster bar in her palm the entire drive to ONExia, Incorporated to turn the volume down. Everything she'd said to Cassie and Willa had needed a jolt of electric pain from her wrist to her shoulder. Loonsfoot, with her uranium and whatever reasons she had for calling Astrid Amy, had needed another jolt. Regis-132 being named after a retired talk show host, another. Willa being Willa but having this or that to do instead of going to the diner or coming to the apartment. Cassie being Cassie, just talking—not talking-talking. Mr. Hogan in the halls at school, treating her like everyone else instead of honors student Astrid.

She'd needed to stop before she ruined Amanda's makeup. And all of it had settled into a deep bone-ache. As if hairline fractures were lacing themselves up and down her forearm, coiling through the white under her biceps, triceps, turning, eventually, to gravel that was only held in place with skin and blood and muscle.

But, sitting in front of Richard Jennings, the pain was softening into a distant cotton afterthought.

Maybe it was because she'd memorized the packet Loonsfoot had typed out and included with all of Amanda's information. Maybe it was because she would have absolutely taken the potential business herself if she were in Richard's shoes because of Amanda's performance. Whatever it was, Richard scanned the plans Astrid had handed over making mmhmm sounds, and ah sounds, and saying things like, "Interesting," and "Fascinating."

Astrid didn't need to flex in her cast for that to sting. Richard spitting an innocuous word that just so happened to be a Spock-ism did it for her.

Cassie was at the diner. Maybe pouring decaf into requests for refills of regular. Maybe not dropping checks off in time before people left without paying. Maybe standing behind the register, elbow on the counter, chin in her palm, staring.

And it was Astrid's fault.

Again.

"I've never seen anything like this," Richard said looking up from the *Rippa*'s plans. "May I ask what it is?"

To Astrid's left, Loonsfoot—Donna King, CFO, a bob of a brown wig on her head, hazel contacts, some mascara, a bit of gloss on her lips—leaned forward said, "You'll have to forgive us, Mr. Jennings, but we're not at liberty to discuss the nature of the project other than its specifications and other assorted requirements such as the expected date of completion, et cetera."

"Right," Richard said. "My apologies. It's just...this thing looks like it could go on the *Enterprise*, and I just can't see how it's practical. At all."

"That is the United States government's business," Astrid said. "We don't even know what it's for. What we do know, however, is that if we can pull this off by the due date, the potential design contract we could nail down would be long term and extremely lucrative. Not to mention, due to such a quick turnaround time, whichever company could get this thing done would, perhaps, see the benefits of such a successful government partnership."

Richard took a sip from the mug on his desk, wiped his mustache with a finger. "And the infrastructure is already built? You would just need—"

"Titanium poly alloy paneling, internal wiring, and heat shielding, yes," Astrid said. "Plus, the lead engine and manifold casings."

Richard click-clacked at his keyboard. Made sounds from deep in his throat. Scratched his eyebrow. Adjusted the way he was sitting, his leather chair groaning under his weight.

"Something wrong?" Astrid said. She would have to get her suit dry-cleaned with all the sweat she was pouring into the coat's pits. The smell from her wrinkled arm once her cast could come off would be damn near lethal. The pit in her guts, the flutter of her heart, the need to pull more air into her lungs than usual, it was all...good. Like stepping on stage as a woman ready to kill to alleviate loneliness in *Arsenic and Old Lace*. Like opening the envelope from Wyndmoor Academy at the tail end of eighth grade, Cassie watching with her hands folded in front of her mouth. Just before the portal exploded and threw Astrid through the door.

"Is there any flexibility with the delivery date at all?" Richard said.

"No, sir," Astrid said. "There is not."

More clicking-clacking.

More throat sounds.

Loonsfoot saying they'll have to push back their four o'clock, holding her phone to Astrid. An article from *Scientific American*, "According to Current Physical Theory, is it Possible for a Human Being to Travel Through Time?"

"Nothing I can't handle," Loonsfoot said. A smirk, a wink.

Astrid pursed her sticky red lips to keep from showing teeth, moved her eyes from Richard to Loonsfoot, from Loonsfoot to Richard. She nodded, said, "Fair enough."

If she could travel through time, she'd introduce Loonsfoot to her 14-year-old self. Have her explain that what then-Astrid was experiencing wasn't everyone else's normal. It was hers. Different, not wrong. And it didn't have to scare her. Those deep-darks, that blackness, it was all a point of view, not a curse or a burden. That there was someone who understood. Someone just like her.

Then she'd watch her future shift. See the bad memories that had turned into monsters in her sleep evaporate—dew burning off the summer morning grass.

Maybe the new-now would allow the current Astrid to see the same things she saw when zooming in and out of the Regis-132 photo in her apartment with Cassie. At school with Willa.

The plaster crackled in her hand.

Richard cleared something from his throat, swallowed. "I can make it work."

"Good." Astrid reached into her coat, pulled out a slip. "We'll need the parts shipped to this address."

She signed contracts, established the payment method. Lightened the mood in the office a bit by loosening her grip on her tone of voice. She smiled, joked with Loonsfoot about being glad they could finally cross this off their list—they were so busy, Richard couldn't even know. It was impossible for him to understand how important this job was for their company.

Astrid's hand in Richard's for a good, strong shake.

Loonsfoot thanking him for his time.

Richard asking, "Do you have a daught—"

"Yes," Loonsfoot said before Richard could punctuate his sentence. "I do."

Astrid kept her eyes stuck to Richard's face. Didn't let her face shift, turn to Loonsfoot with a series of questions stuffed behind her teeth.

"Oh, that's great," Richard said. "But, no, I meant to ask Amanda."

"Me?" Astrid said. "No. Why do you ask?"

"I feel like I've seen you before. Parent, teacher conferences maybe? Wyndmoor Academy?"

Astrid couldn't say the word, couldn't shake her head no.

"My daughter's finishing up her senior year. Lily Jennings?"

Astrid stuttered through telling him she didn't have a kid. Wasn't even thinking about having a kid. Ever.

"Sorry about that then," Richard said with a smile splashed across his face. "Now that I think about it, you do look a bit young to have a teenager."

Loonsfoot broke through the quiet that had billowed up, invaded every corner of the office. Told Richard that it was a pleasure, that they would be certain to come to ONExia again for all of their future projects if everything goes according to plan and schedule.

There was Loonsfoot's hand at the center of Astrid's back.

The office door, the thanks again, and the have a good day. The corridor between the office suites and reception, the air sparkling with dust floating in the sunlight through the glass walls.

The nods to the receptionist, Daniel.

The heat in the parking lot.

The air in the car pressing into Astrid's body like it was an invisible layer of skin itself.

The engine coughing to life.

Loonsfoot saying, "I had a script of my own, you know."

Astrid saying, "What?"

"The whole kid thing." Loonsfoot's eyes kept sliding back and forth, back and forth between the road, Astrid, the road, Astrid. "Everything needs to be as believable as possible when we do stuff like this."

Astrid knew that.

Of course she did.

This only functioned because of a very delicate balance between fiction and reality that needed to be sprinkled with details, details, details. Most of which would never be breathed into the air, but still—it all needed to be ready to go.

"Next time," Loonsfoot said. "I'll give you both outlines. No surprises. Sorry about that."

Astrid nodded because, yes, she believed Loonsfoot. Because of course Loonsfoot didn't have a daughter. Because it was all part of a carefully constructed ruse to ensure the success of their mission. Which was, of course, very, very real.

It had to be.

18.

Willa was under no circumstances going to allow Garrett to sit his boney ass in her car. The black she'd painted along the ridge of his eye socket was more a blend of greens and yellows now, but that change in color was in no way an indicator that the person who'd put it there had changed her mind about anything.

Lily walking next to her, close, their uniform shirts brushing together, making the little blonde hairs on her arms stand up straight, Willa didn't bother to turn her face even slightly to answer any of his questions.

Past the school buses, the only information Willa had was that Astrid woke up not feeling well. Cassie had verified that it was definitely a stomach thing and not some residual effect from Garrett being a complete asshole that hadn't hit her until then.

Past the open gym doors, the squeaking sneakers, the thumping, thumping on the court, no, Astrid would not want to see him again. He'd humiliated her. Made her feel small. She was fine, of course, because women get over pretty-boy man-children faster than said man-children could ever admit to themselves.

Waving off the smoke from the cigarette circle in the school parking lot, absolutely not, Willa had no reason whatsoever to help Garrett get back in Astrid's proverbial good graces because, one, he was a cliché, and two, he spoke in nothing but clichés—who says good graces who's not eighty?

Only when they reached Willa's car did Garrett enter her line of sight. And by then, Lily, standing by the passenger side door, made a face that made Willa want to turn and sprint back into the building to lock herself in a bathroom stall until Lily went ahead and made her way home on her own. She'd seen the same face on Astrid, but without the freckles across her cheekbones and nose, without a sheet of blonde hair that made her left eye lock with Willa's through a golden waterfall.

"Tomorrow instead?" Lily said. "Same place? I'll buy."

Willa nodded, said sure.

And Lily was gone. Melted into the circle of smokers asking if any of them had a spare. Lighting up, keeping it pinched between two fingers on her left hand.

Willa had only ever tasted smoke on her tongue from those couple months she'd kept her trying-smoking habit from Astrid. And the occasional blunt. But Garrett had probably just delayed her from maybe, possibly taking that campfire heat from Lily's mouth into her lungs and tasting it on her lips.

Garrett used his eyebrows, his shoulders to say, "What?" without saying a thing.

Unlocking her car door, pulling it open, getting into her car, turning over the ignition, putting the window down, Willa said, "What do you want, Garrett?"

Bending at the hip, nearly putting his head through the open window, Garrett said, "How can I help? I want to help."

"You could've started by not leaving Astrid in the woods."

"What would you have done?"

"I wouldn't have left Astrid in the woods."

Garrett's voice raised to a pitch that only little boys being dragged from supermarkets and malls use when they're trying to keep it together, just before the inevitable screaming, snot-leaking rant. He had nothing to say. Not that he didn't want to say anything. He just didn't have a set of words that wouldn't have come out of a bad teen movie. It was all, "I'm so sorry," or "I'll be there for you if you let me," or "If there's anything I can do, I'll do it." He left to get them both a drink, that was all. "I was scared," he said. "But I had every intention of going back with something more to offer than a stupid one-liner and a can of warm Coke. But then I'd gotten punched in the eye. Then the party collapsed. Then Astrid was gone."

"I know what you're doing," Willa said.

"Do you?"

"I do."

"What's that, then?"

"You want to have sex with Astrid. Just say it. I'd respect you more for the honesty."

"That's—look, you let me help you find her the other night."

"No, I forced you to help me find her because it was all your fault. There's a difference."

Willa shifted the car into reverse, backed out of her spot. Heard Garrett trying to speak over the sound of tires rolling over black top, drowned him out by switching on the air conditioner. "Get out of the way or I'll run you over."

In front of the car, through the windshield, Garrett said, "Come on, you're not going to do that."

But Willa hit the gas, sent Garrett spinning out of the way.

Hands on the car door, hooked through the window where the glass would be if Willa had been smart enough to put the window back up, Garrett said wait, wait, wait, and please, just a second, trying to keep pace with the car as Willa sped up through the lot.

Running alongside now, Garrett kept calling her name. Kept raising his voice to a squealing whine to say things about really liking Astrid. That he cared about her. How he wanted to make sure she could count on him. And then he went sprinting past the car as Willa hit the brakes and screeched to a stop.

"You don't care about anyone," Willa said, throwing the shifter into park, getting out of the car. "Do you even know what people say about you? They say you're hot, and sweet, and committed, right up until you get what you want—which, I assume, is to get girls naked and jackhammer away at them for thirty or forty seconds—and then you tell them some shit about things moving too fast? You're a John Hughes character, Garrett."

"Who's John Hughes?"

"And you're an idiot."

They had an audience now. The track team jogging through the lot toward the track in their short-shorts and mesh tank tops. A handful of teachers in the staff lot taking tiny steps toward the yelling just in case, but hopefully not, yeah, they'll all be fine. The smokers lighting fresh cigarettes. Lily.

"Do you know what people say about you?" Garrett said.

"I'd like to think I have—"

"They say you're a mean, angry person, who only has one friend, and thinks everyone else is a total idiot."

There were crowd sounds. Like when Ken Nicosia's fibula poked through his furry leg in the fourth quarter of the Thanksgiving game last year. Or when Daniel Bannon got a cleat to the crotch during sudden death overtime in the semifinals that past fall.

Mr. Gillespie, still making his approach from the staff lot slow, slow, called down to them with his hands cupped around his mouth and asked what exactly was going on.

Willa did nothing but grind her teeth hot. Stood there, fists in balls, shaking.

"I know for a fact that's not who you are," Garrett said. "It can't be."

Willa spoke through her teeth. "You don't get to tell me what I am."

"That's not what I'm doing. I'm trying to tell you what I'm not."

Someone out there, in the crowd, called for Willa to beat Garrett's ass.

Two fists in the air, both tipped with middle fingers, Willa scanned the crowd with them so she made sure no one was left out.

But then she stuffed her hands into her khakis. Bit the inside of her lip. Kept her eyes on the blacktop. Watched an ant go about its ant business, not thinking a thing, not feeling a thing. Never happy. Never sad either.

Garrett said, "I blew it. But I didn't mean to. It might be a normal thing for you, having to consider all that stuff all the time, but it's not for me. I got scared."

Willa swallowed.

Cleared her throat.

"It is normal, and I don't deserve it."

She didn't.

Of course she didn't.

But what an awful thing to say.

Selfish.

"I don't think that's selfish, Will," Garrett said.

"It's Willa. You don't get to drop the A."

Leaning against her car now, hands in his own pockets. "What do I have to do to earn that?"

Willa wiped her nose.

The crowd had gone about its business by then. The track team damn near left a cloud of dust behind them. The teachers were in their cars, pulling away. The smokers had left a pile crushed butts on the ground.

Lily waved, gave a little nod.

Garrett. His big, round eyes. The patch of stubble on his chin. His everywhere hair. His neat, disheveled clothes.

"You can keep your mouth shut while I figure some stuff out." She told him to get out of her way, opened her car door, got in.

There were his eyes again. Through the open window. Just staring. Looking her in the left eye, the right eye, left, right.

A car horn, a trail of cars spanning back to the curve in the lot through the rearview mirror.

“Oh, you mean now?” Garrett said.

“Jesus.” Willa unlocked the doors.

No, Willa didn’t deserve any of this.

But still, with Garrett sitting shotgun, rolling through the parking lot slow-slow to inspire more sound, more honking, Willa dug through her brain for the directions to Loonsfoot’s office.

19.

Cassie hated everything about what she needed to do. Need was such an awful word. It implied a handful of nasty things about her. The types of things that people bury underneath layers of smiles and laughter and music and television shows. The things that sneak up when shit tips sideways. Like praying.

Dear God, please make sure the contractor doesn't find black mold behind the bathroom walls.

Dear God, please let the boss take a sick day today to ease the tension in the office.

Dear God, please, if the neighbor's tree is going to fall during this storm, make sure it falls into the street and not onto this lovely, standalone, four bedroom, two and a half bath starter home.

Most people didn't need much else besides a sunny day to help with their self-diagnosed Seasonal Affective Disorder. They didn't need to go to Walmart searching for GPS tracking stickers that can sync with their phones with a QR code. They didn't pack their shopping baskets with this, that, the third, to make sure they didn't get a cocked eyebrow from whomever was running the register. Didn't need to pay for everything with two credit cards because of how many shifts they'd needed to cut short or give up all together recently to cook up plans in plans in plans—just in case.

They didn't need to skulk around in the dark while their daughter slept, scanning stickers, placing them underneath a stack of books in a discounted Jansport. Underneath wallets, makeup, receipts, tissues, and change at the bottom of purses. In the toes of pairs of Chucks, Keds, hideous suede school-mandated uniform shoes. Deep in the back pockets of pairs of jeans, or on the back of a smart phone hidden by a rose gold, sparkling, shock-resistant phone case.

And they certainly didn't need to sit down in the shower with their arms around their knees until the hot water ran cold because that was the only place they didn't need to be whatever was expected of them. Morning Mom with the steaming mug of coffee and a funny, but completely made up story about a customer from the night shift. Dinner Mom with sandwiches in white Styrofoam rectangles, grease-sopped packets of French fries, and a large fountain soda with two straws sticking up through the plastic aperture in the lid. Friend Mom on the couch with a bunch of episodes on the DVR to mow through replete with goofy asides and comments on plot, character motivation, or bad kissing noises television sound engineers seemed to love to put front and center in the mix. No, Shower Cassie just sat. Let the steam and the water pull everything out of her. She was a full-grown, human-sized boil under a hot compress every night at about three in the morning, just without the yellow and green and red muck to show she was finally running her course.

This was her life.

Having to recharge her phone three, four times a day so she could refresh the tracking app to see where Astrid was and where she was going, that was her life. Managing a diner was her life. Keeping on her mom faces, having to keep up her Cassie-isms was her life.

Maybe her daughter not making it past graduation was her life too.

But it had been good.

For a little while.

At least.

It was a Thursday when Chris showed up at the door. Or a Friday.

"It's Wednesday?" Cassie said, leaning her hip against the doorframe, the door only half open.

Chris held up a plastic bag from some sandwich shop where you needed to order on a touchscreen that wasn't Wawa—too expensive for Cassie—and said, "Yeah, seventh—"

"And eighth periods free, right."

"Thought I'd bring lunch. Turkey avocado BLT if I remember correctly?"

Cassie forced her mouth into a smile, said, "Nailed it. Thank you."

"Could I—"

"I actually already ate, though. I'm sorry."

Chris rubbed the back of his head with his free hand. He always looked so nice in his sport coat and tie. A little disheveled, but in a scatterbrained professor sort of way. "Sure, no. I should've texted. Sorry about that."

Cassie clenched her teeth, breathed through her nose, pursed her lips. "You have nothing to apologize for."

"Well, here," Chris said handing over the bag. "You and Astrid can have it for dinner."

Cassie nodded.

Couldn't say anything.

There was nothing but the birds in the trees, cars whooshing by.

"Astrid's doing really well," Chris said. "In school. Not that that's exactly surprising. But, I don't know, kids tend not to tell their parents about school stuff."

Cassie laughed, could hear how fake it was, said, "Must be some good teaching going on over there."

Chirping.

Traffic.

"I'll get going," Chris said. "Department meeting right after last bell."

"Thank you for the food. And the update."

Chris nodded, smiled, turned toward the parking lot. Then, "Hey."

Cassie did her best to look as if she hadn't been watching him go. Reached for the mailbox. Raised her eyebrows but had nothing to say.

"If there's anything you need, just give me a call."

"Thank you." A nod, a toothless smile. "But I don't need anything."

She closed the door behind her without turning back for one more last look.

Eyes clenched tight, she counted to one.

Two.

Three.

Then she stuffed the bag of food into the refrigerator, sat at the kitchen table, and swiped this, tapped that on her phone.

A clump of red dots at the apartment.

One at Wyndmoor Academy.

She closed, reopened the app every five or so minutes.

This was her life now.

20.

Willa wasn't going to let her phone buzzing-buzzing away in her pocket interrupt this. Whatever this was. Lily's face so close their noses were almost touching, her hair splayed out on the pillow. Willa's hand sweating into Lily's, locked together, fingers between fingers. Lily's smoke breath wafting into Willa's mouth, lungs. Bare legs wound up and threaded together, a warm latticework of skin and bone. Lily asking if Willa was nervous. Willa telling her no, of course not, keeping her shaking arm tucked under Lily's pillow so she wouldn't give the truth away.

They'd gone for coffee. But without Cassie, the diner hadn't had the usual set of comforts. No goofy conversations, no references to obscure science fiction shows to shift the conversation away from things that made Willa's stomach act as if she were stuck on a roller coaster with just one massive drop. Just Lily and Willa and two chipped coffee mugs staining brown rings into the napkins they were set on. Willa's eyes had gone back and forth between Lily, the table, the front door, the parking lot through the plate glass, cars zipping this way, that, up and down 309, back to Lily, just to start the circuit over and over again. And Lily had never once looked away from Willa—not that she was able to confirm that for sure considering that at least forty cars had passed by the diner on their way to someplace or another every minute or so.

When they'd finished their coffee, Lily had asked if Willa liked Hop Along or Laura Stevenson. Willa had nodded, said, "I love the guy from Hop Along's voice."

Lily had left a couple dollars on the table, said, "Their singer's a woman."

"Oh."

"I think you'll like them."

Willa had followed Lily to the car. Said, "Okay," and, "Okay," and "Okay," to the directions Lily gave from the passenger seat.

Parked on a street she'd never been on.

Walked into Lily's empty house.

Followed her to her bedroom.

Watched her switch on a Bluetooth speaker and scroll through her phone.

Told Lily she'd been right, she did like them.

And then it'd all happened so fast.

Too fast.

Willa hadn't had the time to pinpoint where she'd smelled the way Lily's house smelled before. Hadn't been able to comment on the sun coming through the bedroom window as a function of, during daytime hours, the sunlight typically being visible through glass. Everything that had happened after that—the sitting on the bed close-close, the hands, the lips, the slow shedding of clothes, that had all been in slow motion. Every movement considered, reconsidered, carried out by cold, shaking fingers.

And now they were here.

Face to face.

With Willa's fucking phone still buzzing and buzzing in her school pants pocket at the foot of the bed.

"I think," Willa said. "I think I should—"

"It's okay."

Willa sat up, scooched herself the edge of the bed.

Then the blood rushed to her face, turned her ears to embers. Searching through her crumpled pants, the skin on her legs, arms, and stomach began to blotch with red at the thought of Lily watching her.

She never should have told Garrett to call only if something important came up, or in case of emergency. The kid was always in crisis. She was smarter than that.

"You're not busy, are you?" Garrett said into Willa's ear.

"Yes, in fact, I am." She turned back to Lily, mouthed, "Sorry, so sorry," made a face she'd never made before, as if it would somehow emphasize and strengthen her apology. She stretched out corners of her mouth, showed some teeth, like she'd stepped in dog shit and smeared it through the house before picking up on the smell.

"Well, I thought maybe this couldn't wait."

"It could've waited, like, twenty more minutes."

"I'm just doing what you told me to—"

"What is it, Garrett?"

Lily stood, went to the window, stretched. Willa would be able to remember that. Lily's body backlit in the sun. Muscles pulling against bone, showing themselves through skin.

"You still there?"

"Jesus. Yes."

"Doctor Barbara Loonsfoot hasn't had any professional publications that date back more than a year and a half or so ago. No research, no interviews, no nothing. But, recently, she's in local papers, she's got her own practice, she's taught courses at a couple local colleges. She's got a page or two of Google searches right up front and center. And it's all super impressive. She's like a local psychology celebrity—if there were such things outside of daytime TV."

Elbow on her knee, forehead in her palm, Willa sighed, said, "I said only call if something's urgent, that's it. This isn't exactly—"

"It's not about what's there that's important. It's about what's not. Everybody's got an online fingerprint. You have to try pretty incredibly hard not to. And it's almost as if, before a year and a half ago, Loonsfoot was really trying pretty incredibly hard not to."

"Are you trying to tell me—"

"I'm trying to tell you that it's almost as if there was no such person named Doctor Barbara Loonsfoot before November 2016."

The sound of compressing springs, Lily's hand through Willa's hair. A fingernail running down the length of her spine.

"This," Willa said, her breath catching in her throat. "This doesn't seem like much of an emergency at all."

Over the phone, Garrett's voice becoming more and more shrill, like he was actually excited about all of this and everything it could mean, he said, "I have more."

Lips on Willa's neck. "Yeah?"

"I ran the plates from the photo you sent me the other day."

"And?"

"So, yes, the plates are registered to Loonsfoot. But the original owner was a guy named Anthony D'Angelo. He lives over on Brent Road in Oreland."

"So the hell what? Maybe she bought it from the guy."

"That's what I thought, but then I was like, why would such a successful psychologist with her own practice, in her very own office space, drive such a shitty car around?"

"She's a weirdo?"

"No. Well, yes, from the things you've told me, sure. But no. Those plates used to belong to D'Angelo, but not the car itself. The plates were registered to a red '96 Ford Explorer Sport."

Lily was behind Willa now, her chin on her shoulder, arms wrapped around her waist. "That could literally mean anything," Willa said.

But it couldn't.

Not really.

And not just anyone could do research like this.

This was Wyndmoor-Academy-grad-bound-for-MIT-in-computer-science shit.

That was real.

"It can't," Garrett said.

"No? Why not?"

"Because there hasn't been a PA state inspection record for that car with those plates since 2014."

Willa whispered she was sorry, pulled Lily's hands away from her. "So that means—"

"It means that D'Angelo and Loonsfoot are either pulling some sort of scam together, or Loonsfoot is a total fraud, and pretty much a criminal."

"Where are you right now?"

"My house?"

"I'll be right over."

Willa ended the call. Began getting dressed.

Lily, still on the bed, shrugged her shoulders.

Willa said she was sorry, buttoning, zipping her pants. Said she would make this all up to Lily, told her she promised.

"Everything's always so serious with you," Lily said, standing, reaching for her own pile of clothes.

"I know. I wish it wasn't."

"I don't know if you do. Wish that, I mean."

"I really do. I just have responsibilities I can't ignore. But I so wish I could. Especially right now."

"Not ignoring a thing is different than being responsible for it."

Willa didn't move. Couldn't. It was a thing Ken had said, not in so many well put-together words, for too long. But he'd said it like an accusation. Like Willa was a fool. Or maybe Willa just hadn't been listening. Maybe Ken had made her not want to listen.

"Sometimes people need to be allowed to figure shit out for themselves," Lily said.

Maybe if Astrid had spoken to Willa outside of school at any point over most of the last couple weeks. Maybe if Cassie had been willing to give her a little more than, "She's doing well, Will, thanks" in her text messages. Maybe if Willa backed off. Maybe if she stayed. Turned off her phone for a while. Went to Garrett's later. Helped out but didn't turn into the only one staying up all night most nights.

Maybe.

Lily stood, moved across the room to Willa. Unbuttoned the top button of Willa's uniform shirt. "Don't you like the music?"

Willa nodded. "I love it."

"Don't you like me?" Second, third, fourth button.

"I do."

Hands on bare belly skin. "Then stay."

Willa stayed.

21.

There was a popular bar in front of Blue Bell Place where many of Cassie's friends used to go, drink, and post half-drunken photos on the internet. She used to show up every now and again when she was able to get a sitter. Then eventually she'd stopped being invited after turning down the invites too many times. Most of those people posted photos from gastropubs and microbreweries anymore. The kinds of places that allow kids and dogs. The last time she'd spoken to Lindsey—actually, literally spoken to her—was when Cassie had gotten a call telling her that unfortunately Lindsey and her then-fiancé didn't have any more open seats left at the wedding venue, and she was so, so sorry about it. Tom texted every so often with updates about a new *Star Trek* series that Cassie couldn't afford to watch because of its streaming service exclusivity. Maura had moved away after some disastrous relationship with a man-child and, as far as Cassie knew, no one had seen her since, outside of photos from Pacific Beach.

The last time Cassie had been out with anyone that wasn't Astrid, or Chris, or sometimes the diner staff was... maybe when *Star Trek Into Darkness* was released in theaters.

Cassie flicked her last, absolutely last cigarette out of the car window into the bar's parking lot on the way through to the independent living home.

The place didn't have the exact smell of Gran's nursing home. No one was dying here. Not that the independent living facilities weren't precursors to the home or the grave. It was more a place where people went to unburden themselves from society's pressures before their fates locked onto them with any sort of certainty aside from, yes, death, but not quite yet—if they could afford such a place.

Probably, most visitors weren't asked who they were there to see. They more than likely didn't need to reference the return address on a crinkled envelope in their purses for the apartment number. Didn't often ask for directions to their visitee's unit. Or need to track the invisible line from the desk attendant's fingers through the wall of windows onto a lovely, grassy courtyard, saying, "Okay," and "Mmhmm," and "Left at the second fountain, okay, yeah, got it."

The walk over the expertly laid paver path that wound, and wound, and intersected with other paths made Cassie add a stop at a convenience store for another pack of American Spirits to her to-do list before her double shift. Jesus, if Astrid were to find the black smears where Cassie had stubbed out smokes on the front step, or the stray grains of tobacco from the bottom of the packs anywhere in the apartment, or get a whiff of Cassie's stinking clothes, a well-placed asteroid would be nothing short of a fiery wreck of relief.

Cassie gave apartment 737B a light tap, tap, tap with a single knuckle.

Waited.

Almost turned back to retrace her steps through the courtyard toward the cigarettes.

She rang the doorbell instead.

Waited.

Pressed her ear to the door.

Maybe he'd passed.

Though this wasn't exactly the best time for Astrid to lose a family member no matter how estranged.

Goddammit, Cassie was a horrible, wet, hot shit of a human.

But the door opened.

And Cassie would have to stuff that thought away in a folder of regret for the time her father would actually go and die.

"Cass," said John Walsh.

"Hi, Dad."

John leaned against the doorframe. "What can I do for you?"

"Coffee?"

His hair was completely white now. The white that made him look like a vibrant geriatric. The type that could be found on a golf course, or a Life Alert commercial. His face had gone droopy. Same for his eyelids, now showing a little bit of the red that holds eyes in place in the sockets. His button-up shirt was pressed, clean, and tucked into a nice pair of slacks with a crease down the center of both legs. A pair of bright white sneakers.

He looked good.

Not quite Patrick Stewart good.

But good.

Cassie told him so, stepping into the apartment.

Apparently there was a gym, a handful of fitness classes run by people probably Cassie's age.

They said nothing to one another while John prepped the coffee in a French press because, obviously, John would only drink coffee from a French press.

Cassie would Keurig at his age. Wouldn't be much time left, so why would she go and waste what little she had left by acting like the people moving into North Philadelphia with their beards and their thick-framed glasses?

She didn't say any of that.

Just sat at the kitchen table looking around at the place

her father had been living since before Cassie had become manager at the diner. She couldn't assign a year to that particular achievement. Probably best not to.

"Place looks nice."

It did. Pictures of Astrid as a baby on end tables, her first-grade photo on the wall. Nice, big television mounted above the mantle. Patty Walsh all over the place. A big, thick hardcover novel on the coffee table next to the TV remote, the Blu-Ray remote, the Amazon Firestick remote, the stereo remote. Fresh vacuum lines on the living room carpet.

John set a glass mug in front of Cassie. "Thanks," he said. "It doesn't always look like this."

"The times I've been here it has."

"You're not here too often."

Cassie blew on her coffee.

John took a slurp from his mug, groaned as he settled into his chair. "You want to tell me why you're here, or are you going to drink half of that and remember you have something you're late for?"

Eyes on the table, fingers tightening their grip around the mug handle, Cassie said, "You know why I'm here."

"It's certainly not money. I've been sending that your way once a month and it never seems to come out of my checking account. I hope you're disposing of the checks properly. Shredding is the best way to be sure you won't get me robbed blind."

"They can tape and paste those things back tog—never mind. You have to know why I'm here."

John cleared his throat, looked through the freshly cleaned window out onto yet another courtyard. "I'm not an idiot."

"I don't know what to do."

"It's happening again?"

Cassie chewed the inside of her cheek, nodded. "At least I think so."

"Cass, I didn't know what to do with you, and compared to Astrid's issues you were playing little league."

"Can you not say 'issues' like some sort of Fox News talking head?"

"You know damn well I don't watch—it doesn't matter. Drinking and sex are typical teenage problems, okay? And your mother and I blew it with you on that front. What makes you think I have any advice whatsoever that would help you here?"

Cassie pulled a napkin from the basket at the center of the table. Wiped her nose, her eyes.

"I tried, kid," John said. "I went behind your mother's back and did everything I could to try to help you, but you didn't want any of it. You were so damn mad at her that—"

"I was mad at you too."

"For getting you started at your apartment? For watching Astrid when I could? For sending money—"

"For not convincing Mom I wasn't the awful embarrassment she thought I was."

John went for the napkins now.

Cassie swatted the basket away. It slid across the table, dumped napkins all over the kitchen floor.

"Your mother loved you," John said. "She hated herself for letting what happened happen."

"Funny. I hated her for that too."

"If she could've gone back and done things differently, I know—"

"But we can't go back and do shit differently, can we?" Cassie stood, slapped her mug off the table. "My daughter is going to die, Dad. She's going to die and it's going to be my fault."

Sniffling, choking back light breaths, John crossed the room. His knees cracked, kneeling where the mug shattered. He picked glass off the floor, dropped pieces into a cupped hand.

Cassie scooped up the napkins. Used one on her eyes.

Stacked them nice and neat by tapping the edge on the floor. Put them back in the basket. Placed the basket back in the center of the table.

John, on the floor, sat, laid the glass shards in a neat little pile next to him. Eyes red, face puffy, he took a deep breath through his nose, let it go from his mouth. "The only thing I ever was able to figure out hit me after you stopped talking to me. Sometimes you've got to trust people to figure things out for themselves. Step in when you can, if you can. But let them do what they need to do, whatever it is."

The roll of paper towels came away from its wooden post with less effort than Cassie needed to dish out. It clattered onto the countertop. She was wrecking his nice, clean apartment. Like she couldn't help herself.

The paper towels turned brown, had to be placed in the trash in coffee flavored clumps. But they did well with the glass. Didn't tear, didn't let glass open up her palms, the soft pads of her fingers.

The floor still smelled of fancy coffee. There were probably little bits of glass hiding on the patterned laminate. But Cassie sat next to John anyway, her back against the dishwasher.

"The way I see it, having to watch you do your thing from a distance turned the worst part of my life into something special. You raised a beautiful, smart kid. Gave her a good life. If nothing else, everything your mother and I did, right or mostly wrong, led to her. And you."

"This is a little different than our shit."

"It's a lot different. But so are you. And that's why I think you'll figure this out. You figured your way into making everything else work. I trust you to not let Astrid go without having some say in the matter."

Whatever coffee was left on the floor had soaked into Cassie's pants. She should just laugh it off if she wound up needing to pull a piece of that mug out of her butt cheek.

"Besides," John said. "If you ever need any help with fucking things up worse than they already are before figuring a way to make it better, you can always call."

Their faces were wet, but they laughed anyway. Half laughed. Somewhere between cracking up and breaking down. That space where people have no reason to laugh at anything but have no better reaction available to them.

Shoulders six or so inches apart, Cassie said, "I'm going to need some help paying for UPenn. Astrid's not smart enough for an Ivy League full ride."

More laughing.

More sniffling.

More need for paper towels or napkins for their faces, but just going without them.

Then, nothing.

John placed a hand over Cassie's on the floor.

They didn't look at one another. They just stared straight ahead at the empty seats they were sitting in a bit ago.

On the floor, next to her father, Cassie said, "Coffee was good."

"Columbian dark roast."

"Nice."

Cassie still bought more cigarettes on her way to the diner after she and John resumed their distance from one another. After she found her way through the maze of the courtyard. Through the lobby, out to the parking lot.

But she didn't open the app that would show her where Astrid was at that moment.

She went to work.

She added her name back onto the shift schedule almost everywhere she'd crossed it out.

22.

Everything was fine.

The thing at the bottom of Astrid's purse was nothing.

The insert in plastic Coca-Cola bottle caps that can be peeled away with a thumbnail.

A QR code for a million-dollar contest no one ever hears about after the first month's marketing push.

It didn't matter whether or not the last time she'd bought a bottle of Coke was a year ago.

Or two.

Or five.

It didn't matter that the purse was on the older side of new—things get caught up in the transfer from old to new. Simple.

She would enjoy the movie. She would watch Jim from *The Office* give stern looks to his family for making too much noise, because aliens. She and Garrett would chat about it over really bad cheeseburgers at Dave & Buster's.

She'd kick his sorry ass in Skee-Ball and buy him a shot glass with a cup stuffed with ropes of tickets.

And maybe, if he'd done a good enough job making up for leaving her in the woods after she'd spilled her guts all over his Birkenstocks, she'd kiss him in the car. See what happens after that—it wasn't as if she'd be getting a full night's sleep.

She'd had to try showering away the bags under her eyes.

Had to brush more than her usual amount of makeup over her graying skin.

Needed to flex every muscle under her cast so her brain wouldn't run circles around and around the reasons why she wasn't sleeping as opposed to just the reality that she wasn't sleeping.

She'd never been the best sleeper.

That's all it was.

Not a precursor to the other thing.

But, at this point, she could sit awake in Garrett's car all night. Listen to him snore behind the wheel. Catch the sunrise over Bethlehem Pike.

She'd started and finished the novelization of *Star Trek: The Motion Picture* written by Gene Roddenberry himself last night—if that hadn't forced her into the slipstream at the backend of consciousness, nothing would now.

She'd gripped the bar in her palm tight. The electric current of pain was there. Weak, but present. But there wasn't much else to it. Her own sheets at the apartment were scratchy, though. Like the ones she'd slept on during her stay in inpatient care. Every conversation with Cassie, with Willa, had been nice. But nearly clinical. All about how she was feeling. What she was thinking. If she needed anything. If she would let them know if something had shifted inside of her.

Nothing had changed.

Couldn't have changed.

But she kept pressing her thumb to the sticky side of whatever the thing was she peeled out of her purse. Kept pulling the skin away, pressing it into the glue again, pulling it away. Even still, Astrid yawned, deep, hard; her thumb thip-thip-thipping away from the gluey surface.

Someone in the dark shushed.

The movie was too quiet. Almost no dialogue. Just footfalls and whispers. Popcorn crunching between teeth. Candy being shaken into palms from cardboard boxes.

Then Garrett asking if she was okay close enough she could feel his breath on her cheek.

He'd sent her text after text. Called her to talk through what he'd done. Shown up at the apartment with flowers. It was all very sweet. Too much, but sweet.

She was leaving soon. It wasn't a time to hold anything against anyone who could blame themselves for Astrid leaving Earth after she'd gone.

She took his hand, squeezed it, said she was good. Really good.

"You just seem nervous."

"I'm good, really." She followed his eyes to her knee keeping time to whatever tempo the metronome in her brain had set.

Another static shush from the dark.

She dug her nails into the plaster bar. Hard.

Almost nothing at all.

Just a bit of an ache.

No sharp bolt firing through her body.

And maybe the men in the suits she'd seen, the same ones who were driving the cars at the edge of the woods, and around the parking lot at school, had broken into the apartment in the middle of the night, or when Astrid was at school, and Cassie was at work. Stuck tracking tags all over everything she actively used, or things they'd figured she would use at some point.

She dug through her purse. Tossed change, makeup, pens, gum aside, scratched at the fuzzy faux leather bottom. Opened her compact, clicked it shut. Riffled through her wallet, pulled out every shiny new card she'd tucked inside, fanned them like they were playing cards. Reached down, went through her shoes.

Nothing in the left but damp heat.

But her nail caught on something stuck to the upside of

the toe in the right.

She was sweating, pushing her nail under the thin plastic. Wasn't breathing when it gave way, fell onto her fingers, the tackiness on her skin telling her what it was before she pulled her hand out of the shoe.

White.

Round.

A QR code printed in the center of the smooth side.

Garrett wasn't whispering anymore.

"I have to go to the bathroom," Astrid said loud enough for people in the theater to turn around and give her dirty looks.

It wasn't anything that couldn't be handled with a phone call to Loonsfoot. She would take care of everything. She always did.

Whoever had been shushing moved on to full sentences, saying thank Jesus Astrid was leaving. Thank God she'd be gone.

Astrid stomped her way down the rest of the theater steps. Made sure she'd be remembered. Didn't matter how.

She was being watched, crossing the lobby to the women's room. The man at the soda fountain filling a large cup, soda spilling over the sides. The woman standing in the concessions line pretending to text, her thumbs moving, but her eyes on Astrid. The man sweeping popcorn into a dustpan leaving a greasy slick on the tile floor.

Astrid typed and sent messages to Loonsfoot in the bathroom, tried to keep her eyes on her screen instead of on the mirror—she couldn't see herself like this.

Someone was keeping tabs on everything she and Loonsfoot were doing.

They were tracking her.

They'd been in her house.

A series of blue text balloons on her screen. Enough to push Loonsfoot's gray texts up and out of the thread.

But there was a lump.

A tiny one.

Almost not even there, but there.

On the back of her phone.

Under the glittery, plastic case.

The phone crackled a bit, but pulled free.

The Apple symbol was gone. Covered in a white circle, a third QR code.

They'd move up the timetable. Leave sooner. It was simple. They couldn't be caught by anyone at all if they were on a planet halfway across the galaxy. Easy. Astrid and Cassie would have dinner together tomorrow night, watch a couple episodes of *Star Trek* and fall asleep together on the couch during one of the episodes that was too ridiculous to pay too much attention to. The next morning, she'd spend the day with Willa. Do whatever she wanted to do. They'd cut school. It'd be a first for them, but it'd be a good first. The kind they would look back on. Willa on Earth, Astrid elsewhere.

Astrid reached up with her casted arm, brought the elbow down on the sink.

The sound stabbed at her eardrums.

The pain was hot and attacked her body in waves. Erased the gooseflesh that had pimpled all over her from all the eyes in the lobby, pinched beads of sweat out of the pores on her forehead. And nothing mattered while it radiated through Astrid's body, the top of her skull to the tips of her toes.

But then it settled.

Dulled.

Brought back the eyes, the suits, the trackers with every breath that didn't need to be pulled in and forced out through clenched teeth.

She raised her arm again.

But it wouldn't do.

Not long enough for the volume on everything to be turned down so she could focus on the things that would help her get what she wanted. What she needed.

Her fingers shook, moving through her purse. Then it was

her whole hand shaking, gripping the Sharpie she'd stored there back when people were still asking to sign her cast.

Astrid inched the marker into the top of her cast, cap first.

The pressure peppered her vision with sparkles and colors at the edges. Turned her breathing into short bursts of in-out, in-out, in-out whistling through her clenched lips. Made her eye makeup streak down her cheeks, pool at the corners of her mouth, mix with the drool she couldn't stop from dripping down her chin, gray, black.

She was making sounds.

Whimpers.

Groans.

But she kept them low in case there was anyone standing just outside of the bathroom or behind locked stall doors.

When her finger met plaster and fiberglass and fraying fabric, Astrid shoved the marker in farther.

She pulled the paper towels from the dispenser to wash her face. Flushed all the splattered black tissue when she was finished.

She reapplied new makeup in the mirror, the pain now constant.

It didn't come in waves. It was steady, sharp, fresh. It was a thumb on a bruised shin. Pressing the tip of a toe into the barb of an ingrown nail. A palm grinding into a sinus infected forehead.

Her brain would compensate.

Adapt.

Eventually.

But for now, she was able to agree to meet with Loonsfoot to talk things over. Come up with a plan. Do what was necessary.

Everything was a matter of fact.

Calm.

And even when she opened the door to Garrett standing, leaning against the wall, she was able to answer his questions in the same way—the pain only tweaking her vision with water every now and again.

Yes, sorry, she was fine.

One hundred percent.

"Scary movies really get to me sometimes."

Garrett smiled. But his eyes weren't matching his teeth the way they normally would.

Even that didn't matter.

Everything was under control.

Astrid would enjoy the rest of her night.

23.

Willa was going to pretend she was asleep. She was still shivering from the rain. Her hair was still wet. Her soaked-through crew workout uniform had chaffed her arms, her legs, where material bunched up at the nape of her neck from the drawstring. The calluses on her hands had ripped open from coaxing the boat through a whitecapped river. Ken could say her name from the bottom of the steps all he wanted. There was nothing that was going to get her out from underneath her covers. From allowing the steady rain on the roof to white noise her into a warm nap before she microwaved leftovers and ate alone at the kitchen table once everyone had gone to bed.

That was until Ken opened her door without knocking, without asking if he could come in. Willa would have begun making him feel as uncomfortable as possible with all sorts of questions about the possibilities of what she could have been doing behind her closed bedroom door, but the grin on his face, in all its confounding stupidity, cut her off after she called him by his first name.

"What?" Willa said.

"There's someone here for you."

"Who?"

"A boy named Garrett?" There was an emphasis on "boy" that would have put Willa back under the covers and kept her up most of the night if it weren't for the name. But the tone of his follow-up statement, the near excitement of it, would certainly do the trick—once she got rid of Garrett. "Maybe run a brush through your hair, this kid looks like you could find him in Pac Sun advertisements."

Willa did no such thing. But she didn't question her father's fragile sense of masculinity either, even though she could've ripped him to shreds if what he'd said hadn't been such a gut punch. Whether it was her continuing, worsening disappointment in him, or bad timing, or whatever Garrett was there to say twisting her guts, she couldn't tell. Still, she walked past Ken with a tangled mess of hair on her head, an oversized Columbia University t-shirt, mesh shorts, and bare feet.

Willa said, "Porch," at the bottom of the stairs. Followed Garrett outside, closed the door behind them.

It wasn't cold. But there was a chill on the breeze, a dampness that cut into Willa's windburned skin. She shivered, crossed her arms in front of her, almost told Garrett just to get in the damn house, that this was a bad idea and she regretted it.

But she didn't.

Waited for him to say something.

"Well?"

"You never showed up to my house."

"That's true."

"You've been ignoring my texts."

"That's also true."

"What about all the Loonsfoot stuff?"

"I've decided I can't be responsible for Astrid anymore."

"But last week—"

"Last week you said yourself that I didn't deserve any of this. You did. And, for once, I felt like something that had dribbled out of your mouth made sense."

The folder in Garrett's hands was dotted with gray circles of rain. He kept passing it off between his right hand, his left hand, right, left. Wouldn't pull his eyes from his shoes. "I brought this because I didn't think it would take any convincing for you to take a look at it. I came here because something happened."

Willa didn't move. But could've gone inside and thrown up. It had been the longest gap between texts from Cassie since Willa could remember. Astrid was always at school. Working at the bookstore. Going to her sessions with Loonsfoot. They talked. They just hadn't talked-talked.

Garrett told her what he'd heard on the other side of the women's room door. The crack of something against porcelain. The crying, the cut-short breathing. He told her about how Astrid went rifling through her purse, through her shoes. Found little white sticky disks that had freaked her out so bad he wasn't even sure he was sitting next to the same person he'd gone to the movie with. "I tried texting you. A lot."

"I blocked you. You're a chain texter. Just put the whole message in one text, not twenty. It's really annoying."

"Willa."

She leaned against the screen door. Wiped sweat from her forehead. Kept swallowing whatever saliva she could. Watched her peripheral vision close itself off like at the end of movies when the curtain slides back over the far sides of the screen. "What's in the folder?"

"Everything I told you I found out about Loonsfoot. I brought it so maybe you could take a look at it and give it to Astrid's mom."

There was no amount of steady breathing, or waving cool air onto her face, or staring at her gray skin in the bathroom mirror that could've stopped it. Willa threw up what little was in her stomach. Mostly water and acid, some flecks of the chicken fingers and French fries she'd eaten during her lunch period.

She brushed her hair after showering the vomit out of the ends.

Dressed in fresh clothes from a pile of folded laundry she'd neglected putting away.

If she'd been in the bathroom with Astrid at the movies, Garrett wouldn't be at her house, downstairs, talking to Ken about football.

If she'd kept in touch with Cassie instead of staying so angry about being frozen out of the situation, maybe she would've seen Astrid's behavior as something more than what it was.

She could've made a list of things she should have done to be a better friend, a better this, a better that, a better Willa.

Instead, she went downstairs, told Garrett she was ready, told Ken and her mother, Sandy, that she'd eat when she got home.

"You guys should eat here," Ken said. "I'll cook up another steak, it's not a big deal. You like steak, right, Garrett?"

Garrett stammered, said um, and uh, and, "I do, yeah, but—"

"We can't stay," Willa said. "We have to go to Astrid's."

Willa watched Ken's jaw clench, unclench, clench again. "You have to go to Astrid's."

"We have to go to Astrid's, yes."

Garrett leafed through his folder at the kitchen table. Sandy's eyes went back and forth between Willa and Ken.

"I haven't heard much about her lately," Ken said.

"Would you even want to?"

"I think I'd like to hear more about you building healthy friendships with healthy people."

"People like Garrett?"

"Sure, people like Garrett."

Sandy slid back in her chair, stood, said Ken's name, then Willa's, then said, "Maybe we should table this conversation for another time."

"Because Garrett's a boy?" Willa said.

"Not sure what you're getting at." Ken crossed his arms over his chest, stood the same way Willa was standing.

"Is this about Astrid or me?"

"Maybe it's about both."

Willa snapped her fingers, said Garrett's name, told him it was time to go. "Well why don't you take a seat and think about it a while, and then we can have an actual conversation."

On the way out the door, Ken called from kitchen, told Willa that was no way to talk to her father. Especially in front of guests. "Astrid probably isn't going to make it, Willa. She's sick. It's a shame, but it's true. People like her need more than just you."

Willa slammed the door behind her, followed Garrett to his car.

If Astrid wasn't going to make it, it wouldn't be from a lack of trying.

24.

Everything in the lab was wrapped in a halo.

A glow.

Like the hazy, buttery glow of a streetlamp in the fog.

Loonsfoot.

The frame of the *Rippa*.

All the windows and doorways.

The tables, chairs, tools.

The radiation suits hanging from hooks nailed into the walls.

Astrid had seen it before. It's what she described in her therapy sessions during her inpatient stint.

It was a symptom.

There wasn't any doubt about that.

Not anymore.

She wasn't stupid.

But it didn't have to mean what it meant the last time.

Didn't have to mean that at all.

She could use it.

Would use it.

To finish the *Rippa*.

To get the uranium.

To reach Regis-132.

And start a brand-new life.

A literal brand-new life somewhere else. Not the figurative sort Doctor Wallace discussed sitting behind the lovely wooden desk that must have been paid for with the exorbitant hourly rates she'd charged. It wouldn't come "from within" as she'd said. It would be the reverse for Astrid.

It would come from the new routines she'd establish on that alien world.

Going for a morning hike through the violet, bulbed grass. Over the shifting, hilly plains that never looked the same way twice. Cracking the glowing bulbs open for the fruit-sweet creatures inside to cook for breakfast over a green flame. Napping on top of the foamy caps of the mushroom trees in the afternoons—they would be simple enough to climb. Her hands would slip inside the soft flesh of the trunk for good, solid grips. Then she could use those holes for footholds before they laced themselves back together; a unique healing ability that all the plant life shared.

Nights, she and Loonsfoot would search for cleaner, safer ways for the *Rippa* to function. The deep purple soil—material Astrid would only be able to compare to the Nickelodeon Floam that Cassie had bought for her on eBay when she was little—would break the laws of Earth physics; the key to a perpetual motion engine. Once the *Rippa* went through a moderate refit, she could come back to Earth to offer Cassie, and Willa, and even Garrett, a new home on her world.

Then they'd sleep under pulsing pink clouds that moved across the sky like thunderstorms, but brought no needle-like rain, no brutal winds. No destruction of any kind.

Astrid could see it.

And it was so good she couldn't help herself but to laugh while Loonsfoot unfurled a tube of blueprints over a cluttered, dusty table. Once she flattened them the best she could, she ran a shoddily polished-nailed finger to loading docks, entrances, emergency exits, hazmat containment. Marked Xs in white pencil here, here, there. Sloppy ovals there, there,

here. A pair of arrows from an X in a space marked "parking" looping around, through the building from both sides, to the docks, to the hazmat containment room.

"Just like that?" Astrid said, stuffing giggles back down into her chest.

"Just like that." Loonsfoot, wide-eyed, grinning, crossed into the room where they'd seen Regis-132 for a split second before Astrid had been exploded through the front door. "You'll run communications from here, listening in on any radio chatter that may be coming through the police scanner. If something goes wrong, and I can't pull this off, the news will spread quick. You'll need to scrub the place down and get the hell home before anything can be traced back here."

Astrid ran her hand across the blueprints. The images more like X-rays than schematics. With the steady ache in her cast, the marker doing exactly what Astrid had jammed it in there to do, the way the cooling towers were put together on the page acted as a reminder that a lady in a cast strolling toward a reactor core may cause questions to billow up in people's brains.

Still, Astrid said, "I still don't know why I can't go with you."

Loonsfoot smiled. Not the usual manic and enthusiastic type Astrid had tried, tried, tried to emulate in the bathroom mirror, but ones she'd seen on Cassie.

Loonsfoot spoke with her hands cupped on Astrid's cheeks, her face close. "You're being watched. You found the trackers yourself."

Lips a bit squished, Astrid mumbled, "I can help."

"There's never been any doubt of that. But I've been, let's say, working outside of the confines of the legally acceptable scientific method for long enough to know when things are getting a little hot. You, here, keeps you safe. You'll still have a life if I get caught."

"Maybe I don't want one."

Loonsfoot pressed her lips to Astrid's forehead, pulled

her into a hung, rubbed her back. Astrid, nostrils full of solder and grease and sweat, rested her head against collarbone.

"We've talked about this," Loonsfoot said into Astrid's hair. "People like you and me always have a place in the world. Doesn't matter if it's on this planet or one lightyears away. We experience life turned up to full volume. That can be terrifying. And isolating. But just because there are fewer of us than everyone else, it doesn't mean you can't live a full, meaningful life. You just have to find your way of living it. It can be whatever you need it to be. Here, there, doesn't matter."

"I don't want you to get caught."

Loonsfoot pulled away, wiped the corners of Astrid's eyes dry with her thumbs. "I have a precisely zero-point-zero percent chance of doing that. Only the arrogant get caught. That's why you'll be here. My safety net. My just in case."

"But—"

"If that happens—and it's a gargantuan, capital-I if—I'll be just fine knowing you're out here, Amy. Out here living."

"Astrid."

Circling the blueprints again, marking the blue up with lines and circles of white, Loonsfoot said, "Hmm?'

Astrid was laughing again.

Couldn't really help it.

"You called me Amy again. Who's Amy?"

Loonsfoot's eyes stayed on the pages, went from mark to mark, followed her finger place to place. The sound of fingerprints over paper like static snowing away at the quiet room. "Sorry about that. Again. Scatterbrained is not a strong enough word for the way my mind works."

"Doc," Astrid said, the laughter dying in the back of her throat. "Who's Amy?"

Loonsfoot stood up straight, stuffed her hands into the pockets of her lab coat, took a deep breath through her nose. Then smiled. This time with just her lips.

"Amy was someone I used to know. About your age. Lab assistant at UC Berkeley. Not as good as you are with the math, but great with tools. You remind me of her very much."

"Sounds pretty impressive to me."

Loonsfoot laughed. "She was."

"Where is she now?"

Loonsfoot's eyes drifted from Astrid's. Went to the floor, the tools, back to the blueprints. "She died. Same way you and I almost did."

Astrid had nothing to say.

Couldn't string together a sentence.

Not a word.

But she crossed the room, wrapped Loonsfoot up in her arms. Let the jolt of pain in her cast dull the edges of having dredged up more awful from a place her friend had no intention of going.

There wasn't much else but silence.

Burnt metal.

Lady Mitchum.

Pain.

"Don't worry about it," Loonsfoot said, patting Astrid's back like she was saying okay, okay, she was okay.

But when Astrid let go, Loonsfoot's hands remained on her shoulders. "Now, we've got lots to do and not a ton of time to do it in before a bunch of jackbooted thugs come and try to put the kibosh on this whole shebang-a-bang. Let's get back to work, shall we?"

Astrid nodded.

Laughed.

They got back to work.

Any time Loonsfoot called Astrid by name, Astrid caught a slight pause before the A-sound. Like the woman running through the house this way, that way, talking, talking, talking, had to stop, think about it for a split second. Almost as if it was work. Almost as if, to Loonsfoot, there was no difference between Astrid and Amy.

The halos keeping every single thing encased in light glowed just a bit brighter.

Astrid would do nothing to fight it.

She would use it.

Loonsfoot snapped her fingers.

"What?"

"Let me show you how to switch out a license plate before you go. Can never be too careful."

Astrid followed Loonsfoot out the front door.

25.

Cassie hated having to sign her name to the back of John's check. It had taken nearly a week to decide it was okay to dig out the envelope she'd hidden in the stack of mail. She finished up a pair of night shifts before it was absolutely, one-hundred percent her choice, not John's, to pull it out of her purse, where she'd stuffed it once she'd found it, with the intent to deposit the check. But signing the thing made all of that justification and consideration seem foolish, an insult to both her intelligence and independence.

Astrid's hospital stay, the rest of the itemized list of hospital charges on the bill, and the amount she would have to cover before her insurance kicked in had changed things. It was no longer a point of pride that she'd refused help for so long. It was one of those nebulous stances that people seem to make during moments of stress—like becoming a vegan without giving any thought to its limitations, or adopting some sort of half-baked political stance without asking a single question first, or deciding to shave bald and wear a robe to a Kool-Aid party without thinking that maybe it was all feeling a bit familiar.

What had made Cassie Cassie was now just a thing that proved she'd been an idiot.

Still, she'd log into her mobile banking app and deposit the check after work.

Better yet, in the morning. It'd be late, she'd be tired. There would be nothing but a slice of old pizza, a cold beer in a hot shower, and her bed—which still, every now and again, smelled a bit like Chris.

The check would clear in a couple of days. She'd pay the bill once she was sure the money was available. Simple enough.

And someone was knocking on the office door—even more of a reason for Cassie to leave well enough alone just a little while longer to make exactly sure it was the course of action she should take and just get back to work.

Cassie heard them through the door.

Something about how there was no reason to just ignore a person. That it was completely disrespectful. That all they were trying to do was help because the people they were trying to help had agreed to allow them to do so.

Willa's arms were crossed over her chest. Her hair was soaked, matted. She carried no umbrella. And whether or not she was listening to Garrett go on and on, or had just allowed her face to become even more annoyed by and intolerant of fools during the little while since Cassie had seen her last, was something she was sure she'd find out soon enough.

"What's he doing here?" Cassie said, waving them inside, standing beside the open door to make room for them to pile into the office and get out of earshot of the old ladies circling the salad bar.

"Trust me, he wouldn't be here if he didn't have a use," Willa said. Her voice flat, deep.

"I resent that, okay," Garrett said. "Use? I've done nothing to deserve—"

"You left my kid in the woods," Cassie said. "Black eye's healing nicely."

"Thanks. And, again, that was a misunderstanding. I'm sorry—"

"Going to have to stop you there, captain," Cassie said, palm raised. "The only reason you were even allowed in my apartment was because Astrid had vouched for you. A lot. So, watch it." She turned to Willa, smiled, said, "Now, Willa. How can I help you?"

"Is that where we are now?" Willa said.

Cassie would have been an even bigger idiot than she had originally assumed herself to be if she'd ignored the possible reasons for Willa looking the way she did. Texts had gone unanswered. Conversations had been cut short. It was the longest amount of time Cassie had gone without seeing Willa—even if it hadn't been that long at all.

"No," Cassie said. "It's not where we are. I'm sorry for that. I'm happy to see you."

Willa's face softened a bit from Cassie's hug. Went from jagged lines to the light beginnings of forehead creases that will more than likely become a point of concern for Willa as she moved into her twenties and thirties. No one wants the creases. Especially not this early.

Willa fidgeted, leaned against the closed door, the desk, the wall, as she spoke. Snatched a folder from Garrett's grip. "So, Garrett's pretty good with computers, and—"

"Pretty good?" Garrett said. "It's, like, an objective fact I'm good with computers, and, by the way—"

"Objective means a thing is factual, that was redundant," Willa cut in.

Both hands up, Cassie told them both to relax, said, "Whatever's going on here, it needs to happen now. I have a shift to run."

Willa took a breath, went on. "According to Garrett's research—which, if I have to admit it, is really, really thorough—Doctor Barbara Loonsfoot doesn't exist. Not anywhere close to here anyway. And, out of the ones who do exist in the United States and Canada, none of them are clinical psychiatrists—most of them are just old ladies. Or dead ladies."

Cassie sat down in her rolling desk chair, rolled back into the wall. They had looked Loonsfoot up. Read articles. Vetted the woman. Did everything that anyone else on Earth would do to make sure the person they were sending their kid to was an actual person.

"Garrett thinks all of the material about Loonsfoot was faked."

"Actually, I'm pretty close to totally sure," Garrett said. "It's not all that hard to create an online identity. Anyone can do it. But I think this lady is super talented. I think she forged degrees, lines of credit, a social security number, LinkedIn profiles, everything."

Cassie's tongue was dry and reeked of smoke, but she licked her dried-out lips anyway. Cleared her sticky throat. Swiped her sleeve across her forehead. "How could you know this?" she said.

"Well, you're, what, forty?"

"Asshole," Willa said.

Cassie said, "Thirty-four."

"Sorry about that. Seriously, I'm—"

"Just—please?"

Garrett shook his head, waved his hands, said, "Right. Sorry. So, at thirty-four, you probably have about eighteen years of an online presence. At least. Screennames, chatroom handles, profiles, user accounts. A trail that can be traced back to your very first keystroke on the internet. Loonsfoot's probably, what, forty-five? Does that sound right?"

Cassie nodded, watched her periphery blur, focus, blur again on the tile floor.

"Well, there's no way she just discovered the internet is all I'm saying."

There was more. Something about a guy named D'Angelo. There was an issue with Loonsfoot's car. A handful of rental properties. All of it was behind a wall of cotton. Distant, like it was being beamed into Cassie's brain on subspace radio from a Federation Starship out in the Delta Quadrant and she didn't have the equipment to decrypt it.

But Willa's voice was coming in loud and clear.

As if she were yelling.

"Where is Astrid now? I texted her, she hasn't gotten back to me."

"At work," Cassie said reaching for the box of tissues sitting next to the computer monitor.

"You know that for sure?"

"I can find out easily enough."

"What do you mean? Are you going to call Barnes & Noble?"

"Not—not exactly." Cassie thumbed through the apps on her phone. Opened the tracker. Told them one or two dots should tell them where Astrid was right then, the rest were going to be in a clump at the apartment.

But that wasn't what the screen displayed at all.

There were tiny spots of red all over the map of the immediate area. All ten tracking stickers in ten different points of light. And Cassie strung together a sentence laced with every permutation of "fuck" she could spit out without repeating herself. Then, "She found them."

"Holy shit," Garrett said. "What did the trackers look like?"

"Small, white, stamped with a QR code."

"Well Astrid pulled one out of her shoe the other night at the movies. She must've found the rest and stuck them all over the place."

"Wait," Willa said. "You seriously put tracking stickers in Astrid's stuff?"

Cassie stood, slapped her hand onto the desk. Hard. "What was I supposed to do?"

"You had me."

Then there was nothing but diner noise through the office door. The desktop computer buzzing and clicking under the desk. The air conditioning groaning to life.

Cassie stood, said, "I was wrong to put so much on you.

You're my daughter's friend, and that's enough. I had no right to put you in a position where you felt it was your responsibility to look after her."

Willa's pressed her wet hair into Cassie's collarbone, soaking through the Michael's Diner work shirt.

Cassie said, "Shh."

And, "It's okay."

And, "It's okay."

And when the sniffling stopped, Cassie pulled away from Willa, untied her apron, hung it on the coatrack. "I'm not asking you to come with me," she said. "But I'd be happy to have the company."

Willa ran a hand through her hair, wiped her nose, nodded.

Garrett raised his hand, said, "Can I come, too, please?"

"Who even is this guy, Will?" Cassie said, pulling open the office door, hooking a right, and heading through the front plate glass doors into the parking lot.

The rain was heavy now.

Cold.

Like it had a point to make.

But the weather wasn't an indicator of jack shit, and Cassie drove as fast as her car would allow to find her daughter.

26.

They pushed open the front doors and the chilled Barnes & Noble air stung through their soaked clothes. Garrett went left toward the Starbucks. They went straight back to the customer service desk, dead center in the middle of the store.

Pushing past browsers, children, around tables of new paperback releases, endcaps featuring series of young adult novels, they stopped when they were asked if they needed any help. Almost with one voice they said, "Is Astrid here?"

Over the intercom, echoing through the store, "Astrid to customer services, Astrid to customer services."

The woman hung up the phone, smiled, asked if there was anything in particular they were looking for? Telling them if they bought a book today, they would receive a coupon for fifty percent off a cookie of their choice at the café.

They were as polite as they could be. But couldn't keep themselves from peeking around shelving, displays, people. Couldn't help but ask additional questions like, "Is Astrid scheduled tonight?" and "Is there a way you can tell if she punched in from here?" and "Has she missed much work lately?"

The woman smiled, said she was sorry but she was fairly

new and didn't have a lot of experience with the computer system as of yet. "But Astrid's a pretty name. Unusual. There's probably a book I could find for you that could give some insights about its origin and meaning. Would you like me to check if we carry something like that?"

One of them said, "Divine strength."

The other said, "Divine beauty."

And before the woman could say anything, they turned to the sound of a familiar voice.

Astrid stood in her khakis and black golf shirt, her nametag pinned on her chest, her cast hugged to her belly in an L. Clean, together, smiling, the opposite of the images of her they had cobbled together on the drive over—ashen, slouched, greasy, her cast melted from the rain and no longer strong enough to keep its shape.

They said hi, asked her how she was.

She laughed a little, said, "I'm good. Are you guys okay?"

They said, yeah, they were, just figured they'd pop in, say hello. They hadn't heard from her in a while. She hadn't responded to their texts. They were in the neighborhood.

"Sorry, we can't have phones on the floor," Astrid said.

"We knew that," they said. "Maybe coffee at the diner after work?" and "We could have milkshakes or burgers, whatever you want," and "Will you meet us there? When you're off?"

Astrid was laughing now, nodding, saying sure, it all sounded good.

She hugged them.

Waved to Garrett once he'd made his way over.

"We're having milkshakes and burgers after I'm done here apparently," she said. "Want to come with us?"

They shot him a look that insisted no, absolutely not, this was not for him.

But he said he'd love that, running his hand through his hair, crossing his arms over his chest.

Astrid kissed his cheek.

Hugged them again.

Said she had to get back to work.

Disappeared into science fiction section.

They stood with Garrett. Let the *Mama Mia!* soundtrack pumping lightly into the store fill the space between them.

"This was good, right?" Garrett said.

They headed toward the front doors. The nearly black, roiling sky through the windows, the flimsy parking lot trees bending and bucking in the wind.

They didn't run for the car.

Kept a steady pace with their shoulders hunched, their hands in their pockets.

Garrett said, "Guys?" behind them.

They'd seen Astrid like this once before.

"What does that mean?" Garrett said.

In the car, he asked again.

They told him.

There was nothing but the rain beating on the windshield. The wipers chunking, chunking, chunking through the water.

They weren't having much of an effect at all.

A Taste of Armageddon

27.

Everything was stuffed in the box she'd brought from the apartment.

A Stay Puft Marshmallow Man with glow-in-the-dark eyes and mouth that haven't glowed since Cassie was a little girl. The one John had bought for her after they'd watched *Ghostbusters* on VHS ten times over a single weekend. Astrid hadn't even realized she still had the thing until she went digging. After Loonsfoot asked if she'd had any stuffed animals lying around for what she'd called "a bit of training."

Perdita from *101 Dalmatians* was in the box too. Cassie had told Astrid they'd gotten that one at Disney World. Astrid could almost see the park, thinking back. The castle. The gift shops. The Magic Castle motel a twenty-minute taxi ride away from the front gates. But not Perdita.

Buttercup, the toughest of the Powerpuff Girls. She was the one who took no shit. Said what she meant and meant what she said. Astrid was too young to know what any of that meant, but Cassie had told her later on that the oval-headed, mean-mugging cartoon reminded her of Astrid from ages two to four.

A plush xenomorph from *Alien*. Astrid had gotten that one for Cassie. The nightmare beast from one of her favorite movies. A perfect Christmas present. But Cassie, one morning, came to the breakfast table shaking, sweating, saying she'd had a dream that she was trapped in a *Groundhog Day*-esque time loop on the *Nostromo*. That every morning she'd wake up, have a monster burst out of her chest, then have to watch the thing kill everyone she knew in the most disturbing ways possible. Willa had gotten an inner jaw through her forehead. John had been pulled in half. Astrid had been melted to the bone with acid blood. From then on, the xenomorph lived in Astrid's closest.

And, last but certainly not least, a barrel-chested, squinty-eyed Captain Kirk. Cassie loved him. Astrid loved him because Cassie loved him. Whenever Cassie needed to take care of things around the apartment, or run out to the Wawa for something quick to eat, she'd plop Astrid down on the couch, tuck Kirk in her arms, switch on *Star Trek* and say she'd be back at Warp Nine-point-nine. They'd watch two, three more episodes before Cassie had tucked the cleaning supplies away, or unpacked the food at the kitchen table, all huddled up together, Kirk between them.

Loonsfoot lined them all up on the workbench in front of the nearly finished *Rippa*.

Said it was a precaution.

Said that, if eyes were so close to shining a spotlight on them, Astrid needed to learn how to defend herself.

Just in case.

Could never be too careful.

Loonsfoot reached into her lab coat, pulled out a gun.

Astrid backed up, hands up, said whoa, whoa, whoa.

"Relax," Loonsfoot said, pointing to the yellow and black striped muzzle. "No bullets are coming out of here. Just fifty-thousand volts of knockout power. But keep in mind that this little exercise is just phase one."

"Phase one?"

"Correct."

A couple days ago, that would have doubled Astrid over,

made the muscles in her stomach ache. But the halos all over everything had faded. They were still there, just with a different quality. As if they were pulsing.

And, despite the marker in the cast, Astrid's arm was healing.

The pain was mostly unnoticeable.

It still would manage to bring everything back into focus if she dug her nails into the plaster bar in her palm.

But it was different.

Whatever her brain was doing, it made the men watching her, the black cars driving around and around, and Loonsfoot stand out. Gave them a shine.

Astrid had spotted them in the bookstore pretending to read through trade magazines. Outside of the school, dressed as the workmen who'd been hired to move the tennis courts. At the diner, scooping up melty sundaes, pretending to enjoy them.

Astrid nodded, took the taser from Loonsfoot.

Backed up ten or so feet away from her targets.

Looked down the barrel at Buttercup.

Sneering a bit, the Powerpuff Girl would want Astrid to know how to defend herself if a situation ever came up that was serious enough to point something at someone.

Loonsfoot adjusted Astrid's grip, told her to make sure she held the handle tight, but not too tight—it could wreck her aim. Told her to breathe in through her nose once she had the laser dot placed square in the center of her target's chest. Breathe out as she pulled the trigger.

There was a pop.

Wires uncoiled from the gun.

Barbs hooked themselves into Buttercup's soft body.

Electric light went on, off, on, off, on, off; a rapid-fire clicking, clicking.

A puff of smoke wafted from the points where the barbs had ripped through the green in Buttercup's costume.

"Good," Loonsfoot said.

She took the gun from Astrid, pulled off the spent cartridge, clipped another into place.

"Again."

Astrid trained the laser dot on the xenomorph's elongated head.

This one deserved the shock.

It wouldn't scare her mother again.

She fired.

Hit where she aimed.

"Good," Loonsfoot said. "Again."

Perdita was next.

The new burns matched her spots.

"Good," Loonsfoot said. "Again."

Stay Puft.

His plastic eyes watching, his plastic smile smiling.

Astrid put the laser dot in the middle of his chest.

The white fabric browned, blackened, peeled away from his cotton guts.

But then his insides caught fire.

Loonsfoot sprayed him down with a fire extinguisher. Coughed, waved her hand in front of her face before giving Astrid a grin, a thumbs up.

Stay Puft was all white again.

But the damage had slouched him, forced his eyes to stare into his open belly.

He was still smiling.

"Okay," Loonsfoot said, clicking another new cartridge above the laser sight. "One more."

Then, Captain James Tiberius Kirk.

His smirking confidence.

His ability to see through any situation and figure a way out of it.

His scratchy material between Astrid and Cassie on the couch, watching his own adventures play out on the television alongside the two of them.

The laser dot fell from the middle of his forehead to the floor beside Astrid's feet.

Somewhere out there, Loonsfoot was asking what the problem was, if Astrid was okay.

Astrid let the taser fall from her hand, clatter onto the concrete floor. "I don't know why I did any of that."

"To learn to protect yourself."

"Most of them were my mom's. I ruined my mom's things."

Loonsfoot picked the taser up from the floor, pocketed it, said, "We're going to a place where we're going to learn how not to ruin anything of theirs ever again."

But leaving would ruin everything.

Astrid would be gone.

Cassie would be alone.

Willa would have no one.

They'd shown up to the bookstore because she'd been careless. Lost track of time. Laughed her ass off for too long while Loonsfoot explained that using a license plate from another vehicle was most effective when registered to an alias and used in close proximity to the car's point of origin, fully aware that a Googe search could have confirmed she was exhibiting all sorts of symptoms. The aura alone had already done that, but she just had to try and put it all to good use. Because that had always worked out so well in the past.

Hands on her shoulders, again, Loonsfoot said, "We are days away from hitting the power plant. And after that, we're gone. You need to start thinking about this differently. Like us being gone will be a break for them. They do so much for you. They worry all the time. But they don't need to, and once we're gone, they won't have to. When we come back for them, they'll be healed from all the hurt we've put on them. And so will you."

Willa always had said she wanted to help, wanted to see Astrid get old.

Cassie had always said she was never happier before Astrid.

"We know how hard it is to deal with our own selves," Loonsfoot said. "Imagine what it's like for them."

She reached for Astrid's hand.

Placed the taser back in her palm.

"You need to know how to defend yourself," she said. "I promise we won't move to phase two until you're absolutely, one-hundred-percent ready."

Astrid sucked back her running nose, trained the laser at Captain Kirk. "What's phase two?"

Loonsfoot snatched the fire extinguisher from the concrete, crossed the room, said, "Live rounds," patting the other pocket on her coat.

Kirk shimmered at the far end of the room, the same shimmer that could point out whoever-it-was who'd been following her, keeping tabs on her.

"Do you trust me?" Loonsfoot said.

Astrid nodded.

"Then do this, and we'll move on."

Astrid licked away a salty bead of water that had slid down into the corner of her mouth.

Took a breath.

They would be better off without her.

She needed to learn to take care of herself.

She would come back for them.

She pulled the trigger.

Kirk was a puff of smoke.

Then his gold uniform shirt burst open.

His face caught fire but was still smirking.

Loonsfoot sprayed Kirk out. Coughed through the blast of chemicals.

Cassie would be better without her.

Willa would be fine.

Astrid would be better too.

It didn't matter that Loonsfoot called her Amy again.

She'd be somewhere else.

Where she wouldn't have to worry about anyone or anything anymore.

Just herself.

Until she was ready.

Even still, her lip wouldn't stop shaking, her nose wouldn't stop running, and all that was left of Captain Kirk's head was a lump of singed synthetic fibers and goo.

28.

Cassie's plan was shit. She knew it. Willa knew it. Even Garrett knew it, and he didn't know much of anything at all.

Sitting in her car, her phone clamped into a plastic contraption jammed into the air vent, Willa's face front and center, Garrett in the background, she told them how it was going to go.

They were to say nothing to Astrid about anything they had dug up. Ever. That would be Cassie's job. Astrid had grown attached to Loonsfoot, and it needed to be handled in a way that would place the blame where it needed to land. On Loonsfoot. Six months of programming didn't just unravel, it had to fall apart. And Cassie would need to be the one waiting to see Astrid through it.

There was that word.

Need.

Again.

Once they were able to nail down an address to whatever property was linked to Loonsfoot—not her office, the other one; the one Garrett hadn't even been able to pinpoint with all of his tech-savant brilliance—they would send it to Cassie, and that was all.

After everything was out in the open, after it would be apparent to the police that Loonsfoot was, in fact, a fake, that's when they would go to the station. Together. And this would be only after Cassie, with Willa's (and Garrett's) help, created a soft landing pad for Astrid.

This wasn't about nailing Loonsfoot. Not all of it, anyway. This was about making certain that Astrid made it through this manic episode alive. Everything else was secondary. Had to be. Otherwise, all of it would have been for absolutely nothing. Sure, Loonsfoot would be in jail, or a psych ward, but Astrid could maybe be...

Cassie couldn't say it.

Instead, she said, "Am I making myself clear?"

Willa's face spoke for her. All angles. But she nodded. Said okay.

"Garrett?" Cassie said, eyebrow cocked, a tone of voice she only wrapped her words in for the insufferable geriatrics who would become indignant over Cassie's refusal to allow them to haggle over their price of their French dips.

"What about D'Angelo?" he said, tinny, distant.

"I am...taking care of that now," Cassie said, flicking her cigarette out the car window, taking in the lovely little house with its well-kept bushes and flower beds and bright green-lawn.

"What's that mean?" Willa said. "Where are you?"

Cassie tapped the red circle underneath Willa's chin, ended the call.

All the horrific fantasies Cassie had cooked up about this guy seemed nothing short of ridiculous now, sitting out front of his house. Sure, he could have a lab in the basement specifically for the experimentation and subsequent dismemberment of all the teenagers Loonsfoot lured to him. He could have kilos worth of heroin in the attic, waiting for Loonsfoot's pick-up and delivery service. He could be some sort of suburban pimp. A serial killer. Loonsfoot's lover. Leather enthusiast. Crime kingpin.

But she'd lived, at most, two miles from Brent Road at

any given point in her entire life. The Flourtown, Erdenheim, Oreland triangle of suburban Philadelphia towns never made the news save for once last year when a punk working at Dunkin Donuts was found skimming card numbers from plastic users at the drive-thru window. The occasional DUI, every now and then an unlocked car gets run through for the change in the cup holders. But a monstrous psychopath dining on children? That certainly never hit the Springfield Township Facebook group.

Halfway through her third cigarette, Cassie said, "Fuck it," and got out of the car.

She crushed the butt under her sneaker, made sure the other two were totally out—wouldn't want to burn down such a nice neighborhood unless it was completely necessary—and crossed the street, walked up the driveway.

The house was small, but nice. Little patch of grass that was just a bit overgrown in the front. Chain link fence to the sides with rust spots here, there. White siding. Beige roof. Windows with Child Inside decals. The perfect house to throw off suspicion. No one would suspect that a human trafficker lived there. No cop in the world would go after a white guy living like this.

She knocked on the front door.

Maybe she should start with a punch to the nose.

Get things moving quickly.

No futzing around.

Maybe she should crack her knuckles, lower her voice, say, "You D'Angelo?"

Maybe she should kick the guy in the groin, yell something about the kick being for Astrid.

But the door opened, and Cassie stood up straight, smiled. "Hi, is Anthony D'Angelo here?"

The woman in the door, balancing a little girl on her hip, blew a rope of black hair out of her face, cocked an eyebrow.

She turned, called his name. Called him Tony.

Tony would be the name of a guy who lures teenagers into

the seedy underbelly of society. Sex, and drugs, and guns, and money. Cassie would tear into the guy. Maybe he'd stolen that kid for whoever that lady was. Maybe he'd stolen her, too. Back when she was young.

But when Tony appeared in front of her, all Cassie could see was that the guy needed a shave. No hideous scar from a knife fight or an attempted assassination. He didn't have a big, fat mob-gut. Wasn't wearing a stained sleeveless undershirt. No gold chains around his neck. No wiry chest hair poking out from underneath a half-unbuttoned French-cuffed shirt. Just a "Punk is Dad" t-shirt. A pair of jeans that had probably been worn one day too many. Chucks.

The scars on his arm and hand were disconcerting though.

Like he'd been burned.

But they were faded. Melted white American cheese.

He smiled, said hey, and, "Can I help you?"

Cassie wasn't exactly disappointed. But she knew his face. Maybe should have just opened a yearbook and made a phone call.

"This is going to sound a little weird, but have you reported a car stolen?"

Tony shook his head, said, "Nope. Mine's right there." He pointed to a navy-blue station wagon in the driveway.

Nice little house. Nice little car.

"Do you know a Doctor Barbara Loonsfoot?"

Tony laughed, leaned against the doorjamb, crossed his arms over his chest. "What kind of name is that?"

"So you don't know her?"

"I didn't even know that was a name until you said it. Sounds made up."

Cassie scratched her head, said, "I mean, technically, all names are made up."

"Yeah, sure, but that sounds like she wasn't even trying."

"Whatever the case, she has your car. A silver Chevy something or other."

"The last car I had was wrecked on a road trip a few years back."

Cassie shook her head. Pulled her phone from her pocket, read the license plate number Willa and Garrett had given her.

Tony's forehead wrinkled. His eyes went just over Cassie's shoulder. Then, "That was my old car's license plate, but I've never driven a silver Chevy something or other. That doesn't make sense."

Tucking the phone away, Cassie said, "None of it does."

"None of what?"

"What?"

"You said none of it does. None of what?"

Cassie couldn't do anything else but chuckle, scoff. "Know what? It's probably nothing."

"I mean, a lady with a name like that with a license plate from a scrap heap? Something's kind of up."

Nodding, backing away, Cassie said, "You're definitely right."

"That's definitely a made-up name too."

"Yeah. Yeah, definitely."

Whoever Tony was, he was nothing he was supposed to be. Cassie was supposed to have solved something here. Made some leeway into understanding Loonsfoot. And Astrid. But Tony was just a guy. Doing everything Cassie was doing, just doing all of it better.

Cassie slapped her forehead. Hard. Enough to hurt.

"Better watch that," Tony said. "Might knock something loose."

"I should probably do it a lot more often then."

There wasn't much to look at after that aside from Tony's scarred arm, the welcome mat, Cassie's sneakers, as she shifted her weight from one foot to the other.

She should just go.

There was nothing here.

"You okay?"

"No," Cassie said, shaking her head. She pointed to Tony's arm. "You?"

"Oh, yeah. Some of us get to wear our hurt on the outside. I'm lucky like that."

Then there was a little girl's voice yelling something funny. A word from a cartoon Cassie used to watch when she was a kid.

Tony had his daughter in his arms.

Green, plastic Ninja Turtles mask covering her entire face, a strip of orange across her eyes.

"Sorry to bother you."

"We weren't doing much today anyway." He turned to his daughter, poked her stomach, said, "Right?"

The girl squirmed, giggled, screeched behind the mask, the plastic muffling the sound.

Cassie smiled.

Astrid used to make those sounds. Laughed a lot. Played a lot. But there must have always been something in her head that was ready to eat away at her. A thing more vicious than any scar. One that nobody could've seen coming.

If that little girl was lucky, maybe she'd been given a little bit of a better shot than Astrid had.

Tony said, "Say bye-bye, Natalie."

Natalie lifted her mask, smiled, said, "Bye-bye, Natalie."

"Might want to tell the cops about your plates," Cassie said.

"What would it do? I left that thing in California."

Walking back to her car, there was nothing but Astrid. In the little girl's laugh. On the home screen of Cassie's phone. On Astrid's voicemail greeting. Cassie said, "Hi, just checking in. Hope you're having a good day. Dinner at Michael's tonight? On me?"

She ended the call.

Drove away.

She and Astrid should go to California one day.

Once everything was settled.

If it ever would be.

They could sit in the sand on Pacific Beach, watch the sun pink and purple the sky as it dipped below the horizon. They would split burritos from food trucks on bus stop benches. Try surfing and give up surfing forever on the same day. Have strangers take photos of them with their arms around each other's shoulders in front of the *Full House*-house, then wait for John Stamos to stroll by because he evidently did that sometimes. Eat peanut butter and jellies sitting in the grass next to the Golden Gate.

Maybe a place where it didn't snow would help.

Maybe just a drastic shift in routine would do it.

Cassie drove to the diner, the spring air thumping through the open car window.

If she closed her eyes at the red lights, it was almost California. The birds, the warmth, the sun on her skin.

But then panic would soak into her brain. And before she was able to do anything about it, a car horn would blare somewhere behind her.

She would drive on.

She would go to work.

She would do it all again tomorrow.

With any luck, Astrid would too.

29.

The dirt road wasn't exactly hidden. If Willa were driving, matching the speed limit, it wouldn't be anything more than a blur of green and brown. But on foot, there was a curb apron, muddy tire tracks, eight, ten feet of driven-over grass and compacted dirt before the tree line blacked out almost everything beyond the first thirty or so feet into the woods. It couldn't be the only way in or out, either. It just also wasn't a patch of woods most people would want to hike. They had looked over satellite map printouts. Marked highways in red, high-traffic roads in orange, more residentially oriented streets in yellow, culs-de-sac in blue, so on and so forth until they had run out of colors in Garrett's little brother's box of Crayolas. The red teardrop indicator hovering over the spot where the house was supposed to be was wrapped in red and orange. Lots of space between, creating a nice big buffer zone between anywhere people were and anywhere they'd want to go on foot. "An almost perfect place to do some shady-ass shit," Garrett had said just before needing to chase down Brayden and beg him not to tell their parents he had cussed in front of him—unless, of course, Brayden wanted Garrett to dole out the ass-whupping of a lifetime.

Willa led the way into the woods.

There was a chill. A ten-degree drop. The treetops reached over the car-wide path, weaved themselves into each other. The sun only reached the ground in blotches of white. Almost hot compared to the air around the sparkling beams.

It was beautiful.

Like the light was bursting out of the ground, the trees, the shrubs, the weeds, into the sky. The Earth powering the sun in rods of light as thin as uncooked pasta, as thick as a tree trunk, every size between.

"Spooky," Garrett said. "Goosebumps." He rubbed his forearm.

Willa said nothing.

Took a photo of the scene in front of her.

It looked nothing like the real thing.

But there was a white spot at the center of the shot. She had to zoom with her fingers to see it. Deep, blurry, buried in the photo, a house.

"Now that's a little spooky," Willa said, pointing down the road. "I'll admit that."

They walked deeper into the woods. The house never seemed to get any closer. The break in the woods where they'd started was a white hole in the dark behind them. It was the type of quiet Willa had only heard on a camping trip she and her parents had gone on years ago. Complete. Enough to make breathing sound as if it were being done into a microphone. Enough to make footfalls and snapping branches perfect, film-quality additions to a horror movie's soundscape.

She would never tell Garrett, or even Astrid, but reaching the circular clearing with the house as its centerpiece forced the hair on her neck to stand up straight. Her shirt was peppered with pit sweat. She'd blame that on the sudden temperature spike, not her nerves. Not on Garrett's silence either. A guy who could barely keep his mouth shut having nothing to say was more significant than she'd willingly point out. So she didn't. Just watched her footing on the groaning, rotten front steps instead. Peeled a leaf of curled paint from the wooden siding. Told Garrett not to touch anything—broken windows meant there would be splinters of glass just about everywhere that could sink into a foot or a finger without any indication other than blood.

The front door was new. Padlocked in two places.

The windows wouldn't budge, swollen into place, covered in flaking paint and jagged wood spurs.

Willa could wrap her fist in Garrett's shirt, punch through the rest of a shattered pane.

"That only works in movies," Garrett said.

They tested the windows along the side of the house, slapped their hands clean after each one. Dug their phones from their pockets with just their fingers, careful not to dirty their clothes with their palms covered in dirt and paint flecks.

Willa took photos of the sagging deck in the back. The support beams that had been chewed to pieces and looked more like a series of ratty old sponges crammed into the dirt than anything that could keep a building from spilling onto the ground.

She sent the series of photos to Cassie.

A blue line stretched across the top of the message, stalled with just a centimeter of white to go.

Then came the red exclamation point.

"Are you getting any—" Willa's breath caught in her throat at the sound of a wooden crack. The blood-rush to her limbs tingled her fingers.

Garrett sent another kick into the back door.

The crunch of splintering wood hit Willa's ears a third time before she hissed Garrett's name, looked this way, that way, this way again into the woods for anyone who could've heard the sound and come running.

"What? The thing looked like I could've put my foot through it." He stepped into the dark of the house. "You coming?"

There was nothing inside that could have suggested Loonsfoot or anyone else was living there. Nothing but a pair of fold-up metal chairs. Tools littering what might have been a kitchen counter. Cobbled together control panels with ropes of tied-together wiring running this way, that. A pair of generators tucked into a corner of the room. Scraps of cut metal on the floors. Scorch marks on the walls, the concrete slab floors. Yellow, rubber suits hanging from hooks.

A filthy sheet over a car-sized lump in the center of maybe a TV room once. Angles and edges jutting in places that suggested whatever was under there wasn't a car at all.

"Looks like a spaceship," Garrett said.

"You're an idiot."

"I'm serious. Has Astrid ever had you sit through that horrible black and white show? *Lost in Space*? Looks like the Rollins's ship, just upside down."

"The Robinsons."

"The what?"

"The Robinsons."

"No, I'm pretty sure it was called *Lost in Space*."

Willa shook her head, crossed the room, pulled the sheet off the whatever it was in one quick tug.

She couldn't put a label to its shape. A diamond sitting on its flat side. But that was where the comparison ended. Riveted, brushed, silver metal so sturdy it barely made a sound when Willa knocked her knuckles against it expecting a deep ring. A hatch to climb through, a pair of seats bolted down inside. Knobs, buttons, diodes, gauges, levers on a panel in front of the seats. A bottle of champagne underneath the console.

"Holy shit," Garrett said. "It is a spaceship."

"It's not a spaceship."

"What would you call it, then?"

Willa backed away from the thing, said, "A spaceship-shaped, oversized science fair project."

Garrett disappeared behind whatever it was, said, "You said spaceship."

"And you should shut the—"

"Willa?"

She ran her fingers along the metal, the rivets, circled around to the backend—or, the side that didn't have a cockpit hatch.

Most of Garret's body was stuffed inside a rectangular opening at the concave underside of the diamond shape. His voice was muffled, echoing from the spots of the hatch that weren't filled with Garrett.

He shuffled his way out of the machine. Phone in one hand, flashlight casting a white cone. A picture frame in the other, the light reflecting off the glass.

"Is that Astrid?" he said. "When she was little?"

Willa took the frame from him.

Astrid had never been to California, much less the Pacific Coast Highway. Nor did she share much more than a passing resemblance to the little girl in the photo according to the framed pictures from pre-school and kindergarten around their apartment. But there was something oddly familiar about the little girl nevertheless. The way she was posing and smiling, standing with her hands on her hips next to a cart with Fresh Strawberries painted across the top in jagged white. Like she was a reflection in a funhouse mirror. An alternate Astrid.

"What is this?" Garrett said.

Willa took a photo of the picture. Turned the frame around, undid the plastic clasps holding the base to the pressed wood.

Her vision blurred a bit.

She nearly lost her grip on the frame as she read the misspelled words that were scrawled in red crayon at a kid-slant.

She took another photo.

Handed the frame back over to Garrett. "Read."

Breathing heavy, Garrett said, "'Dear Mommy. Happy birthday. Your present is strawberries. I bought them with my own money. Can we cut them up and put them in ice cream? I love ice cream. Do you? Happy birthday. Love, Amelia Grace Woods.'"

Willa heard it before Garrett did.

The crunching of tires over gravel and dirt and grass. The squeal of bad brakes.

She snatched the photo from Garrett, shoved him aside, stuffed it back in the empty space where he'd found it.

They pulled the sheet back over the machine, fast, noisy, while they told each other to shut up, and will you be quiet, as padlocks at the front door were clicking, clacking, unlatching.

Willa sprinted through the kicked-open back door first, wasn't so careful not to catch tetanus on anything that might have stabbed at her on the way down the steps.

If they kept on straight through the woods, they would eventually come to a 309 overpass, the abutment. Maybe. Willa couldn't string any words together, could barely tell if she was breathing. But Garrett was keeping pace with her, and she just kept pumping her arms, her legs, faster than her lungs could accommodate.

30.

There wasn't much time left.

Not after what they'd found in the lab.

Kicked-in back door.

Loonsfoot's stuff rooted through.

Astrid nearly had to beg Loonsfoot to let her go through with everything she'd had planned for Cassie and Willa. She'd never seen Loonsfoot like that. White in the corners of her mouth. Eyes wide, red, underlined with sagging pockets of skin. No jokes. No advice. Just that Astrid needed to be ready as soon as it was humanly possible. No more futzing around. Any more lolligagging and they wouldn't be going anywhere.

Astrid hadn't slept.

There was too much to do.

And all the while she'd gotten everything prepped, she'd watched the road outside her bedroom window.

Kept an eye out at school for any new adults who were all of the sudden hanging around the halls.

Checked over her shoulder everywhere she went.

Kept contact with Loonsfoot at a minimum.

A few more days.

That was it.

Willa parked closer to the clearing that led to the woods that led to the Green than last time.

They had too much to carry back and forth, back and forth to do it all from the Walgreen's lot.

Willa carried the screen, rolled up in its flimsy metal casing.

Astrid carried a black box similar to the one Loonsfoot had showed her that would house the uranium—just without all the lead lining—in one hand, hundreds of feet of orange extension cord over her shoulder.

Willa was quiet.

She was never exactly talkative.

But this was different.

After they'd finished the third trip from the car, dropped off the last of the gear, Astrid thanked Willa, hugged her.

"What was that for?"

"Are you free tomorrow night?"

"I can be."

Astrid said, "Good." Walked her back to her car.

There was nothing but feet crunching through brush and old dead leaves, crickets singing away in the empty golf course now too dim for even the most ridiculous golfers.

Willa told Astrid she'd catch her at school. "Or you can text."

Astrid nodded.

Watched Willa open her car door.

Get inside.

Close the car door.

Start the engine.

Then Astrid tapped on the window, used her fingernail so it wouldn't seem aggressive or annoying. She more than likely was the cause for Willa acting this way. That was unavoidable. Everything she'd needed to take care of, everything she had to do to make sure no one was worried about her, all of it did the exact opposite. They wouldn't have shown up at the bookstore if that weren't true.

But there was nothing she could've done about that.

Willa put the window down, smiled with just her lips.

Astrid said, "I'm sorry I haven't been—"

"You never need to apologize for anything, okay? What's the one line Cassie says all the time? 'I am, and always will be, your friend.'"

The breeze picked up, raised gooseflesh on Astrid's arm, blew her hair out of place. She laughed anyway. "'I have been, and always shall be.' One of Mom's favorites."

"Well it's true."

"I'm just—I'm happy for you. Lily is a really nice person."

Willa's face reddened.

She turned her head back to the steering wheel. "Garrett?"

Astrid nodded.

"That kid can't keep anything to himself. I wanted to tell you. I'm sorry."

"You never need to apologize for anything."

Willa smiled with teeth this time, nodded, said, "Tomorrow?"

"Tomorrow."

Astrid didn't wait long to head back to the Green once Willa pulled away.

She had to sneak to Kelly's house just beyond the tree line to plug the extension cord into one of the exterior outlets.

She ran the cord back to the Green as straight as she could, a little snaking to get around trees, bushes, and blowdowns.

She'd borrowed more than enough from Loonsfoot, it'd turned out. Had a clump of tangled orange next to the metal stand where she'd set up the projector, power strip, and DVD player.

Cassie's copy of *Star Trek: The Motion Picture*. Her favorite despite the self-indulgent special effects displays that tried to rival *Star Wars* but just extended what could have been a forty-minute long original series episode into a two-hour monstrosity that only a few people on Earth actually liked. Cassie loved it, of course. The grandeur. Kirk's face upon seeing the *Enterprise* again after so long. The audience was supposed to feel what Kirk felt. People just didn't get it.

Astrid only got it because Cassie did.

It was full dark by the time the speakers were set up and ready to go. By the time the projector was on, the DVD had cycled through all of its previews and made it to the home screen, showing off all of the special features available to people like Cassie. She would definitely want to work through all of those after the movie.

Lawn chairs. A cooler of Diet Coke. Chips, pretzels, popcorn.

And by the time Cassie broke into the clearing, Astrid saw exactly what she'd predicted.

The hopping.

The teenage girl sounds.

She didn't expect the full-blown tears but took the hug that came along with them.

"What's this all for?" Cassie said.

"Because."

Cassie pulled away from her, hands still on her shoulders, said, "Because why?" her voice stern, full of concern.

"Because I'm going to college in a few months and I want to get as many things like this in before I go."

Cassie kissed Astrid on the forehead, hugged her again.

Once they settled into their chairs and started the movie, Astrid didn't watch the screen too often. It was a bloated film, but even if it were well paced and driven by anything other than spectacle, she would've still kept her eyes on her mother.

Cassie had seen this thing at least two dozen times, but the six-minute-long reintroduction to the *Enterprise* always made her eyes go glassy, open wide. She covered her mouth when Spock was unable to recognize Kirk as his closest friend after attempting to purge himself of all emotion once and for all. Let her jaw hang loose when the *Enterprise* cruised into the center of V'Ger's trippy, alien core. Kept having to wipe her eyes when Spock finally understood that the most important thing in the universe was connection. Friendship. Family.

Cassie loved Commander Decker's character arc; needing to sacrifice himself and meld with Ilia so V'Ger could complete its mission of communicating with its creator. Her face lit by the screen, changing color as Decker and Ilia were bathed in light, becoming a completely new being. An infant in a universe where everything was wonder, and awe, and beauty. Where they were above everything, and nothing mattered, but everything mattered.

Cassie smiled, said, "What? I know. I'm a mess, right?"

Astrid couldn't hide her face from the glow of the screen.

Cassie pulled herself out of her seat, went to Astrid.

On the grass, Astrid and Cassie held each other as the movie played out.

Cassie had to keep shushing, shushing, telling Astrid it's okay, it's okay.

They did that as the credits rolled.

After the credits ended.

And even as the disc defaulted back to the home screen.

Lit by the glow of the screen, Cassie and Astrid sat together as the chill set in. And even a little while after that.

31.

Cassie kept her voice as calm as she could manage. But with everything she needed to say, it increased in volume and pitch with every detail she spat at the bleary-eyed, undercaffeinated cop in front of her.

"Wait," Detective Norton said. "So, this Loonsfoot is passing herself off as a psychiatrist to get close to your daughter?"

"Her name is Cecelia Woods," Cassie said, scraping her chair away from the desk, across the linoleum floor.

"And you know this for sure?"

Cassie snapped her fingers at Garrett, held out her hand.

Plopped the file on the desk, opened it.

Pointed to the first page.

A magazine article.

A younger version of Loonsfoot. Long, frizzy black hair tied back in messy ponytail. Thick black frames on her face. She was smiling, shaking hands with a man in a lab coat. "Astrophysicist Makes Breakthrough in Holographic Principle" above the photo.

"'Doctor Cecelia Woods, one of the foremost astrophysicists at University of California at Berkeley, has made major leaps in better understanding our universe,'" Cassie said, reading the first line upside down. She nearly had it memorized, reading it, rereading it, over and over in bed as the sun peeked through the blinds.

"Says here this woman's an astrophysicist," Norton said.

"That's what—" Cassie turned to Willa and Garrett. "That's what I'm saying."

Willa, face red, snapped, said, "She's a fake. She's coerced a teenaged girl into helping her, I don't know, build a machine that looks—"

"Like a spaceship?" Norton said, eyebrow cocked.

"You saw the photo."

Cassie said, "Willa."

Willa said, "Cassie."

Garrett said, "Guys."

Cassie and Willa said, "Shut up, Garrett."

Norton held up a hand, said, "Whoa, whoa. Let's just calm it down for a second here, okay?" He pointed to Garrett. "You found all this stuff?"

The overhead panels of lights buzzed while Garrett stammered through his response. Yes, he'd done the research. Yes, he'd printed out all the material. "But it was a team effort, I'd say."

Later, Cassie would ask him if he'd meant that to deflect any culpability if this didn't go the way it needed to go, or if he was genuinely trying to compliment them on circling Astrid's life like a flock of goddamn vultures to better keep her safe. Though she wouldn't treat him any differently if it were the latter—which, from his sweaty, sad-looking face, it may have been. He'd left Astrid in the woods, may have contributed to her drifting further and further from Cassie and Willa. But maybe she'd float him a free burger at the diner the next time he was in.

"He was able to get her real name from these," Cassie said. She turned the pages in the file. Pointed to "Bitter Custody Battle Leads to What Father Calls Kidnapping" from the *El Cerrito Journal*. Then, "Teen Girl Commits Suicide in Apparent Response to Familial Battleground" from the *East Bay Times*. She flipped to another page, pointed. "Disgraced Astrophysicist Disappears, Wanted for Questioning in Kidnapping Case" from the *San Francisco Chronicle*.

Cassie opened the camera roll on her phone, pulled up the photo of the birthday note in crayon, handed it over to Norton, said, "Amelia Woods was that girl. Amelia Woods was Cecelia Woods's daughter. Barbara Loonsfoot is Cecelia Woods."

Norton sat back in his chair. Scratched the neat part in his hair. "There's a whole lot to this. And it goes back a while. And across an entire country."

"I understand," Cassie said. "But this woman is a talented liar. Loonsfoot can't be her only alias. She's got to have stockpile of license plates from all over the country in her trunk or something. She's building a goddamn spaceship in her house."

"Speaking of which," Norton said, leaning forward, lacing his fingers together, resting his hands on the file. "How did you find out about this spaceship? And I'm using spaceship very, very loosely. I've seen some strange stuff—had to literally chase down a guy who thought he was Batman a while back, and I'm not kidding about that—but a spaceship?"

"We're using spaceship loosely, sir," Garrett said.

"You were the one who said spaceship first," Willa said.

"Guys," Cassie said.

"We may have peeked in a window," Willa said.

Norton nodded, said mmhmm. "You didn't happen to go through that window, did you?"

"No, sir," Willa said. "I can tell you that we definitely did not go through a window."

"That's good." Norton pinched the bridge of his nose. "Look, I agree that there is something very strange and very wrong going on here, so please don't take what I'm about to say the wrong way. I have to run this all through multiple channels, get in touch with a lot of people, and have a very long conversation with my captain about how I came to possess all of this information—"

"Evidence," Willa said. Her eyes went to Cassie, to Garrett, to Norton. She cleared her throat, said, "Sorry."

"This is going to take time, guys, I'm sorry," Norton said.

Cassie sat down. Needed to sit down. Elbow on her knee, forehead in her palm, she said, "What am I supposed to do?"

"I suggest you tell Astrid the truth," Norton said. "That she needs to stay away from this Loonsfoot woman. She could be dangerous. And whatever she's getting into with her could be potentially damaging to her future considering all the illegalities Loonsfoot has taken just to create a viable, believable, and detailed backstory for a fake woman."

Cassie nodded, nodded, nodded, had nothing to say.

Couldn't find a single word.

Willa and Garrett staring at her, Norton waiting for her to respond, there was nothing.

Just the pain in her mouth where she was chewing away the flesh on her lower lip.

"What I think we do have going for us here, in the meantime," Norton said. "Is that this woman seems to be nothing more than an extraordinarily talented special effects artist and forger." He leafed through the file. "All of her work was discredited, right?"

"The articles said the math was good," Garrett said. "But that's the thing about theoretical astrophysics. When you go and design an experiment that supposedly opens a stable wormhole, which then blows up in your face and you can't offer any explanation as to why it blew up besides spontaneous catastrophic system failure, and then fail to offer a shred of verifyable evidence justifying the experiment's purpose in the first place because it had been destroyed in the explosion, people have questions."

"It doesn't seem to me that Astrid is in any immediate danger," Norton said. "But you do need to get her away from Loonsfoot."

"Wait," Willa said, shooting up out of her chair, hands reaching for the file on Norton's desk.

"Sorry about this," Cassie said. "But when she's got something, she's got something."

Willa pulled a page from the file. Said, "Says here that her experiment with the portal exploded. Hurt people. Did anyone ever find out who was driving the car that hit Astrid?"

Detective Norton spun his chair around, rolled it toward a file cabinet.

"The plates we were given weren't registered to any car currently in use, nor did they match the description of the vehicle in question," Norton said.

Cassie slapped his desk, stood, "You didn't bother to tell us that?"

"Miss Walsh," Norton said. "When we get results like that it's generally understood that perhaps the victim didn't actually know what they were seeing and made a mistake. It happens more than you could possibly imagine."

"So no follow up? No phone call?" Both hands were on the desk, her hips pressed up against the flimsy frame.

"It is still an active case and if there happened to be any new and pertinent information, you would have been notified. Now I'm going to ask you to please sit down, or I'm going to have to ask you to leave." Norton stood, crossed his arms over his chest.

"I think you're missing the point here," Willa said. "Cassie, you and Astrid love space and science fiction more than anyone I've ever met. What if Loonsfoot knew that and recreated the experiment for Astrid?"

Cassie turned to Norton, raised her eyebrows as if to say, "Well?"

"I'm not a criminal pathologist," he said. "I couldn't make an accurate—"

"Humor me," Cassie said. "Please."

Norton cleared his throat, said, "There's a certain logic to that sort of thing if, in fact, Loonsfoot is Woods, and if she did have some sort of connection with Astrid based on something that reminded her of this Amelia Woods. Best way to make a connection with a person is to appeal to their sensibilities. Now, and I don't mean to sound insensitive, but there isn't a single bit of that that I could use to force any of this past the necessary channels I need to go through. I'm sorry."

Cassie slung her purse over her shoulder. She thanked Detective Norton. Said, "We need to go."

"Talk to Astrid, Miss Walsh. I'll do everything I can to get this sorted out."

She barely looked back at Norton as she shooed Willa and Garrett out the office door, down the hall, through reception, and out the front doors of the police station.

Willa said, "Cassie, wait, can we talk about this?"

Garrett said, "Miss Walsh, wait."

But Cassie was already in her car.

She didn't wait to make the turn out of the parking lot, just swerved into oncoming traffic.

There weren't any car horns. There weren't any red lights. There was nothing but the street signs, the turn signal tick, tick, ticking, the engine whining under the pressure her foot was putting on the gas pedal.

She didn't realize where she was going until she got there.

There were footsteps behind the door.

Slow.

Light.

Just loud enough for Cassie to hear.

Or convince herself she'd heard.

She could throw herself into the door once it opened, half of Loonsfoot's face, an eyeball in the empty space. She could wrap her hands around the woman's throat, watch her eyes lose focus and drift over Cassie's shoulder as that last bit of air gurgled from her mouth. But there would be nothing for Cassie after that. Nothing for Astrid.

She couldn't do any of that.

The voice through the door asked Cassie if she needed help.

She belched up a laugh because, oh, she very much did need some help. Said so, too. Made it sound helpless. Or maybe she was being honest. There was no way for her to tell. Her heart in her ears, her breath catching in the back of her throat. Going back and forth between sinking her thumbs into Loonsfoot's eye sockets or threatening in a commanding tone and promising to back up those threats with violent imagery. All of it a jumble. All of it making her eyelid twitch, her stomach groan.

Loonsfoot opened the door. Didn't try to hide. Stood there with a smile on her face in a black suit that told Cassie maybe she was wrong about the whole thing. Maybe it was all a complete coincidence, a total misunderstanding.

Loonsfoot began formally, called Cassie Miss Walsh.

"Cassie's fine. Can I come in, please?"

Loonsfoot stepped aside, swung her arm into the home office with her hand outstretched like, absolutely, come on in, be her guest, take a seat.

Cassie could have been wrong about that D'Angelo guy after all considering the way Loonsfoot's place was kept up. Bright. Furnished with the good stuff—not Ikea's end-of-2006 closeout sale—leather sofa, an entertainment center made of actual wood, all of it closed off behind a set of French doors, the glass so clean it almost wasn't there at all. Nice commanding desk where she'd sat and lied to Astrid about being a psychiatrist, wrote bogus scripts for medication she maybe didn't need to be on. Leather chaise lounge where Astrid learned to trust this woman, before she told her just enough of who she really was to hook her through the heart.

Loonsfoot closed the door behind Cassie, asked if she'd

like anything to drink. She had sparkling water, tap, Coke, whatever she'd like.

"I'd actually like whiskey," Cassie said. "If you have any."

"I do," Loonsfoot said. She put her hand on Cassie's arm. "Right through here."

Cassie scanned fake degrees hung from the walls in ornate frames. The honors. The photos featuring handshakes, the sort of clear jagged awards people receive when they actually do something of note.

Loonsfoot was good.

Those same awards stood on stylish floating pipe shelving, not a speck of dust anywhere on them. Maybe she bought them at pawn shops. Or murdered the original recipients, had new placards made to make them her own.

Cassie sat in the only other chair that wouldn't force her to lie down, or push past Loonsfoot to get behind the desk before she did.

Loonsfoot pulled a green bottle from her desk drawer, two glasses. It was the type of whiskey with a cork stopper instead of a twist-off cap. "I take mine neat, would you like ice?"

Cassie wasn't stupid. Naïve maybe. Too willing to trust, absolutely. But with Loonsfoot in her suit, drinking room temperature liquor, and Cassie in her Michael's shirt, black workpants, broken-in sneakers, she'd take her drink the same.

Loonsfoot sniffed the bottle, said, "This is my favorite."

"I'm a Jack Daniel's kind of girl, myself."

"Then this'll be a real treat."

The ring of their glasses meeting, the sound of Loonsfoot's pull on the whiskey, the silence before the burn in Cassie's chest, it was all meant to deescalate. She knew why Cassie was there, at least in part. Had to.

"So what can I do for you, Cassie?" Loonsfoot said, taking another sip of her drink.

"Know what? On second thought, you can call me Miss Walsh." Cassie turned her glass over, poured the whiskey onto the lovely white carpet.

Loonsfoot set her glass on the desk, raised her eyebrows, said, "May I ask why you did that?" Voice calm, together.

"I know who you are, Cecelia." Cassie scratched away at the pattern etched in her glass with her thumbnail. "Like I know you're not a psychiatrist. Like I know you're a liar. Like I know you're going to drop this...whatever this is you're putting on right now."

Loonsfoot's hands disappeared behind the desk, her throat bobbed up, down hard enough that Cassie could hear if from where she sat. She nodded, brought her eyes back to Cassie's.

"You're going to stay away from Astrid," Cassie said. "You're going to tell her you can't see her anymore. You're not going to say anything more than that. If you're going to shatter her world, you're going to do it the way I tell you. And that's all."

"You have no idea what you're saying. This is ridiculous. I'm going to have to ask you to leave now before I call the police."

Cassie laughed, crossed her legs. "I already paid them a visit today, actually. Told them everything I know. About you. About Amelia."

"Amy."

"Say again?"

"Her name was Amy."

"Well my daughter's name is Astrid. She's not your daughter. Your daughter's dead."

Cassie threw the glass before Loonsfoot was fully standing, clipped her forehead with it. There were three sounds then; a crack of shattering glass, its tinkling all over everything solid, and the taser clattering onto the desk. All at once. All in slow motion. All taking place in the time it took for Cassie to reach for the taser, and level the laser dot sight on Loonsfoot's bleeding face.

"Wait," Loonsfoot said.

But Cassie had already pulled the trigger, couldn't have helped herself if she'd wanted to.

A wired barb caught Loonsfoot in the cheek. Another in her chest. A third in her shoulder.

Flashing white light.

Electric crackle-crackle.

Loonsfoot's teeth clacking together.

Cassie wiped her eyes with her free hand, stuttered, took her finger off the trigger. Said, "I need you to tell me the truth. And then I need to never see you again."

Bleeding, breathing in short bursts, Loonsfoot said, "My name is Doctor Barbara Loons—"

She was writhing on the floor behind the desk again.

Cassie took a breath.

Took her finger off the trigger.

"What's your name?" she said.

"Doctor Cecilia Woods."

"That's the truth, right? I won't go digging some more and find out you're Linda Reynolds from Sheboygan or anything, will I?"

"There's a wire sticking out of my face."

"You already tried to lie with a wire sticking out of your face."

Loonsfoot's breathing was heavy, ragged. She pulled herself into her chair, leaned back into the leather. "Astrid loves you very much."

More lights.

More crackling.

More teeth against teeth.

And then there was a smell.

Cassie let go of the trigger.

Nearly laughed, almost screamed.

Loonsfoot's pants were drenched at the crotch.

She had to purse her lips, breathe.

"Amy was so much like Astrid," Loonsfoot said through

her teeth, stuttering, wincing, breathing badly. "Too much like me, though."

Cassie swiped her sleeve across her nose. "What do you mean, too much like you?"

"My husband didn't understand mental illness," Loonsfoot said. "Couldn't. I'd hidden mine. Gotten good at it. But Amy wasn't talented in that way. He'd told her to buck up. Told her she had to be faking the depressive episodes. All sorts of horrible craziness that just continued to get more and more hurtful. I'd told her I understood her, that everything she was going through were things that I had gone through too. That I was going through. Then she started to hurt herself. Something I was familiar with. But my husband, he didn't believe anyone would do that to themselves for any other reason than for attention. So, I took her."

Cassie let her hand fall to her side, kept the taser tight in her grip. "You took her."

"My husband told the police I'd kidnapped her. I'm not saying I was in the right mind. I've never really been in the right mind. But she couldn't stay there. And when you're already considered a criminal, you learn a thing or two about how to become someone who's not."

"Could've picked a better name," Cassie said.

Loonsfoot laughed, said, "You think this is the first name I took?"

"Well we thought it was your only one, so, sorry for not picking up what you were putting down."

There was nothing between them.

Just breathing.

Breathing.

The smell of piss and burnt clothing.

Then, "Amy was sixteen when she hung herself in our motel bathroom."

Cassie said nothing.

"I was trying to help her and she killed herself."

Cassie clenched her jaw.

"She was so talented. And smart. When she wasn't looking up at the stars with me, she was dancing. And when she wasn't dancing, she was wondering what else was out there in all that black. Something amazing, she'd insisted. Something better. I choose to believe she was right. I know she was right, actually."

Cassie pulled a handful of tissues out of the box on the desk, handed them over to Loonsfoot—she couldn't watch her lick blood out of the corner of her mouth anymore.

"What's the thing in that house?"

"That's the *Rippa*," Loonsfoot said, hissing, pushing the barb further into her face, pulling it out at a different angle, blotting the bleeding flesh with a tissue.

"Like, Boston for 'ripper,' or as in Kelly Ripa?"

"I'm from Oregon."

"Name a spaceship after a talk show host, that's not weird or anything."

"Kelly Ripa is a delight, and it's not a spaceship. It's the vehicle that was going to boar a hole through spacetime to take me and Astrid to Regis-132." Bloody tissue after bloody tissue, Loonsfoot talking, talking, and Cassie should've gone to a doctor about this woman, not the cops. "We were going to come back for you," she said. "Once we'd settled there."

"This—this is real to you?" Cassie said.

"It is real. I've seen it. It's got a pink sky, and grass with these beautiful spinning bulbs of light. Trees that perfume the air with something that smells like champagne. It is endless wonder. It's a place where people like me and Astrid will never need to feel that there's nothing new to discover, or never any dream that can't be realized. Doesn't that sound wonderful?" Loonsfoot used the tissues for her eyes this time.

Cassie nodded, said, "It does. But why my kid?"

"I almost hit her with my car. It was a while ago now. She was dancing down the street. Amy used to dance."

"Astrid hasn't danced since—"

"I know." Loonsfoot pulled herself to her feet, went to work on the barb in her shoulder. "She told me."

Cassie swallowed, waved her arm to the awards, the degrees hanging in the hall. "You based all of this on Astrid?"

"I based this all on a hologram of Amy. Her reflection from the event horizon of a blackhole made human. Dropped at someone else's feet." Loonsfoot pointed a finger to her chest, to Cassie, said, "You and me are the same. Maybe you're my reflection."

The taser landed on the carpet with a soft thump. "I need you to tell Astrid you can't see her anymore, and I need you to do it soon. Otherwise I can't leave this alone. I'm giving you a chance here."

"A chance at what? I don't have anything else."

"Astrid does. I do."

"I don't want to go alone."

"I'm not giving you a choice here."

Loonsfoot pulled the last barb from the burn mark in her shirt. Nodded. "What would have happened if I'd pulled an actual gun?"

In the hall, Cassie stopped, turned, said, "I probably would've ruined everything for all of us."

"If you really are my reflection, maybe everything I told you about today happened to me so it wouldn't happen to you. You're lucky. I didn't have that option."

Cassie said nothing.

Closed the door lightly behind her.

Crossed the street to her car.

Lit a cigarette.

Had to pull over to throw up out the car window.

Kept having to blow her nose, wipe her eyes.

Couldn't not see Loonsfoot convulsing in her own urine. Couldn't not see Loonsfoot's head breaking open if Cassie had gotten a gun pulled on her. Kept running through conversation after conversation with Astrid about what Loonsfoot may have stuffed into her brain.

That there was something better and it wasn't here.

That she didn't belong here.

Cassie wretched up nothing but bile that drooled from her lips in thick ropes of sour slime behind the diner.

Nothing else came up.

She had nothing left.

She spat, grabbed whatever was left clinging to her mouth with her palm and flicked it away.

She knocked on the back door for someone to let her inside.

32.

Willa couldn't come up with a single thing she would've liked to do when Astrid suggested they go wherever she wanted. Wasn't all that hurt, either, when Astrid couldn't put anything together on her own like she had for Cassie.

Before, there were trips to the Philadelphia Museum of Art, and Willa had to practically be dragged out of the place to go get something to eat. Eastern State Penitentiary was another place that she had never passed up an opportunity to tour. Libraries too, didn't matter which one—the smell was what did it. She'd walk around, leaf to the back of books looking for the one that hadn't been borrowed for the longest amount of time, and then check that one out. Didn't matter what it was. Just that it needed her.

And maybe that was her problem.

"I haven't thought about anything I want in a long time," she'd told Lily just before Astrid walked up, asked if she was ready to go.

They sat in the shaded grandstands overlooking the river, the crews rowing past with a whoosh of the oars through the water, the clunk of the fiberglass turning over in the oarlocks, the coxswain counting down each stroke until they could paddle for a short bit before the next sprint. Sneakers slapping the walking path behind them, runners going in both directions breathing in heavy but controlled breaths. Cars blowing east, west on Kelly Drive, the sound of engines and wind displacement bouncing off the jagged rock wall on the far side of the road, back into the runners, the grandstands, and out over the water.

"I figured this is the last place you'd want to be," Astrid said. "You're here all the time."

Willa kicked a stone down to the next level of the stands, said, "I've been telling coach I'm sick."

"How come?"

Willa could have rattled off a dozen reasons. Traipsing through the woods to a shack with a mystery machine inside. Losing the ability to sleep for more than an hour or two at a time. Sitting in a police station before school trying to present evidence in order to have a nutcase arrested. Carrying projector equipment back and forth, back and forth from her car for Astrid. Listening to Garrett talk and talk and talk about Astrid. Sitting in the diner with Cassie discussing what was going on with, and how they could step in and help Astrid. Sitting on Lily's couch with nothing to say when asked what it was she liked, or wanted, or hoped to do.

Instead, she picked a pebble off the cement, tried to flick it all the way to the water, said, "Just been pretty wrapped up with Lily, I guess."

Astrid gave her a light nudge with her casted elbow, said, "How's that going, by the way? Good, I guess, right?"

"Really good. I like her a lot."

"Is it love?" Astrid dragged out the O as if she'd added lines and lines of them to a text message.

That made Willa laugh. "No. Yes. I don't know, maybe."

"Have you told Ken yet?"

Willa shook her head, said, "He'll find out prom night I guess."

It was a back and forth about Ken for a bit. About him being kind of dumb, pretty racist, scared of gays, balding, and getting soggy around the midsection. Moved on to other things from there. A little bit about finals creeping up. A little bit about how hot it had been recently. A little bit about what it was like being with another girl, but not much because Willa wasn't about to go into any of it with any sort of detail.

But she would have.

Before.

Then it was the boats. And the runners. And the cars. And how much farther Willa was able to flick a pebble than the last time she'd flicked a pebble before the talking had started.

If Lily were there, at the very least she and Astrid could fill the silence when Willa couldn't find anything to say.

If Garrett were there, he wouldn't have stopped himself from saying every single thing that popped into his brain, and Willa wouldn't even have been there anyway. Not really. Watching Astrid had taught Willa that physical presence doesn't mean much of anything if there's something being held back, trapped in a skull.

"I'm sorry I couldn't think of anything special to do," Astrid said.

"I already told you, you don't need to apologize for anything."

"I feel like I do."

"You don't."

Astrid leaned over, picked up a pebble, flicked it, made it to the water. Because of course she did. Astrid could do anything, and nothing would stop her, and she didn't have a single clue.

Still, there was too much noise for the pebble's bloop to register.

"I'm sorry you feel like you need to take care of me."

"You'd do the same for me."

"I've never had the chance."

"Do you want one?"

"You're just so put together all the time. Sure of yourself. Sturdy. I feel like—"

Willa didn't mean to laugh. But there was nothing stopping it. Nothing stopping her belly from aching from the spasms continuing to double her over where she sat.

She barely heard Astrid asking what was funny.

But her laughter shifted to something else when she said, "Do you know I can't even think of a single thing I like to do anymore? I've spent most of my life with you and Cassie, and I thought for so long that I was interested in what you guys were interested in, but I'm not. And I can't think of a single thing that's mine that I didn't get from the two of you."

The fingers poking out of Astrid's cast were red.

Her face was pinched.

Her jaw muscles were bunching, bunching, bunching at the corners.

"I didn't mean that the way it sounded. But I can't imagine Lily wanting to hang around me for too much longer if I can't talk about anything other than crew and school—and I'm not even doing one of them much anymore."

"Because of me," Astrid said through her teeth.

"Not because of you. Because I love you, stupid. I'm just realizing that that may not be all I need anymore. What am I supposed to say in college? 'This one time my friend Astrid did this really funny thing, but you had to be there?'"

"That's my fault, I'm—"

"No, it's not. It's mine. But did you even have any idea what I might want to do today? Because I didn't. That's why we're sitting next to one of the most polluted rivers on the east coast, flicking fucking pebbles into it. Like, why are we even here?"

There wasn't much left to say after that.

They stayed where they were for a little while longer. Laughed at a runner who was huffing and puffing particularly loudly. Then stood, brushed themselves off, and began walking to the car.

Halfway home, Astrid said, "I'd wanted this to go differently."

Willa kept her eyes on the road, said, "I'm sorry about that."

Astrid smiled. No teeth. Her eyes stuck to her hands in her lap. "You don't need to apologize to me for anything."

So, Willa didn't.

And she wouldn't.

Not anymore.

33.

Everything she needed was packed in a duffel bag.

She checked and double checked her toiletries, made sure she had a couple of fresh toothbrushes, a handful of tubes of toothpaste. Neosporin, talcum powder, tampons. Toenail clippers, hairbrush, spare bars of Dove. Band-Aids, eyedrops, toilet paper. A week's worth of underwear. T-shirts, shorts, jeans. A couple sweatshirts, a blanket, a spare pair of sneakers. Socks, socks, socks—Loonsfoot had told her socks were probably the most important things she could bring. Keeping her feet dry and healthy would be the difference between a nice, long mission, and one that needed to be cut short because of injury and infection.

She emptied her Jansport, stuffed in the sleeping bag she'd bought, packed in a plastic vacuum-sealed sleeve to save room. Placed the mangled Captain Kirk plush on top. A pillow crammed under the Velcro straps of her duffel. Astrid was ready to go.

She made Cassie's bed, placed the note she'd written on her pillow. Switched off lights, closed doors, made sure the thermostat was set to Cassie's taste—a frigid sixty-eight. Her mother wouldn't be able to keep it like that for too long, but as long as she was comfortable when she read Astrid's letter, that was all that mattered.

The apartment was beautiful this time of day. The sun filtering through the blinds, making the flecks of dust in the air shine like stars over the couch, the television, the coffee table, the rolled blankets in the basket at the corner of the room. The photo Astrid took of the empty room didn't do it any justice, but she'd have it to look at every night before drifting off to sleep under the deep purple time-lapsed sky.

Just before Astrid walked out the door, she leafed through the mail, found the bill, and used Cassie's laptop—and the Word file aptly named passwords.docx—to pay off the balance for the most recent hospital stay with a credit card in a made-up woman's name. Then did the same with the electric, the gas, the car insurance. The credit card bills, whatever was left over from the rest of the year at Wyndmoor, and, last but not least, the rent.

She gave her former home one last look before turning away, closing, and locking the door behind her.

She'd decided to walk to the lab.

Get a last look at the donut tree, the telephone wires passing through the opening that had been cut through the branches and leaves at its center. The pond behind Phil-Mont Christian Academy that always was full of geese. The jujitsu dojo that used to be the bookstore where Cassie and Astrid used to go on Saturday mornings for kids' hour. The Erdenheim community pool they only ever ventured to a handful of times each summer—they'd get so sunburned by neglecting to slather on a bit of sunscreen that it'd take weeks for the stinging and peeling to subside, proving, once again, that the price of membership was never worth it. Donato's Pizza that was now a bank. Flourtown Bakery which had sat empty for the past five years. The Dollar Tree where they'd done their grocery shopping when Astrid was little.

Astrid hadn't gotten that butterfly flutter in her belly recently without using her fingers to zoom in and out on the photo of Regis-132, or watching Loonsfoot weld the *Rippa*'s frame into place, or learning to operate the makeshift communications console she would be sitting behind in just a short bit. But there was that flutter now.

Maybe it was the anticipation of leaving later that night. Maybe it was the acknowledgement that she likely wouldn't walk those streets again any time soon. Maybe it was being able to use the future tense when referring to herself.

It didn't matter.

The butterflies were there.

And before she made her way to the path and stepped through the tree line, she snapped photos of the basketball courts, the townhomes, the 309 overpass, everything she'd lived around her entire life without noticing how pretty it all looked under the setting sun.

She pulled in a breath through her nose.

Released it from her mouth.

And took to the path that would take her to the lab.

That would take her to Loonsfoot.

Who would take them to their future.

But Loonsfoot's car wasn't parked out front.

Astrid dropped her bags on the porch, reached up above the front door. The dust, the grit, the hollowed-out bug corpses raised the hair on her forearm. Tucking her fingers into the hole carved into the wood siding raked up the gooseflesh. But finding the keyring Loonsfoot had hidden up there stretched the corners of her mouth into a smile.

She unlatched the padlocks, pocketed the keys.

She called for Loonsfoot.

But there was nothing but groaning floorboards under her sneakers.

Sounds of the house continuing to settle—or sink into the ground, whichever happened to come first.

She stuffed her bags into the *Rippa*'s back hatch.

Crossed the room to the radio.

Headphones on, fingers dancing over knobs and switches,

the only sound in her ears was static.

She texted Loonsfoot.

"I'm here," she typed and sent away.

"I'm ready," she sent with an exclamation point.

⟐

Everything was dark.

Astrid had only gotten up from her seat once to use the composting toilet in the space that must have been a bedroom at one point. She'd done it enough. Gotten used to scooping sawdust onto whatever she'd left behind. Experience didn't make it any more appealing, but it had erased the consideration of whether or not she should hold it and use a proper toilet at home.

She wasn't going home. Would have to take advantage of far more rustic circumstances soon enough.

But Loonsfoot hadn't responded to a single text message.

Hadn't picked up any of her calls.

And Astrid could only stop her knee from bouncing, bouncing when she put her hand on it, stared at it. Could only make the pain pour adrenaline over her brain when she dinged her casted elbow against the chair's metal frame hard enough for the marker's added pressure to make a difference.

Loonsfoot had gotten held up.

That was all.

Astrid would wait for her as long as she had to.

She was in no rush.

Cassie would be at the diner deep into the night if Astrid needed her.

Willa was out there somewhere. Probably with Lily.

Garrett texted hi with exclamation points and emojis nearly every hour, but that was okay. It was nice. It was good. She was able to text a bit and not create scenarios in which Loonsfoot had been gunned down before she ever reached the power plant, or was in a holding cell somewhere being interrogated and treated like some sort of terrorist, forced to pee in a bucket and maybe even have to sleep with her face just feet from it.

Astrid couldn't keep her phone's flashlight on forever, though.

Wouldn't be able to deal with the spring chill that would set in soon enough without a sweatshirt. Needed to save her cold weather gear for Regis-132.

Maybe Loonsfoot had left her.

Went back on all of her promises.

And maybe if Astrid went ahead and used her concrete arm to smash the radio console to pieces, that would show Loonsfoot that she wasn't going to be left behind by anyone. It would have a two-pronged effect: Loonsfoot would see that Astrid was deadly serious about completing their mission—enough so to endanger the entire thing just to prove a point; and it would wash her brain down with chemicals that would alleviate any idea that Astrid wasn't the right person to go to Regis-132 in the first place, that she didn't even belong there, where no one else but she and Loonsfoot were supposed to live.

Astrid stood.

Kicked her chair out from behind her.

There was no controlling her breathing. She was choking on it. Had to lean her back against the *Rippa*, feel the metal against her spine, her ribcage to make sure her lungs were taking in air at all. It wasn't much. But she'd heard that, as long as a choking victim was making sound, there was airflow, and they could survive.

She was definitely making sounds.

High pitched whining in the back of her throat.

Snotty pulls of oxygen from her nose.

If Loonsfoot had left her, or gotten caught though, there was no real point in listening for those sounds. There was no college, there was no job, there was no apartment in the city, there was no anything. Not here. And there would be nothing but here if there was no Loonsfoot.

Astrid heard the sound her cast was making against the titanium polyalloy plating before the pain reached her brain. A deep thump, thump with a quiet ding of metal clanging faintly on the high end of each strike. Then the splintering of the plaster crunching, crunching the harder and harder she swung her arm.

Sweat mixed with the drool hanging in strands from her bottom lip, added enough weight to speckle the concrete floor with black dots in the near dark.

She spat, left a larger splotch of black.

And another.

It had no real effect other than matching the sentiment of her grinding teeth, her heavy breathing, the growl in her throat.

The screaming.

Astrid decided to leave her stuff.

She'd be back for it.

She didn't lock the door behind her.

Ran down the dirt road, nothing in her ears but her pulse and the slapping of her feet.

Her legs burned, but she kept running.

Wouldn't stop.

Couldn't.

She didn't.

⟐

Astrid cracked open the plastic rock out front of Loonsfoot's office. Let it fall onto the concrete once she pinched the key between her fingers. The hinges snapped when plastic hit pavement, and the thing bounced into the bushes in two pieces.

The shake in her hands forced her to breathe, concentrate on pushing the key into the lock. Still, it took two, three tries for Astrid to unlock the door.

She was right.

Loonsfoot had left her.

Or had gotten caught.

Astrid said hello into the dark, flicked the switch to the right.

She blinked away the spots the light left on everything while her eyes adjusted.

The place was no different than the last time she'd been there.

Neat.

Clean.

Made to be inviting, warm.

Loonsfoot had said, every time she and Astrid needed to be something they weren't, that people only needed to think they believed in what was being said. One thing could tip the scales in one direction or the other, but as long as, for at least one moment, the performer could buy into the schtick, the audience would too.

And one step into this place did just that.

The shards of damage she'd crushed into her cast didn't matter. Sitting for hours alone in a falling-down house in the woods didn't matter. Telling Garrett to leave her the fuck alone didn't matter. Walking into this place now offered the same thing stepping into it for the first time had: a bright, safe space where Astrid was told she wasn't crazy, or dangerous. Special was the word Loonsfoot had used.

Astrid was special.

She called for Loonsfoot again, called her Doc. Asked if everything was okay, if she was there, if she wanted her to run comms from the office instead. They'd have to go get the equipment, sure, but she was more than happy to sit on the nice, comfortable chairs she used to sink into during their sessions.

Astrid poked her head into the living area to the left, the French doors spread wide. But there hadn't been a fresh footprint in that carpet since the last time it had been vacuumed.

That very well could have been just before Loonsfoot had gone upstairs to nap and had forgotten to set an alarm. Or, more likely, she hadn't been there for a while since she'd been spending most of her time in the lab working to finish the *Rippa*, sleeping on the cot in the room that had gotten blown up with the portal experiment.

She almost laughed, knocking on the office door at the end of the hall instead of just opening it. Loonsfoot never liked knocking. It was too formal. Like there would be a line of questions that came shortly after a knock. "Just walk right into a place," she'd said. "We're family now and families don't knock."

Astrid opened the door, switched on the light, caught herself midsentence, "Hope you didn't forget about—"

Loonsfoot was behind her desk.

Her head rested on the blotter.

The rectangular calendar where she'd written this appointment, that appointment with people, places they needed to visit in order to get the *Rippa* built was stained red. Like the time Mrs. Gosnell had bitten through her red pen while grading spelling tests in the second grade. It had gotten everywhere. On her hands, her lips, all over all of the test papers, saturating them with deep red.

"Doc?"

Then Astrid saw the spray. The blotch on the wall. A circular spritz of pink, red, and gray.

Then the hole punched into Loonsfoot's temple. Her eyes staring at nothing. The pool of red on the blotter obscuring the shattered part of her skull from full view. The gun she'd alluded to during their training session with the stuffed animals next to the hand that must have been gripping it tight before it pulled the trigger.

The men in the suits must have gotten to her.

But Astrid knew that wasn't true.

Astrid said, "Doc?"

Said, "It's me."

Said, "What do I do now?"

Astrid stood there a while longer asking a series of questions to no one.

She knew the answers to most of them.

But she didn't want to leave Loonsfoot by herself just yet.

Two Astrids staring into the bathroom mirror.

Both wiped, scratched at the makeup that had run down their faces.

Both read the names on their casts, one in reverse.

Cassie.

Willa.

Garrett.

Liz.

Kenny.

Mark.

Barbara Loonsfoot.

Both Astrids tried scratching names away until little bits of their painted fingernails were left on the cast.

They spit on it, rubbed, and rubbed, and rubbed, and rubbed with their thumbs until they burned, stung, bled, leaving red streaks.

They opened a drawer, found nail files, held them like pencils, and scratched, scratched, scratched until the blade bent, snapped.

One Astrid, the real one, stared at her mirror self.

Then put her casted fist through her face, made thousands and thousands of little hers.

She turned on the shower.

As hot as it would get.

She pulled off her clothes.

If something didn't come off easily, she tore it.

She needed to tiptoe to avoid all her tiny naked selves.

The water was so hot she could barely breathe.

But she stood underneath the stream, watched her wriggling toes splash in the water. Blue was in the water, flowing into the drain. Purple too. Then Green. Black. Red.

Her cast was doughy, bleeding ink.

She couldn't make out Cassie's name anymore.

Couldn't make out Willa's name.

Or anyone else's.

Loonsfoot's name was the only one that hadn't turned into a splotch of color or comingled with the other blotches.

Astrid thought of hidden messages written in clear crayon on Easter eggs that had been dipped into every fart-smelling dye over and over until they looked rotten.

Astrid held that bit of the cast as close to the shower head as she could reach. Until the ink was dripping onto her face, neck, chest.

Bits of glass in her knuckles.

Little bits.

But they'd made her bleed enough to turn the cloth padding at the edge of her cast red.

Once Loonsfoot's name was a patch of black, she held the sopping cast to her ribs, picked glass from her skin.

She set each shard down on the soap dish.

When she'd gotten them all, she counted eleven.

She stuck them to the bar soap that neither she nor Cassie had used since they started using body wash.

Bye-bye bikinis. Long sleeves only. Turtlenecks. Pants. A mask.

Otherwise everyone would see the scars all over.

Think, what the hell happened to her.

Think, freak.

Think, psycho.

She wasn't a psycho.

She rubbed the soap into her chest, just below her collar bone.

Red ran down her breast, down her ribcage, belly, leg, toes, swirled around the drain like peppermint.

She sucked breath through her teeth.

Clamped her eyes shut.

Then she rubbed patches of torn skin onto the spot where her ribs meet in the center of her chest.

The soft spot between her belly button and pelvic bone.

Her kneecap, the top of her foot.

Then she started in on her neck.

Over the static of the shower, the high-pitched notes in Astrid's throat, the sound of metal over metal—a shing sort of sound.

Then, "Oh my God."

A hand reached in, turned the knobs poking out of the tiled wall.

The bar of soap fell into the tub, bouncing once, bouncing twice, a hollow, metal tunk, tunk.

Astrid was wrapped in a towel.

Shushed when she said she could explain, that nothing was what it seemed, that there was a rational explanation for everything.

She could almost straighten her casted arm.

The pain blurred her vision.

Then, Cassie's arm around her wet shoulders.

Blood soaked into the towel.

"Oh God," Astrid said.

"I know," Cassie said.

"I'm sorry," Astrid said.

"Stop that. You have nothing to be sorry for. This is on me."

"This was all me. I did this—"

Cassie, hands on each of Astrid's cheeks, staring directly into her eyes, said, "We were together in this and I did everything wrong. But we're going to fix it."

Astrid didn't move as Cassie dried her off, slathered Neosporin onto her bloody patches, taped non-stick gauze to the good skin around the ruined spots.

Cassie was gone for a moment then.

Astrid called for her.

From the other room, Cassie said, "Be right there, I'm not going anywhere."

A ball of clothes in her hands, Cassie said, "Do you need help?"

Astrid nodded.

She wrapped an arm around Astrid's waist, tucked her shoulder into her daughter's armpit. Said, "Left," guiding her good foot over the edge of the tub. "Right," doing the same for the ruined right foot, and gnarled knee. Said, "Careful," while Astrid set her foot to the floor—the blood already seeping through the shiny white bandage.

She helped Astrid guide her sopping cast through the arm of a button-down shirt. Started with the buttons at the tails, worked her way up. Left the shirt open when she reached the bandages at Astrid's sternum and under her collarbone.

She snipped at the foot holes of the sweatpants, pulled out the elastic bands. She rolled the legs, pulled the waistband up over Astrid's bellybutton to keep it away from the bandage beneath it, let the legs fall loose to her feet.

Astrid watched Cassie work.

There was worry on her face.

But not panic.

She'd done this before.

Astrid had made her do this before.

"Mom," Astrid said.

"One sec," Cassie said, opening the hall closet, pulling the pair of crutches they'd saved from the time Astrid sprained her ankle on the bottom step at the movies when she'd had too much soda but didn't want to leave the theater—not until after Chris Pine delivered Captain Kirk's famous "Space...the final frontier" line, and the *Enterprise* stretched itself like a rubber band and snapped off into the stars.

Astrid said, "Mom," again, held out her arms despite the pain.

Cassie dropped the crutches and went to her.

34.

They weren't allowed to go with Astrid.

They hadn't expected to be able to but tried to insist anyway.

The nurse was understanding. Kind.

But stern.

Once the doctor redressed Astrid's wounds, x-rayed and re-casted her arm, they would be called in.

Until then, they would just need to wait.

So, they did.

They weren't able to say much.

Even Garrett, sitting across from them, didn't say anything. Just kept his eyes on his hands, on his phone.

They went to the vending machines. Keyed in the numbers for chips, candy bars, cans of soda. Set what they'd bought in the chair next to Garrett.

"Oh, thanks," he said. "But I'm not very hungry."

"For letting us know," they said. "We wouldn't have gotten to her without you."

He'd texted them once Astrid had snapped at him and stopped responding. Still, he sent message after message after message. Garrett had typed, "Hello?" and "Are you okay?"

and "Where are you?" and "Astrid?" and "Please just let me know you're okay," and sent each one away, one every couple of minutes.

Garrett nodded, said thanks again. He opened the Doritos, crunched away until his fingers were coated in chip dust.

They sat on either side of him after he covered his eyes, smeared the bridge of his nose, his eyebrows with orange.

They said, "It's okay."

Said, "She'll be okay."

Said, "You did great."

Said, "We don't know what would've happened if you hadn't been so annoying."

They all laughed then.

They reached for Garrett's hands.

And they sat there and waited.

They watched the news on the waiting room television.

Every so often, one of them needed the rest of them to tell them that everything would be okay, that Astrid would be okay, that without a single one of them, everything could have turned out very differently.

When the nurse came for them, there was chocolate and salt and crumbs on each of their hands, and each of their backs.

35.

Cassie asked for a minute.

Willa and Garrett said of course, and absolutely, they needed to wash up anyway.

Astrid held Cassie's hand.

Cassie would squeeze.

Astrid would squeeze.

They'd go back and forth, back and forth. Adding patterns of squeezes at varying lengths and strengths. Like Simon, that multicolored musical toy Cassie was terrible at once it reached a certain speed and sequence.

She could never keep up.

The thing would blart out a sound that could only have ever been invented to indicate someone was bad at something, and Cassie would switch it off, walk away pissed off and red faced for being so stupid that she couldn't follow a simple pattern and see through the color and the noise to get it right.

Cassie fucked up the hand-squeezing pattern.

Astrid smiled.

It was a little one.

But, for a moment, it took Cassie's attention away from the bandage on Astrid's neck, the thought of all the bandages under her hospital gown, the new blank cast, the stitches in her knuckles from where the mirror bit into her fingers.

"Was it," Cassie started. "Were you—" She swallowed, kept her hand in her daughter's.

"I don't know," Astrid said.

Cassie nodded, wiped her eyes.

"But I'm going to check myself in."

Cassie nodded.

"Three-day minimum. Go from there."

Cassie couldn't do anything but nod. Couldn't apologize to Astrid for what could have so easily been avoided if she'd just let the cops do what they do, however long it would've taken. Done what she was supposed to have done as a mother and had the conversations she'd been avoiding; scared into a pack-a-day habit from what might have come from those talks. Loonsfoot, Woods, whatever, wouldn't have painted her office wall with her brains, Astrid never would have had to stare at that mess until what had happened had sunken in, never would have tried carving herself to pieces from what all of the stress and horror had triggered in her brain. All of it was on Cassie. Having to go home and pack a bag for Astrid; all the things she might need if she were to get lonely—a couple of books for good measure. Cassie had done that to herself. To Astrid.

She tried to piece sentences together, but nothing came out of her mouth but her daughter's name. She started with um and uh, but ended the train of thought, or lack thereof, by shaking her head, running her thumbnail over the prickly threads of the hospital sheets.

Astrid said, "Mom."

Cassie said, "No. Let me just—I need to say a couple—"

"Mom."

"This, it was my—"

"No it wasn't." A new squeeze pattern from Astrid's sweating palm. "It wasn't."

Cassie cleared her throat. Pinched away the snot from her running nose.

She wasn't going to tell her. It was that simple. There was no justification for it, no logic behind it, it just wasn't going to happen. Sure, she'd tell Willa and Garrett that it was a decision made to protect Astrid, because, if Astrid knew that Cassie had tasered Loonsfoot in the face, threatened her, pushed her to press the muzzle of a gun to her own temple, maybe there wouldn't be an Astrid to keep things from anymore. And then there wouldn't be a Cassie. She'd never seen herself walking into traffic or flinging herself from the top of a building or stuffing rocks into her heaviest winter coat and jumping off the Strawberry Mansion Bridge into that filthy river. But she'd do it. Twice if one didn't pan out the way it needed to. From her motorized wheelchair she'd have to control with her mouth if she was still pulling breath after the second try.

Astrid's hand was on Cassie's cheek, her thumb wiping away the wet beneath her eye socket. Doing what was supposed to have been Cassie's job.

"I'm going to stay with you," Astrid said. "I want to."

"I need that." Cassie shook her head, said, "Jesus. That's a horrible thing to say."

"Why?"

"It puts a pressure on you that you don't need. You need to want it for yourself, and I don't think there's anything I can do that can help you with that."

"Maybe not," Astrid said, running her hand through Cassie's hair, her head on her shoulder. "But I'm going to try to make sure I want to."

"What—what happens if you don't want to again?"

"I don't know."

They were all arms and snot and tears then. There were apologies breathed into hair and onto cheeks. It was ugly, and messy. And Cassie had never pictured her life getting any sloppier than it already had had become, but it was a mess, and it had to be, and all she could do, right then, was cling to her daughter.

Whether Astrid was doing the same or not made Cassie pull her closer.

36.

Willa was absolutely not, under any ridiculous set of circumstances, going to leave Astrid's bedside. Garrett could head on home whenever he got tired. Cassie could offer to drive her home even though she'd driven herself. Willa wouldn't budge until she was literally hoisted over some scrub-clad goon's head and tossed from the building. She would watch sitcoms with Astrid. Chuckle alongside her at the stupid jokes that weren't at all funny. Have no idea what to say to her other than, "Can I get you something to drink?" or "Do you need your pillows adjusted?" or "Can I call a nurse for you?"

Willa tapped Astrid's shoulder every so often—soft, soft—just so she could look her in the eye. She wouldn't let Astrid forget she was there. Her presence would be felt. Really felt. Proximity was only ever a small part of it. The silence, the laughter, the questions, the not talking, the looking at one another every now, then, now, then, that was all closeness. Not closeness-closeness. But maybe closeness was enough right now. The rest could come later. Once Astrid was out of the bed, once her skin had weaved itself back together into tiny patches of raised white, once she was okay. Okay-okay.

Garrett stood, stretched. "Got to pee. Anybody need anything?"

Cassie shook her head, said no thanks.

Willa wasn't about to pass up an opportunity. "Double Quarter Pounder," she said. "Large French fries and a Coke/ Barq's blend, please."

Astrid sat up a bit straighter, her eyes wide and bright despite the bags beneath them. She raised her stitched fingers until the red pulled white. "Me too, please? And maybe twenty McNuggets for all of us?"

"I was ordering for you, dummy," Willa said. "I'd rather eat hospital food."

"Oh. Never mind then," Astrid said with a grin. "Except the McNuggets. I still want the McNuggets."

Willa still couldn't not hate some of Garrett's faces, despite what he'd done for Astrid. He just looked so stupid. His mouth hanging open, his eyes wide, his rat's nest hair looking like he'd needed a shower yesterday.

Garrett and Cassie went back and forth offering, no, it's okay, Cassie would go, and, no, no, Garrett was happy to go, he'd get a chance to stretch his legs a bit, and, really, it was okay, Cassie had no problem doing it, Garrett should stay while he still could, and, it's not a problem, Garrett would make the run, the McDonald's was just on the other side of the parking lot anyway. And then Willa said, "How about you both go if you both want to go so badly?"

She could barely look at Garrett's face then, could almost predict what it looked like while she and Cassie cocked their eyebrows, nodded toward the door, said nothing, but said everything that Garrett would never be able to understand no matter how long the four of them were the four of them.

Cassie stood, smiled at Garrett, put her hand on his shoulder, and directed him toward the door. "I'm buying, how's that sound?" And even once they were out in the hall, heading toward the elevator, they argued it was okay, Garrett had some money, and Cassie said it was her treat, and Garrett said he'd like to do something for them, and Cassie said, "Would you just shut up about it? You've done so much already."

There wasn't much but the laugh tracks from the television filling the space between Willa and Astrid once they were alone. Astrid ran her good fingers along her sewn-together skin, the black needles poking out of the knots holding her knuckles together. Ran her mangled fingers along the edges of tape keeping the IV in place in her good hand.

Willa tap-tapped Astrid's shoulder again. She'd had so much she wanted to say while Garrett and Cassie were still there, but now she was a grinning idiot waiting for Astrid to say something, anything first.

"Still can't even bring yourself to stress-eat McDonald's, can you?" Astrid said.

"The government can't legally classify some of their food as food, Astrid. It's heinous."

Astrid laughed a bit. A little one. The kind used to acknowledge that something supposedly funny was said, but that was all. She turned back to the television. Went back to staring at her stitches.

Willa said Astrid's name.

Then said it again.

Then, "I'm sorry I wasn't being your friend. I got it in my head that none of it was my responsibility—but friends are responsible for each other."

Astrid took Willa's hand. "If I hadn't lied to you or Mom about everything, we wouldn't be here. If I hadn't left you looking through the woods for me, maybe you wouldn't feel this way."

"I shouldn't have let you go in the woods in the first place."

"I was already in the woods, Will."

Willa couldn't help it. Had to pinch back a grin, a snicker. Cover her mouth with her hand. But then Astrid said, "That was really dramatic," and Willa let the laughing fit take her.

Astrid got that talking, talking from Cassie. Could always turn a phrase into a line from a movie that had been packed with meaning. A fit of self-mutilation, big dramatic pause, line of dialogue that would bring the actors to tears, maybe the audience too if it were done well. Here, though, they were laughing. Laughing-laughing. Enough that a nurse popped her head in, asked if everything was okay, and left just as quickly realizing, yes, yes, everything was okay at the moment.

But eventually, they were quiet again. Astrid's eyes back on an early episode of *Home Improvement*, Willa's eyes back on the side of Astrid's face. Her hand where the IV was anchored. Where the bandage just below her collar bone had bled through leaving a dot of red on her hospital gown.

Close.

Her fingers shaking, hovering above the red.

She should have moved her hand away.

But didn't.

Couldn't.

And she was caught.

Astrid said what.

Willa shook her head.

Eye to eye, they said nothing for a moment.

Two.

Three.

Then Willa said, "How come?"

Astrid took a breath. "It made things more vivid. More real. Easier to focus."

"What—what did that do?"

Astrid's eyes went to ceiling tiles. She scrunched her forehead, searched for words in the dotted flakeboard ceiling tiles. Said, "Like, when I felt like I was slipping. Losing my grip, you know? Pain would bring me back. But it's like anything. You build up a tolerance."

Willa nodded. Was drawn back to the red spot on the gown.

There was nothing else to say.

The only thing left was to stare.

Avoid Astrid's eyes.

"Do you want to see?"

Willa nodded.

Astrid used her good arm to untie the knot behind her neck, pull down the front of the gown. Sucked her teeth as she peeled the surgical tape away from her sore skin. Hissed as the bandage came away. Strings of blood and plasma stretched, broke away to one side or the other.

Made Willa think of knees ripped to shreds from tripping on the sidewalk. A scored piece of meat in Ken's special marinade. A hashtag in a Tweet layered one on top of the another, on top of another, on top of another. "Did it work?" Willa said.

Astrid shook her head.

"Can I?"

Astrid nodded.

Willa's hands were shaking. She put her fingertips to the undamaged skin first. Ran them lightly over the red, hot patch right before the blood. Then she put her palm over the wound. Felt its heat. Wet. Sticky. And just below that, Astrid's heart beating. Beating, beating.

She pulled her hand back. Looked at the patch of blood on her palm.

She didn't have to ask.

Astrid pulled down her gown further. Removed the bandage on her sternum.

Willa felt Astrid's lungs fill with air.

Empty.

Full.

Empty.

She wiped her nose with her free hand. Kept the other where the heat was. Where Astrid's skin was stitching itself back together, making scars that may scare people away someday.

Astrid pulled her gown down the rest of the way. Down to where the bandage was, just above her underwear line. She pulled that bandage away too. Astrid's guts rumbled under

Willa's hand, digesting, moving whatever she'd eaten through her. One groan was loud enough for them both to hear.

They laughed together.

Then they were quiet.

Willa wiped her eyes. Pulled her hand away from Astrid, looked at the blood. She showed it to Astrid. "Please don't do this again."

Astrid nodded.

"I don't want to see any more of this."

Astrid was crying.

Then, Astrid's new white cast pinched between them, they held onto each other. Willa listened to her friend breathing, felt her heart beating into hers. Snot. Lips on wet cheeks.

"I'm not going anywhere," Astrid said into Willa's ear.

It was just dramatic enough to make them both laugh.

37.

Everything was rebandaged. Astrid was given a new gown. The nurses were polite about it, but they weren't happy.

Willa had changed into one of the shirts Cassie had brought for Astrid, the one she was wearing had gotten patched with blood.

More *Home Improvement*.

This time with Cassie, and Garrett, and burgers, and fries, and McNuggets.

They stayed until they couldn't.

They'd be back first thing.

There were kisses, hugs, and apologies for squeezing too tightly.

And when they left, Astrid wasn't a part of capital-T them again. Their team. Their little fucked up family. This time only by proximity because she wasn't walking down the hall to the elevator, taking the elevator to the lobby, walking through the parking lot to the cars.

She wanted to be.

But she couldn't be.

She knew it.

For the moment, though, it didn't matter. They would be back for her.

And that was enough.

Astrid leaned back into her pillow and breathed lightly.

The Voyage Home

38.

SESSION 1

Everybody had so many wonderful plans.

Ellie was going to become a nurse, she wanted to help people.

Jim wanted write stories for video games, maybe create a franchise.

Libby hoped to one day run for some sort of political office, said she wanted to contribute.

The moment was shiny. The sort that stick. The kind people look back on and say they felt a real connection to the people they'd spent nearly every waking minute with over four years.

And I would love to say that I walked out of that meeting inspired. Ready. Able to march into the future with my chest puffed out, and my chin up.

But in the hall, the sounds of shoes on tile floors, lockers being slammed shut, people calling to other people by nicknames and last names, laughter, I knew right then I'd lied in that meeting.

I couldn't remember what I'd even said. I just knew it wasn't true.

The hall felt like one of those time-lapsed videos of flowers poking through soil as stems. Opening, turning toward the sunlight. Closing, sagging back toward the dirt when the moon rose. Opening, closing, opening, closing. Sunlight, darkness, sunlight, darkness.

Forever.

But I was the dirt.

I never moved.

I just watched while people pushed past me to wherever they were going because whatever they were supposed to be doing was real. Significant.

But me, the dirt, I knew better.

I was the stuff people grew out of.

Learned not to be.

I knew right then what I was. And it didn't have a future.

Not for any nihilistic reason like there's no point, we're animals playing like we know what we're doing.

People saw sunlight when they thought about what was coming.

I saw the dark.

Deep.

Black.

Nothing.

And what made it worse was that it didn't frighten me. Not right then at least.

It was just truth.

Astrid's room was a box of painted white cinderblock walls. A pair of beds with white sheets, a brown fuzzy blanket, a single pillow that Astrid was allowed to replace with the one from home Cassie made sure she had before she left. A set of shelves for books and pictures and notebooks and pens screwed into the wall that would hang over the right side of Astrid's body while she slept. Two tall, flimsy cabinets with closet space to hang clothes, a set of drawers underneath for underwear and socks and t-shirts. One for each person staying in the room.

Astrid had unpacked before whoever Jessa was had come back from group.

They were properly introduced by a woman in white scrubs. Jessa had shaken Astrid's hand with a skeleton hand, said hello, kept her eyes on the tile floor.

Astrid didn't bother to say much else. Sat on her bed. Ran her thumb over the three names on her new cast.

Cassie might be alone in the apartment. Might be watching *Star Trek* or microwaving herself some dinner. She would be talking to herself, or to the coffee pot, or to the fridge, blaming it for having to need to order Chinese food from the dump down the road—they were cheaper than the nice place. Maybe she'd call Chris. Ask him over. But more than likely she wouldn't.

Willa could be at crew practice. Back on her boat, yelling into the microphone on her headset for a power twenty, a power thirty to the rowers so they would know how long they needed to sprint before they could let the boat settle back into the water for a light paddle before the next set of strokes. Maybe she'd quit the team after all. Spend her time with Lily at Lily's house. Never at her own.

Garrett told Astrid before she left that he'd buy their prom tickets. Get measured for his tux. He'd made a good case for a teal vest and tie to go with the black jacket and pants. But Astrid insisted he go with a white shirt, not black. That would be the difference between aloof irony and looking like a complete douchebag. Garrett's point that the black shirt would cement the irony while the white would enter douchebag territory was well made, but Astrid had persisted. She would get a dress to match once she was released. Or finished her three days. Or however long she would decide she needed to be here. Until then, she was sure he'd text Willa for updates about her from Cassie, and list all the reasons he didn't think he should text his girlfriend's mother directly—he'd get ignored at first. But Willa would eventually text back. Maybe take him to the diner. He'd be fine.

Jessa, sitting on her bed, pointed to her own throat, said, "Suicide?"

Astrid stayed lying flat on her back, turned her head, winced at the bandaged wound rubbing up against her pillow. "What?"

"Your neck. Suicide?"

"Oh. Sorry," Astrid said, moving her eyes back to the ceiling. "I don't actually know."

Jessa breathed out a deep sigh, leaned back on her bed, put her hands behind her head. "Yeah, you do."

Whether Astrid had remembered where their names were, or could feel the atom-thin difference between the ink and the plaster, it didn't matter, she ran her thumb across the surface of the white over and over until a woman who would later introduce herself as her new one-on-one counselor knocked on her door and said Astrid's name like it was a question.

SESSION 2

Doctor Loonsfoot was the first person I'd ever met who could spit back to me the exact list of emotions I was experiencing when I poured the bottle of pills into my mouth.

Doctor Woods, I mean.

At the time, everything she said to me was true. Absolute truth. It didn't matter how crazy any of it sounded because, during our very first session after I was here the first time, she didn't speak like she was reading off a WebMD list of symptoms. Or talk about them as if she'd memorized a script like my first two therapists did—they knew what they were talking about, I knew that. But Loonsfoot—Woods—was different.

She knew.

No one could fake that.

It can be studied.

It can be written about.

It can be explained to people thoroughly enough that they can convince themselves they know something about it.

But no one really knows what it is until they've thought that maybe, if they were gone, everything would be better.

And she knew.

And I believed in her.

Still do, I think.

And it doesn't matter if I know how much she manipulated me into joining her in her psychosis.

She was my friend.

I didn't know anything about who she was before. I never really thought to ask. But I knew her. Knew her-knew her. And she knew me.

The glass was thin and old enough for cricket-song to come through. Almost as if they were playing their violin legs while sitting on the inch-thick metal ledge on the other side of the windowpanes. But they weren't the reason Astrid hadn't closed her eyes for much longer than a few minutes at a time.

There was always the possibility that she still wouldn't be able sleep.

The hospital was different. She was pumped with things that forced her to drift off.

And if the side effects listed on her new medicines had told her not to operate heavy machinery, and she still didn't sleep, maybe it was a possibility the meds weren't working at all. Again.

If Astrid closed her eyes and sleep didn't take her within a couple minutes, maybe she was still fully in the episode. And maybe it would get worse.

Maybe.

Jessa had been snoring into her pillow and farting into her sheets since lights out.

There were a couple things Astrid could try, but none of them could've been done properly with Jessa six feet across the room. Maybe Jessa was comfortable enough here not to wake up with a bloated belly from the half-asleep efforts of keeping her body quiet all night, among other things, but there was nothing that would get Astrid to that point.

But then someone somewhere was screaming. Not nightmare-screaming, or drama-screaming, but the sort that tears a throat apart with its pitch, and from how deep in the guts it gets dredged up.

Jessa sat up, rubbed her eyes, said, "What the fuck."

"Someone's having an attack," Astrid said, her pillow wrapped in her arms in front of her.

"I wasn't actually asking 'what the fuck,' it's just fucking annoying."

Sneakers squeaked across tile, flickering shadows in the light between the bottom of the door and the floor. Orders were barked back and forth between whoever had gone running to whomeveritwas's room.

Astrid used the layout of her room to understand the way the scene was probably playing itself out. The people in scrubs, the night shift, key their way through the door. They check the left bed, find a cowering teenager with her knees pulled up to her chin, her arms wrapped around her legs. Find the girl having the episode thrashing under her covers in the righthand bed. They try saying her name, try pulling her out with words spoken in gentle tones. But that doesn't work. When they go to her, the thrashing gets worse. She's clawed crescent moons into her palms. There's blood on her sheets. She bites into one of the orderlies' forearms, which forces him to say goddammit, he could use some fucking help here. They're forced to jab a needle into her leg, and she screams and writhes and screams and writhes until her screams turn to whimpers, and her movements turn sluggish, like her limbs were lead weights. They lift her gently onto a new bed—the kind with wheels—while they tell her roommate that she's okay now, that everything will be okay. They say the same things to the girl on the stretcher, whose eyes are now white slits in mostly closed eyelids, whose mouth moves like she's trying to speak, but can't, but she keeps on trying and trying as they say shh, and everything's okay, everything's okay. They're saying that to themselves, too. Have to. Seeing this, doing that, it takes a toll. They wouldn't be human if it didn't. And they nod to one another, sweaty, patched with blood—some from the girl, some from the bitten-into orderly's arm. When she's strapped and secured to the bed, and they wheel her out.

The line of light under the door was shadowed out by feet, a long clump of black, another set of feet. The sounds of metal wheels over linoleum faded along with the footsteps the longer the light in the corridor allowed Astrid's eyes to adjust enough that she could see everything in the room like a switch had been toggled to its dimmest setting. The cabinet, the desk, her feet under the covers, the lump of Jessa across the room already breathing heavy again, just before the snoring set in.

Astrid put her head back on her pillow.

Turned her body to face the dark where the shelving unit blocked out the rest of the room.

Cried.

SESSION 3

Regis-132 was real.

To Woods.

To me.

I believed in what we were doing.

It gave me focus.

Purpose.

And even when I knew I was slipping into an episode, there was still that future.

It was so real I could almost smell the alien air. It was sugary. Like cotton candy.

It was the first future I believed I could fit into.

I guess a part of me knew it was fake. If modern science couldn't open a wormhole through space and time, some lady with a box of scraps and a working knowledge of hologram projection and pseudo-science certainly couldn't.

But I wanted it.

And I don't think it's wrong of me to look back at that and think, despite all the lies, that building the Rippa, *spending all those hours with Woods, learning that, yeah, maybe I do have a future, were some of the happiest times I can remember.*

Yes, I was wronged by Woods.

Badly.

I feel stupid.

And used.

And it landed me here.

Mostly everything was fake. I know that.

But some of it was very, very real.

The stuff that probably really mattered was real.

Cafeteria food never bothered Astrid. There was something about it. It was always the same thing, every time. If it was cheeseburger Tuesday, the cheeseburgers the following Tuesday would have the same meat, chemical, and processed cheese flavor as the ones from the week before. Wednesdays at Springfield Elementary featured zeps—a salami, cheese, onion, and tomato sandwich on a soggy Kaiser roll. They were cold and slimy, and any time Astrid burped over the next six or so hours, onion and salami particles were sprayed onto the back of her tongue. Pretty gross. But, once a week, she handed over a dollar and was given a tray with a zep sitting in the center of a Styrofoam plate, a carton of milk, and a wet, salt-pimpled soft pretzel.

There were options here at lunch.

Ham and cheese, or turkey and cheese.

But the room was bright, and white, and smelled clean. Like it was mopped after every use with some sort of lemon-scented cleaner that found its way from Astrid's nostrils and into her food. It was something she would be able to count on.

Girls peppered the cafeteria. Some at their own tables. A couple of bunches here or there. Every long, six-seater table had at least one person unwrapping their sandwich, pulling one slice of bread up to squeeze mayonnaise or mustard onto the colorless meat from plastic packets, making faces, chewing, keeping their eyes on their trays. There wasn't much talking because there probably wasn't all that much to say. And there would be plenty of talking and talking and talking as the day went on because of group, or individual sessions, or saying thank you to the people distributing paper cups of meds, saying, "Open," to check if the girls had swallowed their pills or tried hiding them under their tongues.

Jessa sat across from Astrid.

Astrid smiled.

Jessa was a loud chewer.

Astrid traced the zigzag pattern on the surface of her blue tray with her eyes to block out the sucking, slopping, horror movie splatting going on in the mouth a couple of feet away.

"Sorry," Jessa said, her mouth full of mashed up white bread. "I've been here a while and every time a new person gets assigned to stay with me, I get nervous."

"It's okay. I can't really assume people are looking to make friends here—not that that's what I'm trying to do. It's just, I don't know."

"It is what it is? I hate that saying. It doesn't mean anything. I feel like it's something people say when they don't have anything to say and can only acknowledge that things are shitty."

Astrid laughed, wiped a rope of milk away from her chin with a paper napkin that rolled itself to bits on her skin.

"What?" Jessa said.

"Nothing. You just said a thing my mom would say."

"Is that good or bad?"

"It's good. Definitely good."

"Well," Jessa bit into her sandwich. "If I ever tell you that you remind me of my mother, that's a bad thing."

"Noted."

Jessa pointed to her throat, then to Astrid's bandage. "So?"

Still, even brushing against the bandage made her neck send waves of heat and ache to her brain. But Astrid ran her fingers along the tape, said, "It'll sound crazy."

"Crazy's a bullshit word," Jessa said, popping the last bit of her sandwich into her mouth. "Everyone is weird. Everyone does bizarre shit. Am I any crazier than a guy who bites his toenails, or a lady with a dozen cats who are just waiting for her to die so they can eat her?"

"I don't know if it's that simple."

"Probably not. Definitely not."

"This goes beyond quirks. It's complex, and awful, and I hate it."

Jessa drained her milk carton. "Jesus. I was just trying to be friends with you."

"I know. I'm sorry."

"It's whatever. I asked if you tried to kill yourself within, like, five minutes of meeting you."

Astrid watched Jessa's face. Watched for teeth, a wrinkled forehead, something to tell her it would be okay if she laughed. But keeping herself in check didn't last long. It wasn't a belly laugh, it wasn't hysterical, it was just funny. And Jessa followed suit.

"This food's disgusting, isn't it?" Jessa said.

"I kind of like it. At least we know what we're getting every day."

"Yeah, you're definitely batshit."

They laughed again.

Drew looks from the other girls, some of the staff.

They lowered their volume.

But couldn't keep it low for long.

And when they were shushed, they couldn't help but laugh harder, louder. Astrid's stomach muscles were aching.

The tape on her neck was pulling at her sore skin. Her face was red. Her eyes were tearing. Her breathing was erratic.

But there was nothing behind any of it but the laughing.

She could have broken into tears, that realization soaking in.

But she didn't.

And every time they were shushed, Astrid laughed harder.

SESSION 4

Dancing used to help.

It was stupid, but it worked.

I'd dodge blotches of shadow on the sidewalk to stay in the sun. Sunglasses, earbuds, my shoes hitting the pavement to the beat of electronic drums. Like I was walking through the opening credits of a movie. It was almost like it was storyboarded and soundtracked, and I'd bop down one of the busier roads in town just because.

Lens flare at the top of the frame. The camera keeping pace with me to my left.

There would be cuts back and forth between my shoes on the sparkling concrete, and the breeze in my hair, the smirk on my lips. A single shot would spin all the around me and I was the center of the universe.

I could see it.

I would've seen it too.

Sitting in the Chinese Theater in Hollywood. Watching it play out in front of me, my mom, and Willa.

I would've played myself—I'd directed the thing after all.

Marissa Tomei as Cassie Walsh. Only the best for mom.

Emma Stone as Willa. A stretch because even I could barely imagine Willa with red hair. But still. The freckles, the nose, the eyes that stare into souls.

I'd watch our names appear, disappear on the screen. We'd pass a bucket of popcorn back and forth between us, me sitting between them—the real-life people. I wouldn't be able stop myself from tapping my toe to whatever pop song fit the scene in post-production, watching myself dance down the street.

I'd really start dancing then, once that fantasy had gotten a hold of my brain.

I'd pass the line of cars that were stuck in almost the same spot for three lights before they could turn onto 309. Pass Springfield High just as the kids were being let out. Through a group of runners from Wyndmoor's track team, yelling go Adventurers loud enough I could hear myself over my music.

I'd keep dancing, twirling, laughing, rounding the corner and heading down the hill toward Willa's house. Cars would honk, I would wave. I didn't care about the looks I was getting through passenger-side windows, or from people cutting their lawns, or from kids on the school buses that coughed by.

I was sure no one on Papermill Road those days would ever be able to forget the dancing girl dodging cloud cover as she moved to the beat in her head.

Maybe that was what was most important.

Making certain I'd be remembered.

I don't know.

It was all that was working then, and it only worked when I was doing it. After, it was almost like it hadn't happened at all. Like the movie I'd make in the future—however ridiculous that was—would never happen.

Dreams never did much for Astrid.

They were mostly random, sometimes not.

All the reading she'd done about them mostly proved that, yes, they were reflective of something. But they were nothing that could lead anyone to any great revelations about themselves or about what they should do.

So, waking up with a wet face, hyperventilating and snotty, to Jessa saying, "Hey, hey, hey. You good?" all Astrid could say was, "Yeah, sorry," and attempt to go back to sleep with Woods's broken-open head burned into her brain.

SESSION 5

I really don't have much to say.
I'm sorry.

⟐

Astrid couldn't wait until the girl in the next stall flushed, washed her hands, and left.

She'd been sitting there sweating, her belly gurgling, wincing when each rush of pressure pressed down on her guts.

At home, it didn't matter. She did what she needed to do, didn't much care about the sounds or the smells, went about her day.

Nobody ever used the bathroom up on the fourth floor next to the art room at Wyndmoor. She had all the privacy she needed. Even when her meds twisted her up, made her skip steps all the way there.

She ran the water in the sink at Willa's, made it quick. Yes, it was Willa, it shouldn't matter much, but still. She did it anyway. It was more to be polite than anything else. Nobody wanted to hear the echoes of a toilet bowl through the door in their bedroom, so Astrid made certain Willa didn't have to. And even if she did, at least Astrid had done her best.

She hadn't needed to shit at Garrett's yet.

She'd figure that out if and when it needed to happen.

But here, the medicine supplementing her brain with the chemicals it wasn't producing enough of sent her running to the bathroom from group, from the recreation area while she and Jessa got their asses handed to them at ping-pong. And she'd been lucky so far. Empty room, didn't matter.

But no amount of clenching her teeth until her jaw ached would keep everything from spilling out of her for long. Or the girl in the next stall from asking if she was alright. Or wanting to get the fuck out of there and sign herself the fuck out of this place and call Cassie to have to her pick her up out front as soon as she could.

She used toilet paper for her eyes.

Stayed sitting long enough that her feet went numb.

Until Jessa creaked through the door and asked if she was all right, if she needed anything.

"I'm okay. I'll be fine."

Then there was the hand underneath the stall door. Lines of jagged white like she'd been keeping count of something in hashmarks on her skin.

Astrid reached down, took Jessa's hand.

Jessa ran her thumb along Astrid's hand, like, you're okay, you'll be okay, it'll be okay.

Astrid said it again. "I'm okay. I'll be fine."

"I know," Jessa said. "But a hand never hurts."

SESSION 6

It's one of those in-between places.

Like, I'm fine. I'm good.

I could go to a party and talk, and laugh, and go home and go to sleep without tearing myself apart about something I said, or something I didn't say, or something I said wrong. I could go to the diner and eat with my mom and Willa and feel like I actually, really belonged there, not just that I was around so they were obligated to sit with me. I could sleep in my own bed without staring at the stars I'd stuck to the ceiling when I was little without counting them over and over again because there was nothing else to do but worry, and cry, and worry about how loud I was crying.

But there's always going to be more of those times.

And more of these.

Maybe the medicine shaves the edges off the bad ones. But it's probably blurring everything else, too.

I'm always so tired, even after I am able to sleep. And it's not that busy-all-day-for-a-whole-week type of tired. It's more like having a list of things to do on your phone. And you tap a check mark onto all of things you take care of as you take care of them, but something glitches out when you close the app. When you reopen it, all the check marks are gone, and five, ten, twenty new things have been added, and you can't remember when you'd added them because it almost feels like they added themselves. But the usual type stuff isn't the stuff that's been added. It's not like needing to call the registrar's office to confirm online registration, or needing to pick up a gallon of milk for cereal in the morning. It's like, double check to make sure you took your medicine on time. Or, get in touch with Willa because of the look she gave you when you made that one comment you can't remember making that definitely, maybe could have upset her. Or, stop thinking that nothing matters because that's not true. Or, quit assuming you're going to be successful when you're older, because what defines success anyway, and what makes you think you're good enough at anything to fit into whatever that definition could be? Or, scratch that last entry from the list, crazy—you're okay, you're okay, you're okay, and everything will be okay.

I know it's not the new meds doing this.

That's not how they work. They take time.

It's my brain.

Rounding another corner.

Going where it wants.

Doing what it wants to do.

And that just so happens to coincide with what I want it to do.

But.

If this is a high point, and the meds are going to make the low ones less low, they'll make the high ones less high too. If it were on a chart it'd be a gently rolling wavy line instead of jagged spikes so far in either direction from the baseline even I would probably be pretty shocked about it.

Everybody has those ebbs and flows. And I'm working toward getting closer to that standard sort of life. But as much as I hate those low-lows, I wonder if I'll start to hate those low-highs just as much. Then go on new medicines that produce similar but slightly different results.

Round and round.

Over and over.
Forever.
I'm already so tired.

⌾

Cassie would have snatched the remote from Jessa's hands for not staying on one channel for longer than a single commercial break. Astrid said instead, "Come on, pick something."

Thumb on the Up button, Jessa said, "There's nothing on. I'm trying to find something good."

"If there's nothing on maybe you should just stop trying."

"I think that's probably what got us here."

Astrid didn't laugh, but it was funny.

She nodded, said whatever.

But then Spock was telling Bones that his attempt at explaining a human's natural fear of death was illogical, and, therefore, irrelevant.

Bones said, "Mister Spock, life and death are seldom logical."

"Oh, wait, keep this on," Astrid said.

A collective groan came from all the girls sitting around the television on couches, chairs, the floor.

Astrid's face was warm from the rush of blood.

She shrugged, said, "I really like this show."

"This is like a hundred years old," Jessa said.

"It's fifty-two years old," Astrid said. "And once you get past some of the acting, the special effects, and the occasionally questionable gender politics, it's really a lot of fun."

"You're such a nerd."

"Maybe."

On the screen, the bridge crew shook in their seats, puffs of smoke burst from control panels, Captain Kirk was thrown from his chair.

"How can you stand this?" Jessa said.

Astrid shrugged again. "I've been watching it my whole life. It's my mom's fault."

"Yeah? What did she see in it?"

"Hope."

The sound from Jessa's throat was halfway between a laugh and an attempt at dislodging a wad of phlegm.

"My mom told me they were our only friends when I was born. She only ever saw my dad three times, and once she told him she was pregnant he was gone. My grandparents pretty much disowned us. So, every night we'd sit and watch this. She loved that they could travel at nine hundred times the speed of light. That the only reason they were out there was to discover things and help people. They taught her that everyone has a place. Even monstrous space creatures whose could only communicate in a way that seemed to Kirk and Spock like it was an attack. She found out who she could be by watching them."

Jessa wasn't smiling, didn't make any throat sounds. Just said, "What's it mean to you?"

"Different things at different times, I guess. Sometimes it scares me, the idea we're so small. But mostly that fake, white-speckled black background the *Enterprise* zooms across was home. I'd go out there in a second, if could. It's possibility. It's promise. It's the future."

"You should be an astronaut," Jessa said.

"I wouldn't pass the psych evaluation."

The girls who'd heard it laughed. Astrid, Jessa, too. It didn't last long. But no one complained about the show after that. Not all of them watched, but the ones who did seemed partly interested. Maybe.

Jessa stood, said she'd be right back.

On the screen, Kirk said, "Our species can only survive if we have obstacles to overcome. Without them to strengthen us, we will weaken and die."

From the floor, Bethany said, "Deep."

Maybe it was more than that.

Maybe it could be.

Jessa sat back in her chair, got a grip on Astrid's cast, began to write.

Jessa Harris scrawled in Sharpie.

"Now you can take me with you when you go to outer space."

Astrid laughed a little, her eyelids stinging a bit. "I'll have to get the cast off one day."

Jessa nodded. Then grabbed Astrid's cheeks with one hand. Began swiping the marker across her forehead with the other.

Once she let go, she said, "There. That shit's permanent."

Everyone was laughing.

But Astrid reached across Jessa with her good arm, pinched her cast between them on the couch, put her chin in the crook of Jessa's neck.

"Thank you," Astrid said.

"For what?"

"Letting me watch my show."

Jessa's hands were on Astrid's back. Her hair smell was in her nose.

She held on until Jessa said okay, okay.

And then some.

SESSION 7

I've gotten pretty used to not knowing anything.

Every time I feel like I get a pretty good hold on something, a new thing happens, and it turns that understanding into a complete joke. Like, there was no reason I should have ever thought I understood what I'd thought I did.

That's probably pretty common.

But I think there are also a lot of people who are just so confident that everything will work out the way it needs to, or believe that everything happens for a reason, that it makes my not knowing feel like I'm missing something. I'm pretty certain nothing happens for a rea-

son. Like, everything from movies to television to even Shakespeare puts every life event into a narrative that, even when it gets messy, there's a cause and effect for everything and that gives people some odd sense of comfort. And people assign that structure to their lives. But life doesn't have a narrative. It can't be crammed into three acts or five acts or whatever. And trying to force completely random sets of circumstances into a narrativeless life is just ridiculous. If individual lives were movies, they would be the most boring and frustrating movies ever made. Nothing makes sense. Very few actions go from A to B to C. Sometimes lives just end. Most times they go nowhere for eighty or so years and then end. And talking like this to people who believe that scares them so badly that I'd get labeled a pessimist and ignored. Or called crazy.

But I'm not crazy.

I think I might just see the world for what it really is.

And, yes, that's a really grandiose thought—which is absolutely a symptom of my issues—but isn't it at least just a little bit true?

Most days, I go to school, I go to work, I go to the diner, I spend time with Willa, and my mom, and Garrett, and that sort of purposelessness is like a balm I can spread all over my body that cools the immediacy people feel and makes it seem, I don't know, cute. But then there are some days that not being able to create that narrative structure for myself turns that listless drift through space on a rock into a blistered-fingered struggle to cling to a flaming comet hurdling through the solar system without a target. At that point, cracking a planet in half feels like a better option than rocketing through space only to keep circling and circling and circling and circling for no other reason than that's all I was made for.

But right now, not knowing anything, having no idea where I'm going, or what I'm doing, isn't scary at all. I'm just here. And I'll just go about my business. I'll smile, or laugh, or cry, or want to put my fist through glass, or not feel anything at all, maybe sometimes all in the same day, or maybe even all at once every now and then. And that doesn't seem so bad at all.

Right now anyway.

⟐

Jessa's name had faded from Astrid's forehead, but it was still there.

She had to get close to the mirror, strain her eyes to see it, but it was there.

Which was good.

She hadn't seen Jessa since she was called out of group.

Was told she'd been discharged and that was all.

Went to sleep in an empty room and missed the Jessa sounds.

Not enough to wish that she'd needed to stay here any longer. But being able to say goodbye would've been good. Astrid would've asked her to sign her forehead again so she'd get through a couple more showers with that jagged script pressed into her skin.

It was on her skin still, however faintly, and it was on her cast. She'd keep the cast once it was cut off of her. Same way she'd keep the goggles she'd accidently taken home from the lab in her bookbag. The suit she'd bought to dupe that poor idiot at UPenn.

What she'd seen at Woods's apartment would crawl its way out of her brain eventually, she knew that. The girl down the hall needing to be sedated in the middle of the night would too. Believing she was going to another world. Spending so much money that wasn't hers on suits and hospital bills.

She wouldn't keep any of it to herself once she was home.

Things would be different; they'd have to be.

She put all of her stuff in a bag.

She walked through the hall, nodded at some girls, waved goodbye to others.

She signed of series of papers on a clipboard.

She shook hands with Doctor Evans, waved to some of the staff, made her way to the lobby.

She wouldn't be this way every day—breathing steady, looking forward—far from it. Right now, there was tomorrow, and the next day, and the next day. And the moment it stopped seeming as if there were any more tomorrows on their way, she wouldn't hide it. Couldn't.

Cassie was waiting for Astrid in the lobby.

Gave her a big hug, told her she missed her.

Astrid missed her too. Said so into her hair.

Cassie pulled back, kissed Astrid's forehead. Said, "Who scribbled on your face?"

"Somebody like me."

Cassie hooked her arm through the L in Astrid's cast, said, "Ready?"

Astrid said, "Ready."

They walked outside together.

The City on the Edge of Forever

39.

Everyone was so understanding.

Let Astrid process everything the way she needed to once she got home.

When she needed to speak to the policeman who'd found Woods's body, Cassie drove her to the station. Sat with her as Detective Norton answered all of her questions. Questions that were mostly about what was done with the body. Questions she figured she needed to ask even though she probably, deep down, didn't want to know the answers..

Whenever she wanted to talk about how beautiful the fantasy of Regis-132 had been, Willa would listen. She wouldn't ask her how she possibly could have convinced herself it was even remotely true. Just sat, listened, nodded along because it was a thing Astrid needed at that moment, and that maybe, without the possibility of such a thing, her episode could have been much worse. Bad enough they wouldn't have been able to have these conversations.

Whenever Garrett asked her if she needed anything, she'd smile, say thank you, but no. He'd still bring her a pack of peanut butter cups from the vending machine before class. Carried her school bag from one classroom to the next if he so happened to have a class in the same section of the building. Brought her dinner at work—once a cheesesteak, once a burrito, once a bag of McDonald's fries. And, whenever he felt Astrid was looking a bit blue, he'd talk about prom plans. But Astrid wasn't blue.

She was fine.

She was good.

And whenever she needed to be alone, she got the space she asked for. Whether the trust Cassie, and Willa, and Garrett had had in her before was fully back in place, or they'd collectively figured that she was unlikely to have another episode so soon, there was no way to tell.

But there was also no way of knowing how much longer it would be until the lab was cleared out by whomever had rented the place to Woods.

And it wasn't exactly a conscious decision to step through the tree line into the woods while Astrid was going for her nightly walk.

It sort of just happened.

She had come back to herself walking along the dirt path, breaking through the shade into the clearing.

Decided to stay for a little while once she was standing in front of the lab, house, whatever it was now.

The keys were where she'd left them.

The floorboards creaked in all the same places.

So much had happened.

It was as if nothing had happened at all.

She ran her fingers along the banister, the mantel, the kitchen table/workbench combination. Drew patterns into the thickening layer of dust.

She wasn't going to clean because Woods had never cleaned.

Wasn't going to sit because she couldn't remember Woods ever sitting unless she was driving.

Dictated instructions to herself because Woods would say things like, "Increase power by forty percent."

Or, "Careful, that thing'll burn straight down to bone if you touch it."

Or, "If this works, and we don't explode, the risk of atomization will have been worth it."

Astrid took deep breaths, standing in the middle of the house.

There was a smell.

Musty, but not mildewed.

Like sticking her nose into the middle of a book that had lived on a shelf in a basement.

All the time she'd spent in the place, she never once considered the smell to be something she'd miss almost as much as Woods telling her she'd better not put her face too close to the lasers; or sitting in the *Rippa*'s cockpit going over what did what on the control panel; writing one-word instructions on masking tape, and sticking strips over switches.

If Astrid's home—her future home—smelled like this place, that wouldn't be so bad. Whoever she would one day choose to live with would need to enjoy it too, or she would live alone. She wasn't sure how she could recreate that exact smell. Maybe she'd have to let dust build up enough to see it without needing the sunlight to shine on it. Maybe she'd need to expose hardwoods, keep them unfinished. Or maybe she'd need to keep some windows open to mimic the wind through the broken panes.

She pulled the sheet off the *Rippa*, crawled into the cockpit.

Ran her fingers along the control console, the switches, dials, diodes, the blank LCD screen in the center that would have supposedly displayed power levels if the thing was actually functional.

Flicked on the silver exclamation point ignition switch.

And there was nothing.

There had always been nothing.

The humming was an old house settling.

The blue glow beneath the masking tape labels was nothing, just the sun setting through layers of clouds and shards of glass, casting a strip of the color spectrum onto the controls.

But then the *Rippa* bucked.

Forced Astrid to sit up straight in her chair.

The blonde hairs on her arms stood on end.

Her breath caught in the back of her throat.

Something underneath her seat rumbled, vibrated the cockpit into a steady shake.

And then Woods was on the screen in the center of the control panel.

Lab coat.

Glasses.

A mess of red hair on top of her head.

A lump of scab on her cheek.

Sitting exactly where Astrid was.

Her tinny voice came through, small, far away.

"These sorts of things always start with, if you're seeing this, I'm already gone. I won't say that. Even though I just did. Doesn't matter. Instead, I'll just say I am so sorry." She scratched the back of her head, adjusted her glasses. "I treated you badly. I lied to you. Manipulated you into helping me do things that I shouldn't have. Taught you how to do things you never needed to know how to do. More than likely, the things you know how to do have probably already gotten on someone's radar."

Astrid hadn't been looking for the men in the suits, their black cars driving off once they noticed her noticing. Since getting home, Regis-132 not being an actual thing, there hadn't been much of a reason to keep an eye out. She almost pulled herself out of the *Rippa*. Almost sprinted out of the house, down the dirt road to Haws.

But Woods, grainy, fidgety, readjusting herself in the cockpit chair.

"If you were to walk away from this right now, I couldn't

in a million years hold it against you. But, I have to say, if only for a short time, and despite how it ended, I felt like I had a place in the world again. And, look, there's no denying it, I am not a good person. I was. I just got lost along the way somewhere. So, as recompense for all you did for me while I withheld all I did from you, I give you the *Rippa* to do with as you please. It's ready to go. The coordinates are logged. All you need to do is hit the launch button. Don't forget the radiation suits, they're in the rear hatch, and even though the uranium is just feet from your face as you sit here now, the suit and the lead casing will be more than enough to keep you, and whomever you choose to bring with you safe.

"I am sure that my actions have caused you immeasurable amounts of pain. I hope that one day you can forgive me. And, even if you don't use this thing for what it was made to do, you're a loving, caring soul who doesn't deserve to feel the way I know you do. It got the better of me. Don't let it get the better of you. And I can't say it's not going to be nipping at your heels the rest of your life, because there's a chance it'll always follow you. Just, make a promise to yourself that you'll always go to the people who can help you through the really awful moments. They might not understand. More than likely they'll never be fully capable of understanding you. That sort of loneliness can be crushing, but you're never actually alone if you choose not to be.

"I know I let you down. I'm sorry. But, if nothing else, your kindness brought me a gift I'd never thought I'd have again. A gift I had right until the end. The gift of friendship. No, you never got to fully know me. I never gave you that chance. Don't be like me. Don't shut people out. Be you. And everything you are. If there's one thing you can trust me on, it's this: You are enough.

"Don't let what's following catch up. Ever. Lead it on a merry chase. I left a few things in the back hatch for you. Goodbye, my friend."

The screen went black.

The menu Woods had programmed popped back into view.

"Begin launch sequence?" in green letters. Y and N keys pulled from an old desktop keyboard just below the screen.

Astrid sat with the hum, the vibrations from deep within the machine.

She breathed deep until the air began to smell sparkly. Like there was something being added to it from the engine chamber. A glittery, metallic taste on the back of her tongue.

She reached for the console.

Flicked off the ignition switch.

The blue faded.

The hum died.

The *Rippa* went still, quiet.

And Astrid had nothing left to do but watch her head on the climb out of the cockpit. Run her stitched-up hand along the metal plating, which was warm, almost alive. Kneel in front of the back hatch, pull it open. Reach inside. Feel the rubber radiation suits on her fingertips. Something made of a soft but scratchy fabric. The duffel bag she'd left behind before running off and finding Woods. A small metal box.

She started with the cloth whateveritwas.

Pulled it from the hatch.

She swallowed hard, ran her fingers along the lapels of Woods's lab coat folded into a neat square. Pulled an orange Post-It note from the breast pocket. Ran her thumb along Woods's handwriting: "For the future, whatever that may be."

Astrid swiped away dust, scraps of metal, flecks of concrete floor that had been knocked lose when they were assembling the *Rippa*. Set the lab coat down in the clean space.

Next, the box.

It was heavier than she expected. Weighed more than something the size of a gift box should.

Another Post-It, this one stuck to the box above the latch holding it closed.

"For your return trip, if you choose to take one."

A little drawing beneath the scribbled handwriting.

A circle with three blacked-out slices of pie inside. A smaller, black circle in the center that had nearly torn through the paper with how hard, and how long Loonsfoot had filled it in with pen.

Astrid dropped the box, scraped her ass across the floor, putting as much distance between the uranium encased inside as she could. She pushed herself away with her healing leg pulsing hot with pulling-open scabs and surgical tape, a hand held together with string, through dirt and crumbs of concrete.

It wasn't glowing.

It wasn't putting off heat.

It was just a box.

That was all.

She wouldn't open it right now, no. There was no need. It was left for her. She'd open it when she felt like it.

Astrid pulled herself to her feet. Peppered the floor with everything that had clung to her clothes as she brushed herself off.

There was nothing but the sound of Astrid's breathing.

Heavy, but in control.

In.

Out.

In.

Out.

In.

If anything, Astrid shouldn't be surprised.

This was what Woods did. She made grand gestures. Manipulated people with spectacle, words about self-worth and the power within. All delusions of grandeur. All nothing more than a symptom of the thing that took bites of her brain every day until she put a bullet through it—the same thing that had gone dormant, at least for a little while, in Astrid.

She wasn't angry.

Couldn't be.

Woods had been suffering and Astrid just so happened to be in the way.

There was nothing she could change.

Maybe she wouldn't change anything even if she could.

"You're forgiven," Astrid said. It was little more than a whisper.

"You're forgiven," she said again. This time louder. A conversational volume.

But then she yelled it.

"You're forgiven," again.

Again.

Again.

Until her throat hurt.

She'd delete the video saved in the *Rippa*'s memory banks. She'd tuck the folded lab coat and the lead-lined box into the duffel, zip it shut the best she could. She'd pull the tarp back over the *Rippa*, head right out the front door, lock it behind her, pocket the keys.

But it couldn't hurt to keep something of Woods's that no one needed to know about—not that, if she were asked what it was, she wouldn't tell anybody about it, of course. It probably wasn't even uranium anyway. Maybe.

Astrid walked the dirt path, the duffel hanging from her shoulder, the new, boxy whatever it was in the bag bumping, bumping into her hip with every step.

Taking a piece of Woods with her wasn't an awful thing to do.

It was the right thing.

If Astrid didn't remember her for what she could've been, no one would remember her at all.

And that was the worst possible thing Astrid could think of.

Jessa's handwriting had been washed from Astrid's forehead, but that moment, staring into her eyes as she wrote, that won't be going anywhere. At least, this way, she'd have actual objects to point to and say they belonged to an old friend who'd passed away a long time ago.

So, in the spirit of friendship, she wouldn't forget a thing.

40.

Willa had always said she would never, under any circumstances, be excited for obligatory, ceremonial nonsense.

But she couldn't help it.

And when her name was called, she pushed herself away from the wall, went into the repurposed classroom without looking back at Astrid, or Lily, or Garrett—she couldn't let on that she deserved this. Couldn't say it out loud either.

Still, she deserved it.

Earned it.

Jeff was unzipping a blue gown. Ingrid was running her fingers up and down her honors sash hanging from her neck. Katie was being as careful as she could, pulling the cap up and away from her hair so it wouldn't get any more mussed than it already had gotten underneath the elastic band, the polyester.

Mr. Hogan checked Willa's name off a list on the clipboard in front of him. Tired-looking, clothes wrinkled from standing, sitting, standing all day in classrooms, the cafeteria, doing whatever else teachers did when they weren't monitoring hallways, or shushing noisy students in the library. He reached into a box, set a clear plastic square with Willa's cap and gown inside onto the table. Held up a pen, pointed to where Willa needed to sign. "You can try it on if you'd like."

Willa scratched her name on the line, shrugged, said, "They're one size fits all, aren't they?"

"I mean, they're gowns, so it's a safe bet it'll fit just fine."

The plastic square crinkled, crackled, sounded more like a piece of trash than the packaging holding an accessory to a momentous rite of passage Willa had spent most of the last four years denying such a description.

"Why don't you try it on anyway."

"I didn't hear a question mark at the end of that sentence, Mr. Hogan."

"Wasn't really a question," Mr. Hogan said, smile on his face, tired eyes watching for how Willa would react. "I just think it might be, I don't know, the start of all the new, good things in front of you."

Willa ran her thumb underneath the plastic flap. She'd have to scrub whatever heinous type of adhesive was used to hold the package together off her skin. It would come off in gray rolls, get caught in the limescale-crusted space between the porcelain and the metal drain cover in the girls' bathroom sink.

Whatever the gown was made of scratched at Willa's skin when she slid her arms through. Tickled the back of her neck when it came to rest on her shoulders. Still, she zipped it closed, held her arms out to her sides. "Well?"

Mr. Hogan handed over her cap. "This too."

The elastic squeezed a little as she tugged the cap into place. Itched at her scalp the same way maybe bugs, maybe nothing at all did when she spent too much time outside in the summer heat. She raised her eyebrows, shifted the cap with her wrinkled forehead.

"Congratulations," Mr. Hogan said.

"Thanks. Do you know how to fold this thing back up?"

"Hey, I just work here. You're the one who insisted on trying it on."

They laughed a little while Willa caught a glimpse of herself in the standing mirror pulled from the stage crew supply room in the auditorium. Aside from her shoulders acting like a garment hanger for the gown, her body was gone. She was a navy-blue ghost. Under there. Somewhere. Hidden.

"It doesn't feel real," she said.

"It will."

"No, I mean, it's like a costume."

"Everything's a costume."

Willa unzipped the gown, pulled the cap from her head. "So, you're saying nothing's real, then?"

"Well, yes and no." Mr. Hogan stood, crossed his arms. "You and Astrid probably already know this by now, but most of everything comes down to pretending to be a thing until you become that thing."

"So, everything's bullshit?"

Mr. Hogan laughed, said, "Language."

"Sorry."

"That was me pretending. Pretty good, right?"

"Not bad at all."

"All that counts, I think, is giving a shit. And you give a shit."

Willa said, "Language." Folded, refolded, refolded her gown again before plunking her school bag on the table and stuffing the cap and gown inside. "Thought I'd be excited for this."

Mr. Hogan leaned against the table, said, "You don't need anyone to tell you much of anything. But if I could offer one smidge of advice?"

Willa zipped up her bag, said, "Who says 'smidge?'"

"Is that a 'go ahead with the advice,' or a 'leave me alone, old man?'"

"Little bit of both."

"Fair enough. I'll keep it short. Most people live in a fantasy camp. You weren't afforded that privilege. But everybody you're graduating with is asking themselves the same questions about who they are, where they belong, what they're worth, and most of them won't ever have a chance to find out because they'll stay within the parameters of that fantasy camp. And good for them, man, that's living. It's comfortable. But what you and your friends have gone through can tell you exactly what you are. Learning that at your age is a privilege in and of itself. It's also a major burden. But you are glue, Willa. You hold things together."

Willa slung her bag over her shoulder, pursed her lips, said, "Why are you saying this stuff to me?"

"Because it takes one to know one. I had a friend who needed lots of glue, too. I'd like to think I was able hold some stuff together when he couldn't."

"So, we're glue?"

"We are glue."

"Isn't that exhausting?"

"Sure it is. But I know my worth, and I think I am fortunate for that."

"You think?"

Chris laughed, sat back in his chair, said, "Life is nothing if not complex."

Willa nodded, headed for the door.

But then she turned, said, "Can I offer you some advice then? Glue to glue?"

"Sure."

"Michael's Diner has the best chicken parm sandwiches in the world."

A smile, a pair of eyes dropping to the clipboard, the table. "And you've been all over the world and tried every chicken parm sandwich out there?"

"No. I just can't imagine a better chicken parm sandwich."

"Somehow I don't think we're talking about chicken parm sandwiches anymore."

"Same way we weren't only talking about graduation."

Mr. Hogan nodded.

Willa did the same.

She should never have expected Astrid, or Garrett, or Lily to cheer, clap, celebrate when she stepped out of the classroom. But there was something in her that wished they had. It wouldn't have done much more than embarrass her, but it would have been nice. Like a scene in a movie that she would've called bullshit on because that wasn't how life worked; everything coming together for a moment at the end that would tie a nice bow on things.

But they were bunched up together, facing one another, staring down at something in Astrid's hand.

Mr. Hogan called for Lily. The end-of-the-day teacher voice echoing down the hallway.

Lily didn't even glance up.

Willa said, "Hey."

Nothing. Again.

Willa put her hand where Lily's tailbone curved away from her back, said her name again.

But that was when Astrid looked up, locked her eyes with Willa.

"What?"

Astrid held up her phone. Said, "Read."

A headline from CNN.

Something about every nuclear power plant in the country being on lockdown due to the possible theft of nuclear material. Words like "terrorist." And "coverup." And the responsibility of the media to bring these stories to light because the people had the right to know the truth about what was going on in the country.

Garrett said, "The world's insane, man."

Lily said, "My mom always says there's no expecting this stuff to happen until it happens."

Willa said, "Yeah, crazy."

Her eyes locked onto Astrid's again.

Astrid nodded.

41.

Cassie was going to quit. Absolutely. One hundred percent. She had to. She woke up every morning with a putrid funk resting on the back of her tongue. Her pillow, her sheets, her clothes had atomically bonded with the gray burn. Her guts ached while she sat on the toilet, kept the pressure up until she smoked one, two cigarettes on her way to the diner, which forced her to waddle from the parking lot to the ladies' room. But there was an urgency to flick the lighter, take that first drag of the morning while backing out of the apartment parking lot that couldn't be avoided—it built up in her chest every night before sleep took her.

Christ, if Astrid and Willa were to pull up, find Cassie leaning against the back of the building puffing away at her third smoke of her fifteen minute break, that would only make her look more inept, more irresponsible, more like her own mother. She'd deserve everything that came with that. Astrid walking away because Cassie was unable to not be the mother she'd always sworn she'd never be. She'd smoke a trach ring into her throat, or cancer into her lungs, or a blood clot into her brain. John would find her body, bloated and reeking in the apartment, the home screen of the first season of *Star Trek* repeating the same forty seconds of footage and music over and over again until he switched the DVD player off. Astrid would never visit her grave. Why would she? Why should she? Cassie had more or less murdered Loonsfoot—Woods, whatever—then helped her own body eat itself until billions of microorganisms took over for her once she'd hacked her last wad of phlegm.

Every now and then, when someone drove their car around back of the diner, Cassie passed her cigarette from its place between her index and middle fingers to the pads of her thumb and index finger, and tucked it away in her palm. Just in case. The heat from the cherry pushing her skin past the point of sting, Cassie decided she definitely would squeeze her hand closed if the cars were full of Willa and Astrid, or Astrid and Garrett, or some other combination thereof.

She'd deserve it.

But she brought the butt to her lips, pulled smoke, waved while Chris parked his car next to hers.

She hadn't blocked his number because he was texting or calling too much. It was nothing like that. It was more, when he did those things, Cassie couldn't believe a word of them. Yeah, of course he'd be there for her if she needed him, that was what good guys did—or the guys who thought they were good guys always said they did—but, most of all, the people who said that sort of thing typically had no idea what that could mean. No goddamn way. Nothing was ever going to be okay because okay didn't exist; Cassie's life was varying degrees of panic and stress, and nothing else. And no, no one never just texted hello. Ever.

"Mind if I have one?" Chris said, pointing, smiling.

"You should quit."

"I should. But I don't want to miss my shot to look as cool as you."

Grinding the cigarette out on her cheek would get Cassie

to quit grinning. Instead, their skin touched when the cigarette and the lighter passed from Cassie's fingers to Chris's, and she forced her teeth back behind her lips.

She'd read somewhere that the human brain stores literally every memory, sight, smell, everything. But it wasn't like a computer where anyone could glide their finger over a person's frontal lobe, click on a file labeled Warm & Fuzzies, and watch memories like forgotten videos stored deep in a smartphone. It took more than that. Something specific.

And Cassie smelled Chris's hair on her pillow for the first time again despite smoking and standing close enough to a dumpster to taste a sweet stink at the backend of every breath.

"I heard they've got the best chicken parm sandwiches on Earth at this place," Chris said.

"Is that right?"

"Heard it from a reliable source, too."

Cassie shrugged. "I've had better."

"I've figured as much."

There was nothing to say the first time they'd deviated from a conversation strictly regarding Astrid either. Just the feeling that Cassie should say something, but maybe Chris had something to say first. But Cassie had waited too long to speak to expect Chris to just blurt anything out.

He always seemed to breathe the same way too. Lying next to her sounded the same as leaning against a filthy diner wall to her right.

"Thank you for the cigarette," Chris said.

"You're leaving?"

"I didn't say that."

"Do you want to leave?"

"Do you want me to leave?"

Cassie dropped what was left of her cigarette to the blacktop, crushed it under her sneaker. "I'm just having a hard time figuring out why you wouldn't want to."

"Why? Because you haven't responded to any of my calls

or texts?" He said it the way he'd told her, no, no, he wasn't asking her on a date, but wouldn't mind some company with his first taste of Michael's Diner's famous coffee. Same way he'd asked when the hell Captain Kirk was going to use the Force already.

Cassie scraped the toe of her shoe into the black left from her cigarette. She was laughing. Really. Enough to reach for his hand. But she stuffed her hand into her apron pocket instead.

And then there wasn't much to laugh at anymore.

And then there was that nothing where one of them should've said something.

This time, she went first. "My parents used to tell me I was special."

"I think everyone's parents told them that."

"But I kind of was. Like, in a lot of the same ways I've told Astrid she is. Always at the top of my class. Honors this, honors that. I played softball and field hockey and was really good at both. Then I had Astrid and none of that mattered anymore. But it mattered to my parents. My mom never looked me in the eye again. Like she'd been wrong about me. Like she'd put all her faith in something only to find out it wasn't true. Astrid actually reminded me of my mom when she figured out I was the one putting the presents under the tree. She was so mad. Almost like, without that belief, there was nothing else she could believe in. I swore I'd never let her feel that way again, or, at the very least, get her to understand that, goddammit, I sure was trying my best. But there I went, taking everything she had left to believe in away from her again and again and again. This is going to sound insane, but part of me feels like, if I die, or if she dies, it'd be better than living without her being able to bring herself to look me in the eye. That's a completely disgusting thought, I know. But my mom is dead, and all I'm really upset about in that case is that she failed me so badly while she was alive. So, if I was so special, why is it I'm so able to make nearly the same mistakes a woman who was definitely not special made?"

Chris's face was the same as it had been in the manager's office weeks ago. No shock or horror reflecting what Cassie had said back to her. Nothing to suggest he was about to push away from the wall, get in his car, and drive away. Just a wrinkled forehead, pursed lips, his arms crossed over his chest, the last few drags of his cigarette wisping away from the orange smolder between his fingers. "I can't pretend to know what happened," he said. "But there's nothing about you that tells me you weren't doing anything but trying to help."

"My mother wanted nothing to do with helping me."

"Well that's the difference, isn't it?"

"Maybe we're just taking two different ways to get to the same place."

"Or maybe none of that matters, and you were doing whatever you could."

"Maybe." Cassie put her open pack to her mouth, pulled out another cigarette. "Or maybe I'm just—"

Chris plucked the cigarette from her lips, put it between his own, and lit it with the last bit of cherry from his. He flicked his butt to the ground, handed her the freshly lit cigarette.

"Thanks," she said.

"Old habits."

"Yeah."

There was that quiet again. The air conditioning units on the roof grunting, humming back to life. The cars passing by this way, that way out front of the diner. Someone having just left the urgent care office next door pulling their car door closed, starting the engine.

"Would you want to go to the prom with me?" Chris said.

Cassie pressed the back of her head to the wall, cocked her eyebrow the way she had whenever she'd tried to show him how corny he was when he'd tried to sound cool, or profound. "You're a nerd."

"I'm serious. I have to chaperone the thing, and if I have to keep a bunch of teenagers from getting too handsy on the dance floor, I could really use the company."

"Is teachers bringing dates to prom even a thing?"

"Who cares?"

Cassie closed off a nostril with her finger, plumed Chris's face with smoke.

"That was gross," he said.

"That's the kind of company you're asking to keep."

"I haven't changed my mind."

"I didn't get to go to my prom."

"I know."

"I'll have to ask Astrid."

"I wouldn't dare assume you'd go ahead with this without her okay."

"You're still a nerd."

"Nerdiness is cool these days. Therefore, you think I'm cool."

It was the longest Cassie had gone without looking away from Chris's eyes. "I think you're good," she said.

"Is that a yes?"

"It's a 'We'll see.'"

"Dependent entirely on what Astrid has to say about it?"

"You'll have to find out." Cassie pulled the steel door open, let the rush of cool air feel far more profound than it had any business being. "You want that chicken parm sandwich, or what?"

"I do."

Cassie put her back to the open door, waved her hand to usher Chris inside.

He brushed his fingers against her arm. Wouldn't take his eyes off hers.

She kissed the corner of his mouth.

"You're good, too," he said. "I know that for sure."

Cassie didn't hear the car pulling through the lot before Chris had already stepped inside. But tugging the door from where it sticks into the macadam divit, she watched it glide by. Slow. Deliberate. A black sedan. A guy who could double for a limo driver if not for the car only having four doors. She couldn't tell if he was staring at her or the building through his sunglasses, but she stared right into the lenses.

Inside, Chris said, "Who's that?"

"I don't know," Cassie said as the car passed out of view. "We get a lot of weirdos through here sometimes." She turned to him, winked. Shook her head because who the fuck winks while she pulled the door shut behind her.

Then she took Chris's hand and walked him to her favorite booth.

42.

Astrid stuffed the envelope back into the lab coat pocket where she'd found it. Then she pulled the coat from her shoulders and tossed it into the hamper in her closet.

She had every reason to be jumpy. There was the SUV in Willa's sideview mirror on the way to school. The sedan idling in the teacher's lot during lunch. The van a few cars behind them on their way home. And, even though it was most definitely Cassie knocking on her bedroom door, Astrid certainly couldn't be found wearing that coat while reading a secret note from a dead woman while periodically scanning Bethlehem Pike through her window for black vehicles driven by men in black suits.

And there they went again.

Up Bethlehem.

Down Bethlehem.

Always just a second slower than the pace of traffic.

Never stopping.

Just circling.

Circling.

Cassie's head was poking between the bedroom door and the doorjamb. She asked if Astrid would come out and read something over for her. If she wanted Chinese for dinner. If she wouldn't mind Chris stopping by for a movie or something later on.

"Sure," Astrid said.

"Chinese sounds great," she said.

"Yeah if that's a thing again," she said.

Cassie stepped through the door, kept her hand on the doorknob. "You okay? You seem off."

"Have you ever heard of Apophenia?"

Cassie tapped her temple, said, "Is that another up here thing?"

"Not the way you think. Or maybe the way you think. Maybe it's a holdover from before. I don't know. I'm just noticing patterns in things that might not have a pattern."

"You know what? The thing I wanted you to look over can wait. I'll order the food and we can talk about whatever patterns you think you're seeing over dinner."

Astrid crossed the room, said, "No, no, it's okay. Just hoping it's nothing. I'm fine."

Cassie leaned against the door, blocked Astrid's way out. "What's the pattern?"

Astrid took a breath.

She couldn't lie anymore.

Wouldn't.

"Black cars," she said.

Cassie said nothing.

Stared.

Then, "What kind of black cars?"

"Just black. SUVs. Four door cars. Two door."

"How often?"

"Often."

"What are they doing when you see them?"

"Just driving by. Maybe following."

Cassie left the room saying things about needing Astrid to read what she wrote right now.

Right now-right now.

Cassie's voice was deeper than usual.

Stern.

Astrid could barely remember the last time she'd heard that voice.

When she and Willa were high that one time freshman year. They'd only smoked a little. But that was all it took. They were giggly and bleary-eyed, and Cassie had told them she wasn't an idiot. She'd been a huge pothead—and although she rolled that back a bit later on, she was still very angry.

Though, this wasn't anger.

This was different.

Cassie at the kitchen table. She opened the laptop. Waved Astrid over. Slid the computer to her once she sat down.

"There's a lot of red and green lines here," Astrid said.

"Just—just read. Please."

Astrid could see almost feel Cassie's eyes on her as her own slid left to right, left to right, left to right in the white glow of the screen.

Everything that Cassie had written was true.

But Astrid couldn't help the words from blurring by, disappearing as if she were deleting them as she read.

The hospital bill, the first one, had been paid.

The water.

The electric.

The rent.

The car payment.

Every one an accusation and a plea.

Every paragraph stuffed with superlatives and question marks.

And it went on.

And on.

And Astrid could do nothing else but lift her eyes from the screen.

"I'm not sure how to talk to you anymore, kid," Cassie said.

Astrid said nothing.

"That used to be our thing. We'd piss people off because of how much we'd talk. But you're doing well again. Talking about things you haven't talked about in forever. I don't want to ruin that, and I thought if I said any of this I'd knock you off whatever foothold you'd landed recently. I couldn't say anything. I'm sorry."

"You're accusing me of some serious shit in here," Astrid said.

But she shouldn't have said that.

She shook her head.

Bit the inside of her mouth.

"I'm not accusing you of anything," Cassie said. "But all of our bills are paid. All of them. Things I haven't been able to pay. Things that have been piling up because—"

"Because of me."

"Because UPenn's really expensive. Because we need electricity. Because sometimes I need takeout just because. But I talked things over with your grandfather, we worked some stuff out—"

"I did it because I was leaving. I wanted to leave you with a fresh start."

"The fresh start I got was you. I don't need anything else."

"I did so much so wrong that—"

"No, I did everything wrong," Cassie said. "Made a lot of stupid mistakes trying to watch your back from—"

"Behind my back."

"Behind your back, yes. Look, whatever you did, it came from a place that I can't even begin to understand. Regardless, it was kind. Despite everything, you're always kind. And, if nothing else, I think that's a win."

Astrid reached across the table.

Cassie took her hand.

Astrid said, "I learned some stuff that I thought would

help. Didn't think things through enough. I don't think I could've even if I'd wanted to."

Squeezing Astrid's hand, Cassie said, "How did you pay off the bills, kid?"

Eyes watery, moving back and forth between Cassie's eyes while she worked out what she wanted to say.

"I think I'm in trouble," she said.

"Like, trouble-trouble?" Cassie pointed to her belly.

Astrid almost laughed. Sort of laughed. She wiped her eyes, said, "Seriously?"

"Trouble meant bun-in-the-oven back in my day."

"You're the most inappropriate person." Astrid sniffed back everything leaking from her nose.

"I'm sorry. Tell me."

And Astrid did.

About the credit cards.

The thefts.

The lies.

The cars.

The men in suits.

Regis-132.

Everything.

43.

Astrid's arm was shriveled and pale. The scarring at her elbow was mean-looking, puckered. None of it offered many options for hiding any of it. So, Cassie suggested they pick out a high-neck jersey gown, maybe with sleeves. Something like that would cover the majority of the patch of shredded skin on Astrid's chest. And the bandage on her throat that had kept seeping because of how much human beings actually needed to use their necks in order to do just about anything. And, as Cassie had begun referring to it, Astrid's Igor arm.

But she looked beautiful outside the dressing room, smiling into the mirror, wearing an off the shoulder A-line split with pockets—the pockets being the only sensible part of the dress considering every scar and wound on Astrid was exposed. Neon glowing throat. Circle of scab below her collar bone. A sunset of red in the center of her chest, the bust of the gown some black horizon. It would need a few alterations, nothing Cassie couldn't handle herself. Maybe she could even bring the bustline up a bit to cover where glass had torn into Astrid's sternum.

But when Astrid said she loved it, Cassie said she loved it too.

At home, Cassie asked if Astrid wanted a pair of long gloves, if she wanted her to see if she could figure out a way to cover up the scarring, the arm.

Astrid said, "No thanks."

"Sure?"

"Yeah. I don't want to lie anymore."

"I don't think keeping private things private is lying."

"Maybe not technically. But when whoever is coming for me comes for me, I don't want to hide anything."

Measuring tape around Astrid's waist, Cassie told Astrid to stop. To just stop. Said, "You're not going anywhere."

"I am if I'm forced to."

"Seriously? This was supposed to be a fun thing. Prom. Dresses. Flowers. You—"

"I spent the last few months running around with a woman who might've stolen uranium."

Cassie balled up the measuring tape, threw it. It landed on the coffee table, didn't make a sound. It wasn't nearly as satisfying as she'd hoped it would be. And she said so.

Then Astrid hugged her mother, said, "I'm not afraid anymore. How could I be? I've got you to back me up."

Cassie was all teeth. And foul language. They weren't exactly saints when it came to how they spoke around one another, but Cassie got creative. Used combinations of words in an order that surprised even her. "That woman—"

"Helped me learn how to look forward to something again."

It wasn't exactly what Cassie had wanted to hear. Even in death, that woman was ruining Astrid's life.

"But I have a life," Astrid said. "And I'm planning on keeping it. It's not the one we'd hoped for. But it's still a life."

Cassie laughed a bit. It wasn't the good sort. It was the kind people burped out of their chests when there was nothing else to do but curl up into a ball and sob, or wreck everything they saw, screaming, screaming. She wiped a fleck of drool from her chin.

"I'm trying to tell you I'm not going anywhere," Astrid said. "Even if I have to go away."

"You don't really know me at all if you think I'm not going to follow you to the drop-edge of the Earth."

"Earth is round."

"Drop-edge sounded cool. I'm dramatic, not an idiot."

Astrid kissed Cassie on the forehead. Wiped her cheeks with her thumbs. "You're snotty."

"You think you're smarter than everyone in the room."

Astrid stood, went to the coffee table, brought back the measuring tape. "You think your farts smell like roses."

Cassie wiped her nose with a napkin from the kitchen table. "Your body odor is impervious to deodorant."

They went back and forth at one another while Cassie measured her daughter, jotted numbers onto her hand. Continued to get more and more vulgar with each traded insult. And when Astrid turned, said, "You're the worst, and I find you repulsive," Cassie stood and saw that Astrid had been right about the dress. Cassie could wash the numbers off her hand. She didn't need to change anything. Astrid's eyes were wide, bright, and alive. Her scabs, her scars, her torn skin were part of her, not acting against her. Her eyebrows were arched, like she was waiting for something—even if it was something as simple as a comment, it was something she was waiting for. Looking forward to.

"You know," Cassie said. "When I was out making a mess of things, I met this guy. He had this burned up arm. When I asked him about it, he told me some people are lucky enough to wear their hurt on the outside."

Astrid said, "Well, I've got a lot of it."

"You sure do, kid," Cassie said. "But you wear it really, really well."

Astrid crossed the room.

Cassie pulled her in close.

They said nothing.
And they stayed like that for a while.

44.

Willa outright refused to wear a clip-on bowtie. So she tied, re-tied, and attempted a third go at a proper bowtie using the paper instructions before turning to YouTube. In her bedroom mirror, she cinched her finger into the knot and had to start over again. Made the standard butterfly into a jumbo butterfly which made her look like she could get a job making balloon animals at an Applebee's. And once she was finally able to get it just about as right as she could, it sat a tad cockeyed, showed off a sliver of button above the knot. But, with her hair tied back, two ropes of it hanging to the sides of her forehead, her jacket buttoned at her waist, she looked good. She felt good. She was ready.

She took a deep breath in through her nose, said, "Okay."

Took another one, said, "Okay."

A third, said, "Here we go."

She pocketed a tin of mints, tucked her phone into her jacket, and left her bedroom. Before, she'd always had a reason for shutting the door behind her, but when she reached in and flicked out the light, she couldn't find one. She clumped down the steps in her patent leather shoes, kept one hand on the railing, the other buttoning, unbuttoning, buttoning her coat. Halfway down the stairs, she decided that she'd keep it closed while she was standing, open when she sat for dinner. It always looked sloppy, a suitcoat hanging open, so wearing something even more formal would need extra attention. No one looked good in a tuxedo unless they respected the tuxedo.

Sandy stood at the bottom of the steps, phone in her hand, smile on her face. She said she wasn't sure if she should tell Willa she looked beautiful or handsome. Said, "Because it's both. You look both."

Willa hugged her mother, said, "I'll take both."

Sandy had Willa stand by the front window. The sun was setting and made Willa's skin really glow. And Willa didn't issue a single complaint about all the ways she was positioned. She smiled, and posed, and asked Sandy to turn on the camera sounds so she could give her cheeks a break between each photo. But even after the tinny shutter sound would snap, she couldn't relax her face. She even said, "One more?" after Sandy said, "Okay, one more."

"I've got about thirty," Sandy said.

"I guess that's all you need." It didn't sound like she attached a question mark to her sentence, but there was enough of an upward octave curve that suggested maybe she had.

The shutter clicked off again while Willa watched cars drive past the house—red one, a gray one, a black one, a green one, another black one, none of them Lily's yet. "I thought you said you got enough?"

"Candids tell a better story," Sandy said. "I'm going to print that one and frame it."

Willa's cheeks began to ache in earnest then. But she turned back to the window. Watched. SUVs, station wagons, the DeLorean the guy down the street drove around and always needed to have towed home. A van, black, no windows aside from the ones up front.

She didn't hear Ken come into the room.

But when he said, "Looking sharp," she turned, said thanks.

The three of them stood where they were, said nothing. The television in the back room roared with a laugh track. Willa wouldn't say anything until one of them did. She wouldn't critique Ken's comment, didn't want to wreck what little was left of the sun adding just enough light to the house—that couple of minutes before someone reached for a light switch, or said it was getting dark later and later anymore, summer was around the corner.

Sandy said, "Doesn't Willa look—"

The doorbell.

Willa took a deep breath in through her nose.

Another.

A third.

Then said, "That's Lily."

She pulled the door open. And Lilly was beautiful. Her hair tied back into a bouquet of blonde curls. Her lips shiny but no different than their usual color. Her dress hugging her in all the places Willa had grown accustomed to reaching for when they were alone. Flowers covering up the hands holding them.

Sandy handed Willa the bouquet they'd picked out together earlier in the day, whispered that right then would be as good time as any to say something, invite Lily inside.

"These are for you," Willa said.

Stepping inside, Lily said, "These are for you."

They traded bouquets, laughed, told each other they had really nice taste in flowers, and their mothers helped to pick them out.

And when Willa said, "This is Lily," Sandy went to her and wrapped her up in a big hug. She said how nice it was to meet her. Said she looked beautiful. Asked if she was excited for prom. Told her Willa never had any interest in going to dances before this one. Said, "I'd like to take some pictures in front of the window if you don't mind."

Willa followed Lily and Sandy to the window but stopped. Said, "Lily, this is my dad."

Ken was nice, but he didn't show any teeth with his smile. Just stepped forward, reached out for a handshake, said, "Ken's fine."

"Okay, okay, you don't want to be late," Sandy said. "And I don't want to waste this light."

Willa stood behind Lily, put her hand on her hip. They faced one another, meshed their flowers together. And when Sandy told them to act casual, Willa said, "There is no possible way to act casual after someone says, 'act casual.'"

Lily found it funny. Laughed and laughed. Which made Willa laugh. And then think maybe Sandy should have gone into business for herself as a photographer, because there was the shutter again, snapping, snapping, snapping.

There wasn't much left to do after that but leave. They had to meet Astrid and Garrett so they all could get in line together for the officially-official photos in front of some ridiculous backdrop, to find their seating cards together, to sit and wait for dinner to start together. Willa put her hand on the small of Lily's back and said, "I'll text you when we get to the after-party."

Hand on the doorknob, teeth chewing away at the inside of her mouth, there was nothing but Ken's voice from where he'd been leaning his shoulder against the foyer wall. "You two are meeting your dates there, then?" he said.

Sandy said, "Ken."

But Willa said, "It's okay."

"No it's not—"

"Mom."

She felt Lily's hand on her shoulder. Heard her whisper it was okay, that she can wait outside.

"I'm not going to respond the way I usually do, Dad," Willa said. "I don't want to do that anymore. I don't want to be angry at you anymore. I know what I am isn't what you wanted. And I'm not going to try to convince you of anything. Lily is my date. I am Lily's date. That's it. You have to deal with that. I'd like you to be okay with it, but maybe you're not ready for that right now. I just won't fight you anymore. This is how it's going to be, and you can either be okay with that or not."

"Well I'm not okay with it."

"I don't really care."

Willa pulled the door open, waved Lily though first. Before she turned, left, and followed Lily to her car, she told her parents she loved them. Sandy called her honey, said she loved her too. Ken crossed his arms.

And, just for good measure, one last time, Willa looked directly into Ken's eyes and said, "Vagina."

45.

Everything was exactly as Astrid had expected.

Massive, square dancefloor covered in sheets of faux parquet tile.

Round tables on three sides with tablecloths and napkins to match the school colors—but just underneath the blue and silver, a white plastic Walmart picnic table.

A chandelier that Astrid decided was crystal, even though, most likely, it was not, hanging over the people milling around the place.

A wall of windows that looked out to a fountain ringed with tall bushes to create the illusion it was not actually just part of the parking lot.

Pretty because of its lies.

Beautiful despite them.

Astrid stopped dead in the threshold between the lobby and the dining room.

Didn't want to move.

The first time seeing something was important.

A template for how a thing could be even after the eyes got used to seeing it.

An image to hold on to for later.

When things wouldn't be as good.

When things got bad.

Next to her, Garrett said, "Ready?"

Astrid said, "One sec."

Beams of light from the DJ rig danced across the walls, the floor, made the silverware sparkle. Balloons everywhere, reaching for the ceiling, held down by silver-wrapped weights. Music bumping lightly from speakers nearly as tall as Astrid, songs she hadn't liked before the hospital now sounded more like her speed.

She nodded, said, "Okay, let's go."

She couldn't be sure if it was because of her muscle-less, scarred arm, or the glowing, healing flesh on her chest and neck, but Kelly was kind to her in line for photos. Told her she'd never seen Astrid look more beautiful.

Renna said it was great to see her without the cast.

Casey made a big deal out of her hair.

Luke asked if he could get her anything before asking if she was in any pain.

But Jill wouldn't look at her.

And Mark waved, but didn't say hello.

Still, when the photographer asked if she would like a shawl or something, Astrid said, "No, thank you."

Through the flashes, the robotic recharge tone of the camera, the awkward poses, Astrid stored everything she could in her memory, tucked it away in a place in her brain where she could bring it up any time she may need it.

Willa and Lily walking through the lobby, finding their seating card.

Cassie and Mr. Hogan standing off to the side, keeping a reasonable distance between one another, but making it pretty obvious that Cassie wasn't just a parent volunteer with all the laughing and smiling they were doing.

Garrett's cologne making him smell older than he should smell. His minty breath on the back of her neck, warm, close. His chest pushing into her back with the air he pulled into himself.

The photographer saying they looked great, they looked happy, they looked ready to dance.

But Astrid yelled Willa's name across the room.

Used her Igor arm to wave her and Lily over.

"Can you take one with all four of us?"

It didn't much matter what the photographer had to say. Willa's arm was already wrapped around Astrid's shoulder. Lily tucked her head under Garrett's arm. And after every flash, they posed in some other vaguely inappropriate tableau for the opening moments of a senior prom, laughing, smiling, laughing.

Then it was just Lily and Garrett.

Then Willa and Lily.

Then Garrett and Willa.

And then it was Astrid and Willa.

Willa's tied-back hair and shampoo in Astrid's nostrils.

Her ribcage expanding, contracting under Astrid's hand.

Their palms sweating into one another's.

Through her teeth, Astrid said, "You look perfect."

Willa said, "Shut up."

And then Kelly said the four of them had about enough time in front of the camera. "Just because you went through something traumatic doesn't mean you get special treatment. Move it."

Kelly being pleasant had lasted five minutes longer than Astrid could have ever predicted.

That was enough.

And they almost managed to walk by her, heading for their table, without laughing.

Almost.

Cassie and Mr. Hogan nodded, smiled as they passed. But

their faces were nearly blood red once the four of them whistled and hooted and Ooh'ed and Ah'ed at them.

They deserved it.

Whose mother goes to their daughter's prom.

Whose teacher dates their student's mother.

Astrid gave them a big, wide grin before taking her seat at the table.

Dinner looked like food Astrid had only seen on cooking shows.

Big plates, tiny portions, a glaze of something or other drizzled across the ceramic in a pattern that was supposed to look as if it was done as an exhausted, final bout of flare, but was obviously calculated.

The meat was rubbery.

The asparagus was stringy.

The glaze didn't do much but help her swallow the dry steak.

But the smashed potatoes made her make sounds as she ate.

Of course, a high school prom venue would not offer the finest of fine cuisine.

But she pretended.

If this was an example of fine dining downtown or in New York, she hadn't missed out, and she wouldn't miss out once whoever were in the cars came to get her.

Her hair all done, her dress on, a corsage strapped to her wrist, her feet squeezed into tiny shoes, sitting at that table in front of the wall of windows, with Willa, and Garrett, and Lily, it was everything. Butterflies. Aching cheeks. Everything.

The guys in black could come knock down the apartment door, drag her out of bed in the morning, take her away. She'd had her night and could live with what she'd done in a cell. Or a padded room. Or wherever.

She danced barefoot to every song on the faux parquet.

Strings of hair stuck to her forehead.

She smelled more sweat on herself than perfume.

Her forearms were shiny.

She licked beads of sweat off her upper lip.

Kissed Garrett on the dancefloor until Mr. Evans was forced to come over and tell them to break it up.

She grabbed hold of Willa in her tux, danced close, made faces.

Rested her head on Garrett's chest, left a sweaty makeup stain on his lapels during the slow songs.

Was in the center of a circle, dancing alone; people watching, clapping, cheering.

Cassie stormed the dancefloor for "Footloose" and danced alongside Astrid to a clapping, singing crowd of teenagers, waitstaff, and teacher chaperones.

They took each other's hands.

They bowed.

They laughed.

Astrid would remember all of it.

Wherever she'd end up.

This was everything.

It would be enough.

Catching her breath, she watched Garrett, and Willa, and Lily.

Cassie and Mr. Hogan whispering into each other's ears, then laughing, then whispering again.

Astrid went through her purse for a pack of tissues to dab her face without wiping off what little was left of her makeup.

She used the mirror in her compact to check if her neck was bleeding.

If the scabs under her collarbone had cracked.

If she'd bled on her dress in the center of her chest.

There was a flash of light.

Whoever had taken her photo would have a pretty ugly keepsake. Not all candid shots were artful. Or polite.

But there was no camera.

Just a pair of lights outside.

Through the wall of windows, behind the fountain, beyond the bushes.

Headlights.

But there were dozens of cars in the lot. It could have been anyone. A waiter catching a smoke break. A parent waiting for their kid. Anyone.

But then there was a second set.

A third.

Astrid didn't turn to look.

Just watched from her periphery.

The men stepping out, looking official. Like people who mattered. They were chatting, chatting stone-faced. She had expected sunglasses, but there were no sunglasses. It was dark, these people were important, they were doing important things.

They were coming for her.

She'd run through this scenario a couple of times. Every time, she walked outside wherever she was with her hands up. Got down flat on the ground slowly, slowly, then waited for them to come for her, put cuffs on her. Through all of the various ways she'd imagined it going down, she never once thought of one in which she'd stay where she was breathing heavy, heavy. Listening to her stomach rolling over. Over and over. Sweating like she was out on the dancefloor again.

She had been ready.

Prepared herself for this.

For them.

For whatever it was that was going to come next.

They were still standing out there. Like they were waiting for her. Maybe they didn't want to ruin prom. Or maybe they were planning their approach thinking she was a flight risk.

Maybe they'd follow her home. Bust into her bedroom just as she was falling asleep. Bleary-eyed she'd put her hands up with nothing but halos of flashlights in her eyes.

She'd already seen every possible version of this future.

A future.

And she wanted something else now.

Her future.

She stayed where she was. In her plastic seat, in front of half-eaten slice of cake, a cup of coffee, she barely even moved.

She watched Willa dance. No tux jacket. Just a white shirt with the sleeves rolled up, an undone bowtie hanging from her collar. Hair matted with sweat.

Watched Garrett. Top button unbuttoned. Shirt untucked. Hair everywhere. Smooth, freshly-shaven face shiny with grease.

Cassie, happy, closer to Mr. Hogan. The closest she'd been all night.

Outside, the lights, the men.

And Astrid didn't want to leave.

She swallowed.

Said, "I don't want to go."

46.

Willa wasn't an idiot. She'd heard what Astrid said when she said it, but with the lights, the music, the smell of sweat, she couldn't quite get it to compute. Yes, it may have been a shock, but Willa didn't want to leave the prom either.

"No," Astrid said. "I don't want to go." She pointed to the wall of windows.

There were lights, shadows. A slow strobing effect when the shadows passed through the white glow. Willa was about to say something about a shift in the waitstaff because of how nicely dressed the people outside looked once her eyes focused through the headlights. But she didn't. Astrid's face was dotted with sweat, slightly streaked with foundation and concealer. There was far too much white in her eyes than usual, and the color in her irises was darting back and forth, back and forth between Willa's left eye, right eye, left eye, right eye. Astrid knew whoever they were, they were not a second shift of waiters and busboys.

Willa didn't need much more than that.

Lily was where she had left her. On the dancefloor with

Grace and Sarah. Her arms up, her hips moving, her lips singing along to the music. This wouldn't ruin her night. They had talked about Astrid before. At length. Lily was understanding, told Willa to do whatever she needed to do when she needed to do it. But when Willa put her hand on Lily's shoulder, and once her smile faded, this was clearly the prom, and it was not cool at all, and yeah, Lily got it, she did, but it sucked. It really sucked.

"I'm sorry," Willa shouted over the music.

Lily nodded. Kissed the top of Willa's hand. Then turned back to Grace and Sarah, neither of whom had taken their eyes off Willa. Like they knew she'd blow it somehow.

It didn't matter though.

Couldn't.

So she took Astrid's hand, led her off the dancefloor.

She couldn't make their leaving seem too urgent. She would text Cassie once they were outside, and Garrett once they reached wherever Astrid wanted them to go. But first she had to zig, zag, zig through crowds of their classmates. Smile and say hello, that this person looked beautiful, that that person looked handsome—all things Willa would never ever say under any usual circumstances, but Astrid would want her to say because she believed those compliments were merited and true.

But then there was Garrett. His mess of stupid hair. His damp shirt, unbuttoned at the collar, making him look like a sweaty little brat at someone's wedding who had only been invited because of some familial obligation. He said whoa, whoa, whoa, and was everything okay. "Is there anything I can do?"

Before Willa could tell Garrett to go play in traffic, but then apologize for the comment and tell him what was really happening, Mr. Hogan had made his way to them from where he and Cassie were gazing into each other's eyes. What was going on, was anyone feeling sick, should he get someone on the staff who can help in emergencies. There were more questions, all out of concern, all from that good Chris Hogan place.

And then there was Cassie. Raising her eyebrows, using her hands as if she were asking a question.

Willa almost spoke, but Astrid nudged her in the ribs with her skinny arm.

Willa cocked an eyebrow, used her hands and gestured at Garrett.

Astrid shook her head.

Cassie clapped her hands twice, shrugged.

Willa stamped her foot, clapped, stamped again.

Astrid pursed her lips, clenched, unclenched her jaw, made her eyes wide-wide.

Cassie punched her palm, slapped the center of her chest.

Willa put her palm to her forehead, showed teeth as if she was about to growl.

And then Garrett said, "Are you guys actually talking to each other?"

Cassie went to Mr. Hogan, said she was sorry. "I'm not sure what else I can say. I need to go. And I have no clue what's going to happen once I do."

Mr. Hogan nodded.

Willa said, "We're wasting time."

Mr. Hogan said, "I'll keep the chaperones off your back."

Willa led the way, and didn't look back to see how anyone was handling what was happening. She had just one job.

They weren't about to go out the front, not with what was waiting for Astrid there. And it was stupid to assume whoever-they-were wouldn't be covering any alternate ballroom entrances and emergency exits. So Willa kicked her way through the swinging kitchen door. Metal utensils clattered against cutting boards, plates fell from hands and shattered on the maroon tiled floor, staff dressed in aprons and caps cursed. And Willa didn't offer up so much as a sorry. Just pulled Astrid by the arm, who had Garrett by the arm, with Cassie not far behind. High heels and stiff dress shoes click-clacked, skidded across the floor behind Willa as she kept up her pace.

People in white coats told them they couldn't be back there. What did they think they were doing. They could get hurt and the kitchen staff would be held responsible and punished for whatever happened. Were they even listening. Who did they think they were.

Willa yelled that everybody should shut up.

Then she screamed exit.

A voice from the crowd of chefs, and line cooks, and busboys said, "Jesus."

"Well?"

Several arms pointed in the direction of a poorly lit hallway.

They followed the pointing fingers past stainless steel utility sinks stuffed and overflowing with dirty dishes. Past confused employees Willa hadn't yet yelled at, rewrapping, restocking unused food into the massive refrigerators. Down a reeking hallway that smelled of stagnant water and fish. And when Willa looked back to check on Astrid, she had stopped, was holding Garrett's hands, looking up into his dumb eyes.

Cassie stepped by them, shrugged.

"What's going on?" Willa said.

"He's not coming," Astrid said.

"I fucking knew it."

"It's not that," Garrett said, stepping back, hands up.

"Then what is it?" Willa pushed past Astrid, shoved Garrett hard in the chest.

Cassie and Astrid yelled her name. Told her to stop.

Garrett stumbled backward, caught himself against the wall, said, "I don't know exactly what's happening here, okay? But I do know that it's way harder to find people when there are a couple hundred other people running out of the same building."

"Are you going to pull the fire alarm?" Cassie said, stepping forward, nodding her head.

"How did you—" Garrett said.

"That's awesome," Cassie reached into her jumpsuit pocket, pulled out a lighter. "Here. Pulling the alarm won't do anything but make noise. Get up on a chair, hold the flame to the sprinkler."

Garrett nodded, and smiled, and pocketed Cassie's lighter.

"Thank you," Cassie said pulling him into a hug. "Proved yourself once again not to be a total dick."

"Wait," Astrid said. "Why do you have a lighter?"

"We do have to get moving," Willa said.

Garrett kissed Astrid, told her to be safe. Said she could call him if she needed anything. They may have begun pawing at one another, too, if Willa hadn't cleared her throat.

But just before Garrett took off down the hall, Willa said his name, then, "I'm happy you've been following us around."

He smiled.

And then he was shoes echoing in the opposite direction as Willa pulled Astrid and Cassie toward the door.

Astrid said, "Okay, we wait until we hear the alarm. As soon as the bells go off, we're gone." They had to stay out of view of main roads, streetlamps, and anything else that could give them away. It would be easy enough to spot three women sprinting through the night in dress clothes, so they needed to take away any advantage whoever-they-were had to at least make it a chase.

"Wait," Cassie said. "These guys have cars. You can run all you want, but the alarm is only going to slow them down."

"You have an idea?" Willa said.

"I have a car."

"You don't think they know what you drive by now?" Astrid said.

"I have a boyfriend who has a different car."

"That's not a terrible idea," Willa said.

"We're not done talking about why you had a lighter," Astrid said.

"Of course we're not," Cassie said. "And I have a perfectly legitimate reason for that, and I swear that once this is all—"

The fire alarm blaring to life made Willa tense her neck, clamp her eyelids tight. But the shrieking that followed gave her a little chuckle.

"Time to go," Cassie said. "Make your way toward the Northtowne shopping center, that's where I'll be." She kissed Astrid's forehead, told her she loved her. Kissed Willa's forehead, told her she couldn't thank her enough. Then she was gone.

Willa rammed her hip into the metal bar holding the door in place, shoved the door the rest way, told Astrid to move it.

They crossed the loading only lane in just a few strides, climbed their way up a short lump of browned pine needles into the woods.

Willa led the way. Pushed, pulled branches, bushes out of the way. Made sure she could still hear Astrid behind her before moving forward. Then, "Life's confusing when you don't want to kill yourself."

Willa turned, said, "While I would love to wax philosophical with you about this, we can't do this right now. I am really happy to hear you prefer this side of existence though."

"You don't have to come with me," Astrid said. "You can go back."

Willa grabbed her by the good arm, said, "As far as I'm concerned, what happened at the hospital means we're married, or blood sisters or some shit, so, no, I can't."

Smiling, Astrid said, "Can't or won't?"

"Take your pick."

They kept themselves away from streetlights in a nice, new housing development. Sprinted into the dark whenever a motion sensor popped a light on. Walked mostly through dewy grass, across parts of driveways obscured by trees. Willa had to roll down her sleeves, use the cuffs to wipe the sweat from her face.

Once they reached the glow of the McDonald's arches, they snuck around the back end of the building. Kept to the mulched areas in the dimly lit sections.

But then they stopped when they saw a car idling in the lot between them and the bus stop.

A lit cigarette butt pinwheeled across the lot from the driver-side window. A hand waved.

"That's not Mom," Astrid said.

Cassie put the window down the rest of the way, said, "You're late. You coming or what?"

"Are you smoking?" Astrid shrieked.

Willa grabbed Astrid by the hand, dragged her toward the car, said, "Can we deal with this another time, please?"

47·

Cassie parked the car down the road from the apartment. Telling Astrid, "Going back to the very place where the people following you know you sleep isn't the best idea," hadn't had an effect. Saying, "We have to start driving and have to continue driving until nothing looks familiar," had done nothing. Whispering, "It's crazy to skulk through our own apartment complex in promwear," went completely ignored. Still, Cassie crouched behind cars in the parking lot with Astrid and Willa. Looked over her shoulder, around bumpers and fenders, up ahead a ways to try to catch any movement in the dark. Decided it'd be best if Willa was the one who went to the front door first. She was the least-wanted out of the three of them.

"Least important, you mean?" Willa said.

Astrid said, "Willa, you know that's not—"

"Guys," Cassie said. "Can we please?"

Willa kept herself crouched, nearly crab-walked to the row of hedges lining the small, square patches of grass in front of the apartment units, said something under her breath.

Cassie said, "I definitely didn't hear that."

Willa shushed, stood, said, "I'm acting casual now."

Cassie had never seen Willa so light on her feet. She was a tiny thing but did nothing quietly. Since she'd known her, Cassie had gotten used to her chewing, her snoring, her stamp-stamp-stamping around the apartment that rattled the silverware in drawers, pictures against drywall. But, alongside the hedges, nothing.

Astrid was staring. Not at anything in particular. Almost through everything. As if the cars, the apartments, the entire complex weren't there at all. Or had become transparent. Cassie reached out, rubbed Astrid's her bare back above where the dress began.

Quick smile. Just lips.

"Willa will be fine if we just go," Cassie said.

Astrid shook her head. Whether it was a "No, she won't," or an "I can't leave her," Cassie couldn't tell. This was an Astrid that hadn't been around for a while. She'd gotten used to ups, downs, dead-center monotone, but whatever her brain had cooked up, Cassie couldn't guess what it would have her do next. It was exciting. And frightening.

Like a breakthrough.

Like an Ah-ha.

Something that had changed the course of things but brought with it a heap of new questions that she couldn't expect or predict.

"What are we here for, kid?"

"Our way home if we need it," Astrid said. "Hopefully."

"I don't know what that—"

The sound of a key sliding into the deadbolt, the lock pulling back into itself, the creak of the front door.

Willa stepped inside, waved.

Astrid stood first, kept her shoulders slumped, her head low.

Cassie almost reached out, but stopped herself, afraid she'd snap the just-healed arm in her grip.

Instead, she said, "Shit," and followed her daughter.

They kept the lights off inside, just in case—a couple hundred soaked, furious teenagers would only work as a distraction for a so long. They used the flashlights on their phones. Pale white rings of light zipping this way, that way across the carpet that, apparently, Cassie needed to do a better job of vacuuming in the future. If she and Astrid would be allowed to stay there anymore. With ankle bracelets, on house arrest. Maybe they could work out that deal.

Willa asked what they were looking for.

Astrid, again, said something about a thing they'd need for a way home, and headed back into her bedroom.

Cassie said, "Yeah, still don't know what that means."

In the dark, phone pointed to the floor, Willa whispered, "Why are we doing this? Shouldn't we be running?"

Cassie crossed the room, tucked her phone into her pocket, but not before making sure she knew where Willa's shoulders were. A hand on each shoulder, Cassie said, "We should be running, yes. But you don't need to be. Why don't you head on home."

Cassie could hear Willa's teeth grinding in the dark before the white light hit her under her chin, cast shadows on her face that made her more...Willa. "I'm not going anywhere," she said. "She needs me, and this is what I am."

"But you don't need to be part of this. This is serious."

"I am part of this, Cassie. I love her."

"I know you do. And I love you for that. But you have a future that—"

Astrid came back into the living room in jeans, a t-shirt, Keds. Her hair pulled back, a backpack slung over her shoulder.

A black box in her hands.

"You guys okay?" she said.

Willa said yep.

Cassie pointed, said, "What the hell's in that thing?"

Astrid went to the kitchen table, set the box down, placed

the school bag beside it and unzipped it slow, quiet. "If it works, if it's real, this can bring us back if we need to come back."

"Okay, yeah, I'm going to need you to elaborate a little bit further."

"Just come over here, please. I'm almost ready."

Cassie switched on her flashlight, crossed the room, said, "Open the box, Astrid. Tell me what this is."

"I can't."

"Why not?"

Willa stood, said, "Jesus, that's not—"

"I think it is, yeah," Astrid said. She pulled a lab coat from the school bag, an envelope from one of the coat's pockets, and a sheaf of papers from the envelope. Then she handed the papers to Cassie.

First, a heading labeled Post-Launch Cool Down. A list, a series of hand-drawn boxes numbered one through twelve. Switches to switch off. Toggles that needed toggling.

The second page, straightedge-sketched diagrams of the refueling process. Cylinders and where to place them, how to secure them, how to make sure the passengers were safe before releasing the fuel pellets. Gauges that would all need to be in nominal green before refueling could begin.

The third page, how a radiation suit needed to be fastened before launch. The risks to the human body if they weren't worn properly when breaching the Coulomb barrier.

Cassie said, "Astrid, what the fuck is this?"

Willa said, "Are you fucking kidding me?"

Cassie could feel her pulse in her temples. Her heart in her chest. Her vision blurred a bit—like standing too quickly after watching too much *Star Trek* on the couch.

"This is why they're after me," Astrid said.

"I thought they were after you for credit card fraud and theft," Cassie said slow, making sure she was still breathing once she finished her sentence.

Willa said, "Holy shit."

"It's for the machine Woods and I built. I was convinced for a while it was real, and then everything happened and pointed to it maybe not being real at all. But I went to the lab and turned it on, and it's ready to go. If it works, and I'm hoping it might actually work, it's how were going to get away from those people. And she left this for me in case I ever wanted to come back."

Cassie was holding her breath. Was trying to make sure her face wasn't wide-eyed, gaping-mouthed, shaking. She breathed in through her nose, out through her mouth. In her nose, out her mouth. "What if it doesn't work?"

"Then we'll figure something else out."

"And what would that be?"

"I'm up for to trying anything because I'm not willing to give up."

Astrid wasn't just saying those things. They weren't hollow statements that would have absolutely worked on Cassie just a few months ago. It was her eyes. They were wide, afraid, but not because of an uncertainty. There was something to lose.

Astrid wanted to run.

And that was enough for Cassie.

"Okay, then," Cassie said. "Lead the way."

So Astrid did.

And Cassie followed.

But not without taking Willa's hand and pulling her out the front door behind them.

48.

Astrid had Cassie park out back of the Walgreen's. Behind the dumpsters where she'd seen the cooks from the Chinese restaurant smoke.

They crept up Bysher through people's backyards.

Used the same path Astrid had used to get to the lab from the Green.

It wasn't a short walk.

They'd stopped talking altogether once Cassie and Willa had stopped questioning Astrid about her plan and simply started following her.

On the way, she saw the looks they were trading back and forth.

She knew what they were, what they meant.

Knew, at the moment, that they were only out of concern.

Maybe they were thinking they'd been wrong to assume that Astrid's mind was in a good place. Maybe they were wondering whether or not they'd have to have her admitted.

Again.

Or maybe it was simpler than all of that.

It was a crazy plan. It would've been insane for either of them to believe any of it outright. But they were following her anyway.

They kept to the tree line at the edge of the golf course.

Passed behind the Acme, the community pool.

Underneath the 309 overpass.

Through the Oreland Inn parking lot.

Over the train tracks.

Across street from the basketball courts.

Cassie and Willa were right behind her the whole way.

Astrid didn't look back, tromped right into the woods behind the house a couple houses down from the one on the corner that marked where, if they were in a car, they could begin searching for the hidden driveway.

Cassie said something about it not being exactly wise to once again be going directly to one of the places for which the people hunting Astrid most definitely have been searching.

Willa said something about them maybe already being there waiting for them.

But when Astrid stopped to get her bearings—they weren't far, but she'd only ever walked these woods in the pitch black the one time—both Cassie and Willa went silent.

Willa said, "We're almost there, right?"

Cassie said, "I think she's just doing a quick morale check. I'm at about a seven-point-five because of the humidity."

"Oh, yeah. Totally," Willa said. "I think I'm more an eight. But these patent leather shoes are fucked."

Astrid turned, smiled, said, "Thank you."

They weren't far.

Astrid could almost hear the house.

Creaking in the breeze the way it did.

And once they crossed into the clearing, there was nothing but crickets and darkness and the moon spilling pale light onto the lab. Broken windows, gutters hanging from their brackets, wooden planks of siding that could be pulled away by hand.

Cassie said, "Jesus."

Willa said, "Yeah.

And Astrid said, "It's safe. It just wears its hurt on the outside."

She had them follow her around back.

It didn't matter which door they used, not really.

If they were there, they were there.

It wouldn't matter.

Also, it didn't matter.

Astrid would see for herself, figure what was next when she needed to.

Inside, nothing had changed since her last visit.

At least nothing the light from her phone touched.

The house groaned, creaked, and moaned under their feet, and Astrid pointed to places where they shouldn't step, where they needed to be extra careful, where they probably shouldn't stand.

And there it was.

The sheet with the *Rippa* beneath it.

"So," Cassie said. "That's it?"

"Is the sheet part of the design?" Willa said.

That made Astrid laugh.

Considering the circumstances, she didn't expect to laugh.

That made it funnier.

Still, Astrid got to work, asking Cassie and Willa to help her out while she prepped the ship.

Cassie didn't go to her, call her kid, ask her what she was thinking. She just pulled the sheet from the *Rippa* and dragged it into the other room to avoid the launch heat setting it on fire, just as Astrid had asked.

Willa hadn't started stomping around the house saying the whole thing was crazy, that Astrid must have known it was all nuts. Didn't say that they had already been through all of this a bit too recently. No, Willa pulled the radiation suits from the back hatch and draped them over a pair of sawhorses. As she was told.

All of it was very different for Astrid.

She was looking forward.

To what was next.

To the next whatever.

To Regis-132.

Or wherever this thing was going to send them if it was going to send them anywhere at all.

A little while back, Astrid had set out all of her prescription bottles on the desk in her bedroom. Knew that, if she had done nothing then, she would've only believed what she hadn't done was even more necessary the next day. There had been nothing in front of her. Everything had been off. Nothing was right. She was a burden to her mother. Her friends felt sorry for her, kept her around. Her achievements, her plans, were nothing. Meaningless. Useless. Being anywhere else, even in the black of whatever was next—if there was anything next at all—had seemed better than whatever her life was. So she'd poured a handful of white pills into her mouth, chewed them up, washed them down.

A handful of reds.

A handful of blues.

And she'd repeated the process until the room was liquid and shimmery. Until her guts were cramping, painful but somehow numb. Until her brain was quiet. Until every orange bottle was empty.

But standing in front of the *Rippa*, she wanted to see something.

Anything.

And it was exciting.

She flicked a switch on the control panel in the cockpit, twisted a knob, switched on a series of diodes.

Then, "What if none of this is real?" Willa's arms were crossed over her chest. She was standing, staring, shifting her weight from one ruined shoe to another. "Look at you," she said. "You're a mess."

Astrid went to her, said, "I'm not. Really."

Cassie said Willa's name, but that was all.

"We don't know if any of this is real," Willa said. "We don't know who's after you or why they're really after you, or if it's all just a bunch of huge paranoid coincidences, right? Right?"

"Willa—"

"What if you blow up? What if nothing happens and you have to go back to a regular life with college and boyfriends and jobs and money and kids and whatever, and you hate it all even more than you already do because there's nothing special ever, and there's nothing to look forward to?"

"I don't hate it," Astrid said. "I never did. I just needed to figure out that the meaningless stuff might be the best stuff. And I have no idea if that'll last. The way my brain works, I can't guarantee anything."

Willa pulled herself into Astrid. "I can't go with you."

"I wouldn't want you to."

"I want to."

"No you don't. No one deserves to need to walk away from everything when everything is great even though they can't see it."

Cassie was there then. Her arms around the both of them.

Then, without saying anything else, Willa pulled away.

She wiped her face.

And walked out the back door into the woods.

Astrid didn't move until she couldn't hear Willa's footsteps in the dry leaves, through the bushes, over sticks and fallen branches anymore.

Cassie, from across the room, stepping into her radiation suit said, "Are you sure about this?"

Astrid turned to Cassie, smiled, nodded, said, "Yeah. I am."

She was.

49.

Cassie zipped up the back of Astrid's radiation suit. Tried not to cloud up her own plastic face plate with her breathing.

Then she said nothing.

Didn't have anything to say.

She couldn't speak even though she and her daughter were about to lock themselves into a homemade spaceship and maybe, possibly, but probably not, go to another planet. Before, it was Cassie, still too young herself to dole out any advice to a kid only half her age. Now, maybe there wasn't a soul who knew what to say. But she probably should've worked up the guts to say at least something after all they'd been through.

Astrid said, "What?"

Cassie shook her head in her plastic helmet. Had so many things she needed to say, but said, "Nothing."

"Ready?"

"Yeah."

Cassie helped Astrid back into the cockpit, held the hatch door up and over their heads. It was heavier than it looked.

Astrid, buckling herself into her launch chair said, "Need help?"

"No, no, I think I'm good," She climbed in.

Whatever it was Astrid and Woods had built together, it was sturdy. Cassie's feet didn't bend a thin metal sheet for a floor with each step. She didn't fall through the bottom when she sat in her chair. Didn't pull the safety straps from their anchors. "This thing is pretty legit," she said.

"Woods and I did a pretty good job," Astrid said, clicking her last buckle into place.

"Yeah," Cassie said. "You did."

Astrid flicked switches, told Cassie to press this, pull that. And Cassie listened, did everything her daughter asked her to do. Everything her daughter needed her to do. And when they were done, there was a hum, a blue glow beneath the dashboard or the control panel or whatever it was. Astrid knew what she was doing.

But then, she just sat there.

Cassie had to turn her whole body to make sure Astrid could see her face through the plastic. "You okay?"

Astrid shifted in her seat, faced Cassie. "Yeah. I just...I don't know if this will actually work."

"It's worked pretty well so far."

"No," Astrid said. "I mean, what if there's nothing there?"

"We'll be there together."

"What if this thing doesn't work or explodes or something?"

"We'll do that together too," Cassie said.

Astrid's breath fogged the plastic in front of her face. "I'm scared," she said.

Cassie nodded. "What do you need me to do?"

Astrid pointed to a silver lever, told Cassie, when they were ready, push it forward, but slow. After that, Astrid pointed to a black switch, told Cassie to flip the rubber safety to the side, push the button underneath.

"Okay," Cassie said. "Ready?"

Astrid fogged up her mask.

Did it again.

And again.

"Okay," Astrid said. "Ready."

Cassie reached for the lever, pushed it forward, heard the hum from the machine get louder and louder until she and Astrid were vibrating in their chairs.

She reached out for the switch.

Flicked open its safety.

Took a breath.

Pressed the button.

Cassie turned back to Astrid, searched for her eyes in the intensifying light.

She found them. Her daughter's eyes. Staring right back at her.

Then everything was blue.

50.

Willa was in the bushes nearby when the cars pulled up, flooded the front of the house with their headlights. Her legs were burning from crouching too long, but she couldn't be sure that the engine noise or the hum from the house would drown out her shifting positions. So she didn't move. Waited for Astrid and Cassie to come up behind her, tell her that they all needed to get the hell out of there together. Now. But men with badges were talking, talking, hands on their hips, figuring out an entrance strategy. Figuring out a something. A whatever. It didn't matter.

Astrid and Cassie wouldn't be there no matter what.

Somehow.

Then, sounds.

Rustling.

Footsteps.

Breathing.

Willa turned her head. Slow. Didn't want to give up her position if, maybe, whoever it was hadn't seen her yet.

Then, whispering, Garrett said, "Hey."

"Jesus Christ," Willa said. "What are you doing here?"

Clothes damp, the matted hair on his head beginning to dry and regain its messy-ass shape, Garrett knelt next to her, said, "I love you guys. I just want to help."

"Well you probably just got us all caught."

But none of the men talking by their cars even looked in their direction. They were turned toward the house.

The hum had grown into a deep rumble.

Willa could feel it in her feet even from this distance.

Had to turn away from blue light overtaking the headlights.

"What's that?" Garrett said.

"Will you shut up."

The noise grew, and grew, and soon Willa had to cover her ears with her hands, shut her eyes, grind her teeth. But the hum hurt through her hands. The blue bled through her eyelids. Her teeth were rattling.

She knew it. She was going to explode. Be nothing.

Then, nothing.

No sound.

No light.

No pain.

She opened her eyes, blinked away the photo-bleached spots on everything her eyes focused on.

Garrett was dazed, said whoa.

And the men at their cars were blinking, blinking, shaking their heads.

Until one of them ran to the now black house, kicked in the door, ran inside.

"Oh, shit," Willa said.

They waited.

Watched.

Until the man came back out onto the porch, said something.

Willa couldn't make it out, asked Garrett what he'd heard.

Garrett shrugged.

Then, from the cars, someone asked, "What do you mean there's no one in there?"

They argued. A few others went inside to seemingly double check. Exited with no one.

Then they piled back into their cars, drove over the gravel and dirt in front of the house as they turned around, became nothing but red lights fading into the woods.

"Wait, what just happened?" Garrett said.

"They did it," Willa said. "They're gone."

"Where'd they go?"

"I don't know."

Willa stood, felt the pain in her legs fade.

"Wait," Garrett said, still crouched, still watching the house. "Will they come back?"

Willa said nothing. Had nothing to say. She swallowed. Took a breath. Pursed her lips. Held back what was welling up in her chest. Then, "I think maybe they shouldn't."

"What do you mean?" Garrett said. "Astrid needs to be here. This is everything she knows."

Willa choked back what was in her chest again, said, "I'm pretty sure she knows a lot more than most anyone does."

Then she held out her hand to Garrett.

"What?" he said.

"I'm going to walk you home."

Garrett took her hand, stood.

And Willa led him down the dirt path, out of the woods.

It wasn't long before Garrett started asking questions again.

So many questions.

But Willa kept hold of his hand and walked with him.

"I wanted to be part of what you guys have," he said.

"You are."

"Then why won't you answer any of my questions? I feel like I'm never going to see you again or something."

"If you shut up right now, I promise I'll answer all of your questions tomorrow, okay?"

"Tomorrow?"

"Yeah. Michael's for lunch."

Garrett nodded, said, "Okay. Tomorrow."

Every now and then a car drove past them. There were cicadas in the trees, and crickets in the grass. And under any other normal set of circumstances Willa would outright refuse to walk all the way to Garrett's and then back to her house. But Garrett needed her.

She listened to the scraping of their fancy shoes against the sidewalks, over loose stones, and fresh cut grass. She could walk faster, but she kept Garrett's pace. She would take him to his front door, remind him of when they were meeting tomorrow, and then she'd walk home.

There would be plenty she'd need to piece together the next day.

She would be happy to do it.

51.

It wasn't what Astrid expected.

The world.

The trees, the grass, the sky.

They weren't what Woods had promised. They weren't what they were supposed to be. They were just trees, just grass, just the deep blue-black with the same sparkling shapes Astrid had tacked onto the apartment ceilings when she was a little girl.

That was all.

Still, it all felt new even though it was the same old world.

It was new-new.

Beautiful.

Shiny and wonderful.

And she was running through it, taking it all in.

Her hand was in her mother's, and she was running, and she was taking it all in.

She was a few steps behind, but she was keeping pace.

She could run forever right then.

And maybe, if she kept on going—her hand in her mother's, the wind in her face—it would all be more than enough.

Nick Gregorio is a husband, father, writer, teacher, dog-dad, punk, nerd, teeth-grinder, and mall-walker living and writing just outside of Philadelphia, Pennsylvania. He is the author of five books, and his work has appeared in many print and online journals. *Launch Me to the Stars, I'm Finished Here* is his second novel.

For more, please visit www.nickgregorio.com.

Acknowledgements

As always, thank you to my dear wife Lizz for the time and patience—and our sweet buddy Miles too.

Thanks to the Starbucks staff at the Montgomeryville, PA Barnes & Noble who worked the summers of 2018 and '19. Not only were they kind and cheery every morning, but they knew my order by heart (trenta strawberry açaí refresher), and many times had it ready and waiting for me before I arrived to write early drafts of this here novel.

A great deal of gratitude must go to Nathaniel Kennon Perkins and Trident Press for giving *Launch Me to the Stars* a home. Many people said such nice things about it but couldn't quite figure a way to sell it (which I get, by the way, so thank you for the kindness regardless), but Nate didn't much care about that and did the damn thing anyway.

Thanks to my friends Christina Rosso-Schneider and Claire Hopple for reading my early drafts and lending the honesty a fella setting out to write a story about three women absolutely needed.

Thanks to the following writers for writing books that taught me the immense responsibility required to even attempt to write women: Juliet Escoria, Elle Nash, Lauren Groff, Sarah Rose Etter, Madeline Anthes, Christina Rosso-Schneider, Claire Hopple, Jane-Rebecca Cannarella, Megan Milks, Tara Stillions Whitehead, Gayl Jones, Joy Williams, Kristen Arnett, Meghan Phillips, Katherine Faw, G. Willow Wilson, Sloane Crosley, Emma Glass, Raven Leilani, Amy Saul-Zerby, Cherie Priest, Mela Blust, Jean Kyoung Frazier, Jeanette Winterson, Marisha Pessl, Chelsea Bieker, Carmen Maria Machado, Monica Drake, Lannie Stabile, Andrea Seigel, Jaime Fountaine, T Kira Madden, Amy Hempel, Lidia Yuknavitch, Amber Tamblin, Sarah Schulman, Maria Dahvana Headley, Alissa Nutting, Danzy Senna, and Hannah Pittard—most don't know who I am, and most will never read this, but their words have changed me for the better and I am beyond grateful. I hope I did right by y'all. (Read their stuff immediately, by the way. You'd be a fool not to.)

Thanks to my family, thanks to my friends, thanks to Joshua Isard and Arcadia University's MFA program for literally everything, and thank you for carving out some time and headspace for this story.

Oh, and thank you to my old pal Tony D'Angelo. He was just so much fun to write the first time 'round (he's the wildly flawed protagonist from my first novel, *Good Grief*, who I felt needed a bit of closure...for now) that I decided to expand his world and tell stories about the folks around him. Here's hoping I'll be able to spend some time in the Tonyverse again and again.

Be well. See you next time.

-Nick Gregorio, 1/17/23

OTHER VERY FINE TITLES FROM
TRIDENT PRESS

Blood-Soaked Buddha/Hard Earth Pascal
by Noah Cicero

it gets cold
by hazel avery

Major Diamonds Nights & Knives
by Katie Foster

Cactus
by Nathaniel Kennon Perkins

The Pocket Emma Goldman

Sixty Tattoos I Secretly Gave Myself at Work
by Tanner Ballengee

The Pocket Peter Kropotkin

The Silence is the Noise
by Bart Schaneman

The Pocket Aleister Crowley

Propaganda of the Deed:
The Pocket Alexander Berkman

Los Espiritus
by Josh Hyde

The Soul of Man Under Socialism
by Oscar Wilde

The Pocket Austin Osman Spare

America at Play
by Mathias Svalina

With a Difference
by Francis Daulerio and Nick Gregorio

Western Erotica Ho
by Bram Riddlebarger

Las Vegas Bootlegger
by Noah Cicero

The Green and the Gold
by Bart Schaneman

Selftitled
by Nicole Morning

The Only Living Girl in Chicago
by Mallory Smart

Tourorist
by Tanner Ballengee

Until the Red Swallows It All
by Mason Parker

Dead Mediums
by Dan Leach

Echo Chamber
by Claire Hopple

www.tridentcafe.com/trident-press-titles

CPSIA information can be obtained
at www.ICGtesting.com
Printed in the USA
BVHW040106070623
665322BV00001B/3